PEARL
TONGUE

PEARL TONGUE

A Dallas Diamonds Novel

Tyrone Bentley

KENSINGTON PUBLISHING
www.kensingtonbooks.com

DAFINA BOOKS are published by

Kensington Publishing Corp.
119 West 40th Street
New York, NY 10018

All Kensington Titles, Imprints, and Distributed Lines are available at special quantity discounts for bulk purchases for sales promotions, premiums, fund-raising, and educational or institutional use. Special book excerpts or customized printings can also be created to fit specific needs. For details, write or phone the office of the Kensington special sales manager: Kensington Publishing Corp., 119 West 40th Street, New York, NY 10018, attn: Special Sales Department, Phone: 1-800-221-2647.

Dafina and the Dafina logo Reg. U.S. Pat. & TM Off.

ISBN-13: 978-1-4967-1519-7
ISBN-10: 1-4967-1519-5
First Kensington Trade Edition: October 2017
First Kensington Mass Market Edition: June 2019

ISBN-13: 978-1-4967-1520-3 (ebook)
ISBN-10: 1-4967-1520-9 (ebook)

10 9 8 7 6 5 4 3 2 1

Printed in the United States of America

PROLOGUE

"Up next to the stage is your all-time favorite performer here at Pearl Tongue. After a hiatus, she's
back, and as fine as ever. Get the big faces out, because anything else will not do. Please welcome
the beautiful, talented, pole professional, Lotus."

Aphtan's heart beat ferociously in her chest as
her lungs desperately begged for air. Her fingertips went numb as the long black trench coat she
wore swept the marble floor underneath her now
sweaty feet. Her butter-colored skin sparkled
under the lights as her stomach thumped uncontrollably with mixed feelings.

"Fuck." She took a triple shot of Ciroc to help
calm her nerves. "You got this," she told herself.
"It's like riding a bike. You got this."

Aphtan slowly transformed into Lotus the closer
she got to the door that led to the stage. The bass
from the music boomed through her ears as a feeling of nostalgia took over her. She looked down at
her red-bottomed heels as she leaned against the
pale blue door that separated her from her past.

She couldn't believe that she was about to strip again. It had been six long years since she had been inside Pearl Tongue, which had been her only home at one point in time. It had been all she knew when she was seventeen, and although she hated to admit it, it felt good to be back.

Aphtan leaned her back against the door as the crowd's roars intensified in anticipation. Her straight, red-hair wig hung gorgeously over her shoulders as she signaled for the DJ to play her signature song. She smiled as the familiar tune filled the building and brought back into her mind bittersweet memories that she had tried to forget.

All she could think about was Scooter as she opened the door and walked through it, strobe lights flashing in her eyes. The crowd went crazy once they saw her. The love in the room made her feel good, but making enough money stained her brain like bleach mixing with colored clothes in a washing machine.

She put her finger in the air, telling the DJ to run it back and start the song over. The scratching of the turntable flushed away her thoughts as she focused on only the pole. She removed the trench coat, letting it fall to the ground, revealing her two-piece custom-made gear that she hadn't worn in years and which complemented her small, well-built frame.

Money covered the stage seconds later. She knew she would give the crowd exactly what they came for. Aphtan grabbed the pole, swaying her body up and down against it as she made her ass cheeks clap to the beat. She released one hand's grip, spun around slowly to build up speed with the other, and climbed the pole with ease until her head was at the very top, almost touching the ceiling.

She posed on the pole, using her upper body strength to change positions. Money kept flying onto the stage as the crowd's cheers and praise competed with the volume of the music. Aphtan continued to make her ass cheeks clap as the door at the entrance of the club swung open wildly. A hint of worry stole over her face. Her eyes grew to the size of golf balls as Scooter and his crew walked in.

"Oh, shit," the DJ spat into the microphone. "Y'all get ready. Here's Lotus's signature move."

Aphtan watched them slowly. Her eyes met Scooter's. Fear immediately came over her. She could see the hate in his eyes; the desire to take her life. She positioned her hands, then her legs as they split in the air. She never stopped looking at Scooter as she slid all the way to the ground into a split on the floor.

Scooter stared at her from across the room. He just stared; nothing else. Aphtan could feel his pulse beating in her ears from across the room, blocking out all other sounds except the breath that was raggedly moving in and out of her mouth at regular, gasping intervals. If she could hear it from all the way across the room, she imagined it was deafening in his own ears. Their eyes locked, so now it was apparent that she too was staring.

Aphtan could not take her eyes away from the other set of eyes across the room that were staring her down. Nothing else mattered. The connection had to be held. If it broke, she would die. He would die. Maybe both of them would. Aphtan had never felt so certain of anything else in her life. Aphtan discerned that Scooter could no longer control his hands; they were shaking in an odd trembling rhythm as the color drained from his face. Yet still he stared. He looked as if he was willing himself not to run, willing the connection to hold.

"There it goes." The DJ spun around, tangling himself into his headset. "That's the move that has been imitated by many, but only Lotus does it right. She is the one and only Lotus."

Aphtan eased herself off the ground. Scooter and his crew were now in the front of the crowd. All she wanted to do was get away. She put two fingers in the air to let the DJ know to end the song. She ignored the crowd's disappointment as they yelled for their money back while she gathered the bills from the ground.

Grabbing her trench coat, she put it on and walked quickly off the stage. She could feel Scooter's eyes follow her every move. She opened the door and rushed through it. She paced to the dressing room. Her feet sped up with each second that passed. She ran to her locker while shock consumed her body. Her heart beat inside her throat as she gathered all of her belongings. All of the strippers looked on with wonder as beads of sweat formed all over her face.

Aphtan hadn't thought Scooter would come for her that quickly. It had only been a few hours since he'd accused her of something she had not done. She thought for sure that she could make a quick few grand and be on her way, but as the door closed behind her in the locker room, she knew that wasn't going to happen. She was caught, and there was nothing that she could say to save her life.

She turned around; the smell of his cologne confirmed that it was him before her eyes ever could. A loud ringing formed in her ears as he smiled at her. He winked at her, antagonizing her. A scarce stream of pee rushed out of Aphtan as Scooter removed the gun from his waist and pointed it at her.

"Ladies," he yelled, getting the other dancers' attention in the room. "May we have a moment?"

The dancers screamed as they ran like a herd of bulls at the raise of a red flag. The sight of Scooter meant something bad was about to go down, and they didn't want any part of it. He walked over to Aphtan. Tears rushed down her face without a sound exiting her mouth. He rubbed the small dimple on her cheek while they glared into each other's eyes. He pressed the gun into her chest as she closed her eyes, inviting her end.

"Why?" He pressed the gun as hard as he could into her bare flesh. "Why would you betray me? I gave you everything, Aphtan. I upgraded you. I took you out of this place." He pointed around the room. "Still you betrayed me. I guess a bitch will always be a bitch."

"I didn't steal from you." Aphtan shook her head.

"You don't have to lie, my love." He leaned over and kissed her.

"What do you want from me?" she screamed as she opened her eyes. "Stop playing with me. Kill me if you're going to kill me."

"Can I have a moment to remember you as you were?" He kissed her lips. "I do love you, despite this moment."

"Then let me go," she cried. "I'll leave, and I won't come back."

"You know this game." Scooter pulled the trigger and released a bullet into her chest. "I just can't do that."

As the sweat dripped down her forehead, she pleaded for her life. She pleaded, but her cries weren't good enough. Before she'd even had a chance to pray, she'd heard the bullet scream out of the gun. The connection of metal and her skin was quick.

As the hard, cold, evil lump of metal penetrated her chest, she sighed. She sighed feelings of anger, anguish, and agony. She could feel the life being sucked out of her, and her eyes began to shut. Shut for good. Her life was over. And it didn't even flash before her eyes. It was just gone. Finished. She was about to die.

Scooter caught her body as it was falling and went to the ground with her. He let her rest in his arms as blood gushed from her wound onto his freshly ironed button-up. She looked around the room, her eyes wide with fright; no, not fright, but wonder. Was she in the light? Could she see the light at the end of the tunnel?

Her skin turned a pale, opalescent color. Her hair stuck to her forehead. As he laid her head down slowly, she looked above her, at the dull roof. And before she closed her eyes, she smiled and took her last breath in the arms of the man she once loved.

PHASE ONE

CHILDHOOD

CHAPTER 1

"S-I-X." Aphtan released the black-and-white dice from the palm of her hand, hoping to hit her number.

"You gon' crap out," Byron, a fifteen-year-old neighborhood hardhead, told her as sweat fell from his forehead while the dice bounced off the wall and onto the concrete pavement.

"Hell yeah." Aphtan's mysterious eyes sparkled from the essence of the Texas sun while she turned her baseball cap frontward. "Pay me, nigga," she said as the dice equaled her number.

Most girls were off in packs, eyeing little boys, but that wasn't what ten-year-old Aphtan Epps had in mind. She was the daughter of up-and-coming drug lord Lester "Boss" Epps, which made her rough exterior shine through with ease. She was a natural born hustler, and being raised by a gangster was nothing more than an enablement.

She wasn't your average ten-year-old; she couldn't afford to be growing up in Oakcliff, the slums of Dallas, Texas. Being in the slums would make her one of two things: hard or soft—and there was nothing marshmallow about her.

"You cheated, bitch." Byron used the dark red-brick wall of a building to get up. "You can't use the wall, my nigga, you cheated."

"Stop bitching, nigga, and just pay me my bread." Aphtan held out her yolk-colored hand.

"I ain't paying you shit." Byron smacked her hand down. "You can suck my dick." He grabbed at his jeans.

"Nigga, that's Boss's daughter you talking to," Peanut, another neighborhood hardhead, reminded Byron as he grabbed his arm.

"I don't give a fuck whose daughter she is. Fuck this bitch and fuck that nigga Boss. That nigga ain't anybody special. He sells just like the rest of our pops."

"Fuck who?" Aphtan held her hand up to her ear.

"Fuck you and your pops, bitch." Byron grinned.

Aphtan balled up her fist and, without thinking, punched Byron in his nose. They fell to the floor as blood gushed out of Byron's nose and onto Aphtan's crisp white t-shirt. Byron forced himself on top of her. He punched her like she was a boy off the street. Aphtan fought back, and they went blow for blow.

"You want to act like a nigga, then I'll treat you like one," Byron yelled at her as he wrapped his hands around her throat, choking her with all of his strength.

"Get off of her," Peanut said.

Aphtan's face quickly started to change colors. Before Byron could react to what Peanut had told him, the butt of a pistol busted him in the back of his head, causing him to release Aphtan's throat. The pungent hit caused his vision to grow blurry. He fell over on his side with his hand holding his head, which poured blood profusely.

Aphtan caught her breath and opened her eyes to see a skinny boy with the skin tone of rich caramel hovering over her holding a nine-millimeter. His eyes looked as though they had pain behind them, and she could tell he was a dope boy simply by his appearance. His gear, his stance, and the way he carried himself gave it away. His presence reminded her of her father's, which intrigued her.

"You okay?" The boy reached his hand down to help her up.

"I'm cool." Aphtan grabbed his hand as she got up off the ground.

"You stupid motherfucker," Byron yelled as he stood up. "I'll kill you."

"Nigga, go home before you get something hot put inside of you." The boy pushed Aphtan out of the way.

"Byron, that's that nigga named Scooter we been hearing about." Peanut pulled Byron by the shirt. "Let's get the fuck out of here."

"Hell naw." Byron looked into Scooter's eyes. "I should handle this little nigga."

It was as if Scooter was repenting for his sins, from how tight his grip was on the gun. The smell of gunpowder lingered as his finger pressed the trigger. The sun's blaze made the bullet shine like a kaleidoscope as it was ejected from the gun and entered Byron's chest, killing him instantly.

"Get the fuck out of here," Scooter yelled at a

shaking Peanut, whose eyes were glued to Byron's lifeless body as it now joined the cracks of the warm concrete ground.

Aphtan looked at Byron and then at Scooter. All she wanted was for Byron to pay for choking her out. She didn't want him to lose his life. Despite her dismay, she walked over to Byron's body and checked through his pockets to get the money that she'd won from the dice game. She took everything in his pocket, feeling no remorse for him whatsoever. Her father's blood that ran through her veins wouldn't allow her to.

"You should have just given me my motherfucking bread." Aphtan kicked Byron's corpse. "Bitch ass nigga had the nerve to choke me? Fuck you." She spit on him.

"Let me take you home." Scooter grabbed Aphtan by the arm and forced her body to walk.

"How you know which building I live in?" Aphtan pulled away from Scooter's grip.

"I work for Boss, and he told me to keep an eye on you." Scooter put his hands in his pockets before he walked off.

"How old are you?" She caught up to him.

"Older than you," he answered dryly.

"I know that, but how old are you, though?"

"Seventeen."

"Seventeen and you're already ruthless like that?" she asked in an impressed tone.

"It's not a choice. It ain't like I got shit else going for my life. I got to eat, sweetheart." Scooter's eyes pierced hers. "This is your building, right?" he asked as they approached a building with the letter "Q" written on the front of it.

"Yes." Aphtan took her baseball cap off, revealing her long, sandy brown hair. "Thanks for walking me home."

"No need to thank me." Scooter turned around and paced off slowly. "It's business."

The crisp summer air blew in her face as she watched Scooter disappear into the creases of the buildings. She had never felt anything for any boy in her life, but from the way her stomach fluttered, she knew that she had developed her first crush. She smiled at the thought of them being together one day as she made her way into the building.

There was one family in each of the four apartments in every project building, except for the building Aphtan and her family stayed in. Boss used the bottom two apartments for distribution of his product. One of the bottom apartments was for pickups and the one next to it was for deliveries. The one at the top was for growing his product, and the one next to that one was the one they called home.

Aphtan entered the building, and the smell of freshly burned Mary Jane let her know that she was home. She eased up the staircase with her baseball cap in her hand, which ached from the fight that she'd had earlier. She pulled her house key out of her pocket in order to enter the door to her home, but the voices from across the hall stopped her in her tracks.

She recognized the voices; and with the hunger to know the way of the streets, eavesdropping had become one of her favorite pastimes. Her father wouldn't tell her anything. She got her information by ear hustling. She tiptoed over to the slightly cracked door and listened to the meeting that Boss was holding with his workers.

"It's time we take this shit to the next level."
Boss's six-foot-five muscular frame stood up. His
skin tone was identical to Aphtan's and had that
same high-yellow glow. His voice was deep and demanded respect. He wouldn't be caught without a
suit on or his hair freshly cut. His face was always
neatly shaved, taking years off of his age. His
motto was cleanliness was next to godliness. He
was a laid-back type of man who was about business and business only.

"What do you mean?" Loon "Money" Dixon,
Boss's right-hand man, asked as he sat around the
cherrywood table along with eight other workers.

"This right here." Boss tossed a Ziploc bag full
of white rocks in the center of the table.

"What the fuck is that?" Buggy, the man who
took orders over the phone, asked as he picked up
the bag and felt the crystal-like drug through the
plastic.

"Our future." Boss took a seat. "That shit right
there is going to make us a fortune. No niggas in
the south is pushing this shit. It's more addictive
than weed, and it cost way more."

"What is it called?" Danny, the man responsible
for the growing of the weed, asked as he ran his
fingers through his perm-pressed hair.

"It's called crack." Boss looked back. From his
expression, Aphtan was willing to bet her life he'd
seen her shadow dancing on the hallway through
the crack of the door. "Danny, since you make sure
our Mary grows right, you gon' be the nigga to get
this right."

"I got it." Danny nodded.

"Money knows my plan and my goal. He's going
to explain that shit to y'all niggas while I go talk to

my nosy ass baby girl." Boss stood up. "Soak this
shit up and take it in. I want y'all niggas to learn
this before the week is up. Or I can find some
other cats that will. We're taking over the rest of
the eighties with this one. All of the nineties will be
ours."

Aphtan ran to her apartment as fast as she could
when she saw her father coming. Not wanting to
hear his lecture, she hopped on the couch and cut
the television on as if she had been there watching
it for hours. Boss walked through the door and
smiled at his baby girl's attempt to pretend she was
into the show that was blasting from the top-notch
entertainment system.

"Baby girl." Boss grabbed the remote and cut off
the television. "What did Daddy say about being
nosy while I'm handling business?"

"I don't know, Daddy." Aphtan batted her long
eyelashes at him.

"Aphtan, you can't listen to everything. Some
things aren't meant for your ears, baby girl." Boss
grabbed the white t-shirt on her person. "What the
fuck happened to your shirt?" His nostrils started
to flare.

"Calm down, killer." Aphtan reached down and
untied her shoes. "I was shooting dice with these
niggas from the B building, and one of them didn't
want to pay up. So I decked him."

"He hit you back?" Boss asked in a serious tone.

"Yeah, he started choking me, but this dude
named Scooter came and handled it."

"Good thing I told him to look after you, then."

"So who is he, Daddy? Where is he from? Does
he have a girlfriend?"

Boss smiled. "My baby girl has a crush?"

"Shut up, it's not like that." Aphtan crossed her arms into each other.

"It bet not be. That little nigga a good worker, but I'll cut off his dick if he even thinks about some shit like that."

Boss reached over and kissed Aphtan's forehead as she chuckled at how overprotective he was. Her father was dead serious; she could tell from the stern look plastered all over his face. Boss got up as he adjusted his tie to go back to conduct the rest of his meeting.

"Daddy?" Aphtan stopped him in his tracks. "What were those rocks in that bag?"

"It's a drug called crack, baby girl. It's going to be the thing that gets you the fuck away from this place. This is going to change our lives, Aphtan. Before you know it, we're going to be the fuck up out of here and in one of those rich neighborhoods with the stuck-up ass white folk."

"What's going to be the street name for it?"

"What do you mean?" Boss asked, in shock at the level of his daughter's street smarts.

"Well, we call marijuana, weed, Mary Jane, ganja, and a whole bunch of other stuff. So, what is the name for this crack?"

"That's a good question." Boss walked back over to Aphtan and kneeled down to look her in her face. "They say the first man to sell marijuana named it Mary Jane because it was the woman who meant the most to him in his life. So, since I'm the first cat to sell it around these parts, I guess I'll name it after the most precious thing to me." He gazed into Aphtan's eyes.

"What is that?" she asked.

"You, baby girl." Boss smiled, exposing his pearly

white teeth, which was a rare thing for him. "I guess we gon' call it Aphtan. That shit gon' spread fast, and it's the perfect name for it."

"I don't know if I want my name to represent a drug, Daddy."

"Think about it, baby girl." Boss took some crack out of his pocket and held it in front of Aphtan's eyes. "It's dangerous, but it's worth a lot. When it comes to drugs, it doesn't get any finer than this. It's the most addicting, so it's going to always be in high demand."

"I don't get it, Daddy." A puzzled look took over Aphtan's face.

"I keep forgetting you just a baby." Boss stood back up and walked toward the door. "Don't worry, baby girl, you'll understand one day."

"That's enough of that." Simone, Aphtan's mother, walked through the front door. "Don't be teaching our baby girl about that shit." She set down a slew of shopping bags on the couch.

An unearthly chill fell upon the room as she entered. All voices hushed and movement paused, as if time itself did not dare continue its incessant journey in the presence of such a creature.

She walked so gracefully that she appeared to float through the room, seemingly unaware of the effect her presence had on those around her as she sat on the couch and crossed her legs. Her perfect lips curved into a smile, but her rich chocolate cheeks showed no hint of color to support the gesture.

Boss's mouth opened, but no words issued forth as she pinned him with a look from her coal-black eyes. She thanked him for being quiet and moved on, leaving him feeling simultaneously elated and disappointed. She had spared him a glance, albeit far too brief. Though she struck the fear of God into him, the feeling he would die for one more moment drowning in those bottomless pools of darkness remained long after her attention had dwindled.

Her beauty was both unnatural and breathtaking. A nightmare in motion, yet poetry personified, and no one could tear their eyes away from her. From the first moment anyone saw her, they were ensnared. They stood no hope of escape. She was the finest woman in the hood and every man wanted her, but she belonged to Boss.

"Whatever you say, Simone," was his delayed reply.

Boss closed the door behind him, unaware of the can of worms he was about to open. The drug he was about to start distributing would be a blessing for them, but a curse all the same. The drug would be the biggest thing to sweep the streets of Dallas, Texas, ever.

CHAPTER 2

The sun beamed rays of gold onto the public pool that was located across the street from the projects. It burned like a perfect circle of melted butter in its blue sky dish. The breeze whistled through the turning leaves of the solid oak trees. A blue sparrow flew anxiously above the tops of the willows.

The smell of chlorine tickled Aphtan's nose as the laughter from the other kids from the projects boomed throughout the gate separating the pool from the busy street. Aphtan fixed her bathing suit as she walked around the pool looking for a familiar face. When she saw no one she knew, she thought it was a bad idea to sneak out against her father's will. Boss would never let her go to the pool by herself, if at all.

The brand new Jordans on her feet scuffed against the scorching concrete ground as she approached the edge of the pool. She looked down at the rectangle with its edges smooth and rounded. It was filled with glittering water as clear as the sky, not murky anywhere.

Aphtan noticed how the bottom of the pool sloped gently, going far enough down that she couldn't guess the depth. Some parts were tiled, and the tile glinted in the sun, making the water shimmer even more. Like a silvery blue sidewalk, it was straight and formal looking.

"Them Jordans nice," a girl said from behind as Aphtan was about to jump in.

The sun dazzled in Aphtan's eyes as she turned around to look at the girl who stood before her. Aphtan could tell the girl was around her age as she examined her outfit. She sneered up her nose at her and turned back around as if she'd never said anything at all.

"Fuck her ass." The girl walked off. "Scooter's fine ass and his crew coming in right now, anyway."

Aphtan turned around as Scooter entered the gate to the public pool. Her heart sped up as his eyes met hers. He smiled at her, and she wondered if it was because she didn't have on a baseball cap, because it was the first time he'd seen her without one. Although she was younger, her body told a different story. She was more developed than any girl her age.

Aphtan sat on the edge of the pool; the sun's ray's bathed her with her natural oils. Water from kids playing in the pool splashed on her as a shadow hovered over her. She knew it was Scooter. She could smell him, but still, she ignored him as she removed her socks and shoes.

"Does Boss know that you're here?" Scooter asked.

"Yes." Aphtan handed him her socks and shoes before diving into the pool.

"Stop lying." Scooter bent down as her head came out of the water. "Man, if your pop knew that I saw you here and didn't take you home, I'll be in some shit."

"I won't tell him." Aphtan leaned back on the water and started floating, pushing her curly hair out of her face.

"Get out," Scooter ordered. "I can't take that chance."

"How about you get in?" She splashed him twice.

"Girl, this Tommy Hilfiger," he protested as he wiped the little droplets of water off his shirt. "Get out, Aphtan."

Aphtan obliged; as she held her hand out of the water for Scooter to help her get out of the pool. He leaned his hand down, his gold watch fighting with the sun's oasis for the brightest light at that moment. Aphtan smiled as she grabbed his arm, and before he could mouth a word, she pulled him into the pool.

"Fuck, Aphtan!" Scooter exclaimed as he wiped the water out of his face.

Leaping downward through air, Aphtan immersed herself in the element that felt like soft velvet to her skin. She glided through the pool's luxurious depths, trying to get away from Scooter's reach as she laughed between strokes. Breath flowed through her body, giving her legs and arms the power to stroke and kick, as she watched Scooter swim after her.

The sun shone down on Aphtan's face as she

hopped out of the pool. She rushed up the underwater stairs as she felt her pursuer getting closer. She looked back as Scooter grabbed her, his body colliding with hers as the heat roaring from his body made the water on her skin evaporate.

"Apologize." He squeezed her. "You ruined my watch, you menace ass little girl."

"I'll get you a new one." Aphtan giggled between each word that she spoke.

"You're ten." Scooter released her. "You can't buy me a piece of gum."

"Scooter, who is this?" A girl approached them. Her eyes stuck on Aphtan's while her nose flared and her hands rested on her hip bones.

"She is my boss's kid." Scooter stood in front of her, blocking the girl's view of Aphtan. "Go home, Tiny. I'll come through later."

Tiny looked past Scooter, and if looks could kill, Aphtan knew she would have been dead. She winked at Aphtan as she kissed Scooter passionately for all to see, holding his waist. A look of frustration took over Aphtan's face as Scooter held on to the small of Tiny's back seductively while their bodies moved in unison.

"Is there a problem?" Tiny asked Aphtan after her lips released from Scooter's lips.

"I was about to ask you the same question," Aphtan responded as the pool grew quiet. All the kids from the projects looked on to see what would happen next. They were probably just hoping for a fight.

"Tiny, she's ten," Scooter interjected. "You're fifteen. You don't have shit to argue with her about."

"I don't give a fuck," she said to Scooter as she

got in Aphtan's face. "This little bitch better recognize who the fuck I am. I'll cut her fucking throat."

"Don't fuck up my paper," Scooter warned her as he pulled her by her arm. "This is my boss's kid, Tiny. You can't trip on her like you do these other bitches."

"You better count your blessings, little bitch," she spoke menacingly to Aphtan as she looped her arm into Scooter's.

"I'm not counting anything," Aphtan called out as she started to walk behind them. "I don't want Scooter, bitch. You can have that nigga."

"Bitch?" Tiny balled her fist up and turned around. "I'm about to show you why you should have kept your mouth closed."

Aphtan swallowed hard as her throat accepted the saliva going down it. She looked around at the crowd and knew that she would have to fight to prove herself. She wasn't scared at all; she just didn't know what she was fighting for. She looked at Scooter for answers, but the way he shook his head told her that the fight was inevitable.

"I don't hit girls," Scooter told Aphtan to let her know that he couldn't save her from Tiny. "You better handle your business."

"You." Tiny's voice dripped with hatred. She looked Aphtan in the eye with a stabbing glare.

The way Tiny raised her eyebrow and gave an amused grin of satisfaction let Aphtan know that she thought she had already won the fight. She took two very confident strides toward her enemy, not wasting energy or breath, and looked as fearless as anyone, but Aphtan remained unfazed. Suddenly bursting with an uncontrollable rage that couldn't be calmed, Tiny hacked at her with her fist relentlessly, but Aphtan parried her every move, seeming to absorb every shock with a single hand.

Aphtan spun around after her fist glanced off Tiny's cheek. Aphtan's ring had drawn blood, and Tiny cursed, charging forward like a bull. They crashed against the pavement, scattering around as they went blow for blow. Tiny's grunts filled the air as she punched wildly with both fists, only making contact once, while all of Aphtan's blows landed upon her skin.

Aphtan managed to get on top of Tiny, and she pinned her arms down with her legs. She shook as her fist made a beat with the flesh of Tiny's face. Blow after blow, she delivered as she watched the blood break loose from its normal place and onto the heated concrete ground.

"That's enough, killer." Scooter pulled Aphtan off of Tiny. "Go home." He handed her shoes and socks to her. "You handled your business."

Aphtan approached the gate to leave as the girl from earlier blocked her. She huffed in an annoyed manor as she tried to push through her. She bit her lip feeling as if she would have to fight again. She tossed her shoes on the ground and balled up her fist.

"Wait a minute." The girl held her hands up, the blow pop in her mouth stuck inside the skin of her cheek. "I'm not trying to fight you."

"What do you want?" Aphtan slowly released her hands from the tight balls and picked up her shoes.

"I'm trying to be down with you." The girl took

the blow pop out of her mouth and pointed it to herself. "I'm Jamila, but everyone calls me Mila."

"Why me?" Aphtan left the pool and continued to walk. The heat rising from the concrete irritated her bare feet.

"Because Boss your daddy. I know you gon' be the head bitch in charge one day." Mila grabbed Aphtan's shoulder for her to turn around. "I'm from where you from. I just want to be friends."

"How old are you?" Aphtan crossed the street with Mila tailing behind her.

"I'm ten." Mila bit into the outer shell of the blow pop.

"I don't do well with friends," Aphtan said as they approached the entrance of their projects. "But I guess I can try."

"I think we can be the best of friends," Mila suggested as they walked through the projects side by side.

"Before we can be friends, we need to make sure we like the same things," Aphtan said.

"Let's ask each other some stuff, then," Mila replied.

"I'll ask something and we'll answer it at the same time." Aphtan sat on the front stoop of her apartment building after they made it there. "Then you can ask and we'll both answer."

"I'm down" Mila agreed and sat down next to her.

"What's your favorite color?" Aphtan asked as she squinted her eyes at Mila.

"Purple," they said at the same time.

"What's your favorite candy?" Mila asked.

"Suckers," they both answered in sync.

"What is your favorite shoe?" Aphtan leaned back on her hands.

"Jordans," they said together.

"I guess we can be girls." Aphtan made a fist and held it out for Mila to hit.

"I think we can." Mila made a fist and hit Aphtan's.

The girls sat on the stoop and talked as the sun's beauty faded slowly and the light provided to the earth disappeared. On the stoop of Aphtan's project building, a bond stronger than blood formed within a few hours. They promised to be girls for life and be down with each other through whatever.

CHAPTER 3

The fiery ball of light was shining ever so brightly. The cloudless sky was as blue as the sea below it as Boss, Simone, and Aphtan stood in front of their project building. The sun was so bright that its reflection off the thin rope necklace around Aphtan's neck made the view blinding for all passersby.

A black limousine pulled up to the curb. The driver exited and rushed to the back door to open it. Boss walked toward the limousine with his family following close behind. He signaled to the man looking at them from afar with a rifle in his hand to let him know that everything was cool.

A new car smell met them at the door. They all slid one by one into the black leather seats. Darkness fell with the close of the door; an open chest with refreshments and snacks waited for them. The limousine drove off smoothly as Aphtan sat up in her seat to watch the view of the projects get smaller with each second that passed.

"Where are we going?" Simone laid her head on Boss's shoulder.

"It's a surprise." He kissed her forehead.

"I love surprises." Aphtan turned around and sat down in the seat.

"I know." Boss pinched her cheek.

The small subdivision of South Lake came into view after thirty minutes of driving. Beautiful brick homes filled the streets as the owners walked around merrily without a care in the world. The yards were huge and as green as they could be. Luxury cars filled every parking spot. Dogs played free as kids danced around them with smiles on their faces.

Simone looked on with awe. She had never seen a neighborhood so lively in her years of living. There were no crack heads, boys sagging on the corner, or prostitutes walking around with missing teeth and too little clothing. This was an actual neighborhood. She couldn't believe her eyes.

Simone watched Aphtan roll the window down and hold her tongue out as if she wanted to taste the air to see if it was different. Although her husband had power in the hood, she didn't have the same sense of calmness this area alone brought. Her face lit up as the limousine stopped in front of a two-story Victorian-style home.

"What are we doing here?" Simone's eyes focused on the house in front of them.

"It's a party here for us." Boss signaled for the driver to get out and open the door.

"Why would there be a party for us?" Simone placed shades on her eyes.

"To celebrate us moving into our new home," Boss said as the door opened.

"Boss." Simone grabbed his face. "You bought

this house for us?" she asked before a smile spread across her face.

"Yes." He kissed her lips. "I've been hearing you complain about being in the projects. I hear you when you say you don't shit where you eat. I get it, and I want this to be our family home."

"I love you," Simone screamed.

"I can't wait for my friend Mila to see this house." Aphtan bolted out of the car.

They walked up to the mansion, because it was exactly that, with gravel crunching underfoot. Soft, distant conversation reached them from inside. The tinkling of conversation was like the fine crystal glasses that were abundant in the hands of the wealthy that they passed; the wealthy that surrounded them on their ascent to the estate.

The chauffeur wore a crisp white suit; his head bowed respectfully ahead like a routine machine, oozing professionalism. Simone caught his eye, and he offered her a small smile that she took gratefully, her confidence ebbing dangerously.

Simone couldn't help but smile as she walked next to her family. It was a rare moment for them to have Boss's full attention. Looking up, Simone's eyes searched Boss's, adding warmth to the designer-label dress that she wore. Every step she took closer to the mansion, every time she noticed another window, another butterfly joined her stomach and fluttered ferociously.

It was only when they were several paces from the door that the true size of the house hit them. It was a huge, graceful structure of plaster and glass, brick and slate. So many of the windows were lit up, but for each that was lit, there were three that they could see unattended.

It was a beautiful home that connoted majesty and dignity. They approached the door and awe once again flitted to anxiety through Simone's body. So unaccustomed to this alien environment, Simone didn't know what to expect. So foreign to it, she didn't know how to act.

They entered the mansion as people that they knew and some that they didn't clapped and cheered. Women ran up to Simone to give her hugs. Boss was greeted with handshakes and nods. Aphtan spun around in the foyer in excitement as she dashed off to check out the house.

"Congratulations, brother." Money fixed the collar on Boss's suit. "This is a nice house."

"Thank you, blood." Boss looked up at the high ceilings as Simone leaned into him. "You're next."

"I'm not rushing it." He held up his hands. "It'll come when it comes."

"It will happen sooner than later." He grabbed his shoulder.

Money picked at his goatee as Simone caught him stealing glances at her beauty. She knew everything about her drove him crazy. She thought about how all of them had met as kids. She remembered their first kiss and their last. She could see Money's anger because she belonged to another man building from a couple feet away. It was the same song and dance every time they were in a room together.

Boss and Simone walked off as Boss went and engaged in conversation with some of the new neighbors. Money made his way through the crowd toward Simone, who had joined some of her friends. His eyes were locked on Simone's. All the women in the room, and she could see he was only looking at her. He only had eyes for her. He was in love with her. She was certain he would move mountains for her if she asked.

Simone saw him coming as she smiled in the circle of women around her. She felt the same about Money. She loved him just as much. He wasn't Boss, though. He didn't have the drive. He didn't have the ambition. Money had become full, and Boss stayed hungry and wanting more.

"Simone." Money grabbed her hand and kissed it. "You look as beautiful as ever," he said as the woman having a conversation with Simone walked away slowly.

"Do I?" Simone adjusted her long black hair behind her ear. "You don't look half bad yourself."

"Better than your husband?" Money looked behind him to make sure no one was looking before he guided his fingers up the opening of her small dress.

Simone's chest felt tight at his touch. It was a dangerous joy that she knew all too well. An overwhelming, fluttering pain shot through her that made it difficult for her to breathe. Her stomach felt queasy, making her feel as if she would throw up at any moment.

She slapped his hand repeatedly in vain. She worried that Boss would kill them both in cold blood if he ever found out about their escapades. It was a risk that she didn't mind taking at the price of pleasure that Money provided. It would have been worth it to her.

"Stop, Money," Simone begged.

"You don't mean it." He worked his finger up her thigh a little more as her eyes closed.

She thought to herself that she should have

avoided him at all costs. Every time they made eye contact, she got scared and excited at the same time. Her hands became clammy as Money played with her sweet box in the middle of the party.

She felt dizzy, as if she would pass out. She looked into his red eyes as she creamed on the knuckle of his middle finger. She watched him seductively as he took his finger out of her, licked the cream off, winked at her, and walked away.

Simone watched the man who had her heart as the light from the chandelier above her shimmered on the jewelry she wore. Looking around the party, she searched for something that made her happy, yet she couldn't find it. A mansion wasn't anything if you had to lie next to a man you weren't in love with.

Simone walked quickly to an empty room and closed the door behind her. She rummaged through her pocketbook until she felt the pipe that she used every so often to let her mind escape from the world. She took out a lighter as she leaned against the door to block anyone from entering.

She held the lighter under the pipe, flicked it with her thumb, and put her mouth on the opening to get her first high of that day. She closed her eyes and exhaled the thick, white clouds of smoke as her legs buckled from how good it felt.

"Mama?" Aphtan called from the other side of the door. "Are you in there?" She knocked softly.

"Yes, baby." She put everything in her purse in a hurry. "One moment."

Simone pulled out her pocket mirror and lipstick to touch up her face. She couldn't look anything other than beautiful. She was the wife of the head of an empire and she had to look the part at all times. Anything else would have been unacceptable.

She opened the door and put her arm around Aphtan's neck. They walked back into the heart of the party, the crowd even bigger than before. Simone didn't know it, but the good life that they were just introduced to would be short-lived. You had to give something to get something, and what they were trading would be too much to bear.

The texture of the red couch felt good to Money as a red strobe light from the ceiling of the room flashed in his eyes. The stripper entered the private room of Pearl Tongue, the hottest strip club for hundreds of miles, and danced for him. A stack of money sat next to him, and he threw some when he saw fit. The blunt in his hand slowly shortened a little more with each hit that he took.

The stripper gyrated on him real fast, making his manhood rise. He was enjoying her company so much that his erection could be seen through his slacks. Wanting to get the ultimate tip, she unzipped his pants and wrapped her mouth around his penis. She sucked it ferociously as faint moans left his mouth.

"Make it disappear," he ordered as he held her head in place with a firm grip.

The curtain separating the private room from the rest of the strip club opened as a man walked through. He was a tall white man with short dirty-blond hair. His cold blue eyes checked the room out as he stood still in one spot. Everything about him screamed that he was a cop. Anyone from around the way could tell that in a heartbeat.

The man closed the curtain behind him. He adjusted his blazer, waiting for Money to acknowledge him. The stripper continued her work as Money watched the man. He could see the frustration on the cop's face, but he didn't care.

"Money." The man tapped the watch on his wrist with his hand. "We need to talk."

"I know what the fuck we need to do." Money controlled the woman's head to go faster. "Don't you see me getting my dick sucked?"

"I do see you participating in oral activities." The man raised his voice. "But I'm risking everything by coming here in broad daylight to talk to you." He pointed at Money.

"Don't spit." Money's body tensed up as he released his seed into the stripper's mouth. "Clean me off, and you can bounce."

"Do you hear me, Money?" The man put one hand behind his ear.

"You talk too fucking much," Money spat. "In front of too many people. Let this beautiful bitch leave the room first." He slapped her ass.

The man folded his arms in frustration as Money lay back and let the stripper clean off his weapon. She placed it back inside of his drawers, fastened his pants, grabbed the stack of money, and disappeared through the curtain. Money patted the seat next to his own, giving the man permission to sit down.

The man sat down and helped himself to the bottle of top-shelf dark liquor that sat on the table in front of them. He grabbed a cigar from the open box next to the liquor and put it into his mouth.

"You're early." Money handed him a lighter.

"I'm not on your time." The man dipped the cigar in the liquor, then lit it. "I'm trying to do you a favor."

"Is it really a favor?" Money sipped from his already full glass. "Favors don't cost two hundred and fifty thousand dollars."

"You want the department to arrest and prosecute a man that we have no evidence on? Lester Epps is innocent to us. He's as clean as bleach." The man leaned back. "We have more dirt on you than him."

"You don't now." Money snapped his fingers, and Scooter walked through the thick cloth curtain with a folder in his hand.

"Jesus, is that a kid all mixed up in this?" the man asked as his eyes almost popped out of his head.

"He has more blood on his hands than me." Money grabbed the folder from Scooter and tossed it onto the man's lap. "Don't let his face fool you. Everyone who has is no longer with us," he advised as the young soldier stood there with his arms crossed.

The man looked over the folder. Countless pictures and documents stared him in the face. It was enough evidence to bury Boss underneath the prison. He stood up and grabbed the briefcase that Money pointed to on the side of the couch.

"Do we have a deal?" Money asked as the blunt hung sideways from his mouth.

"I'll get it done." The man walked to the curtain, the briefcase in a tight grip in his hand. "We will get right on it."

Scooter sat next to Money after the curtain closed behind the man. Scooter was fond of Boss. He took him off the streets and put cash in his pockets. He looked out for him and made sure he was good. He remembered what Boss had told him as he sat there. Business was business, and he had to keep reminding himself that to make the guilt go away.

"I'm going to make you a lieutenant when I become boss," Money told Scooter as two strippers entered the room.

"Why not just kill him?" Scooter asked as one of the strippers sat on his lap.

"He's like family." Money flicked the end of the blunt into the cup in his hand. "That would be cruel."

CHAPTER 4

The fury of the dark clouds loomed over the fields, slowly engulfing the world in its magnificent artwork. The people and animals scurried to the comfort of their homes while the trees swayed with the wind. Slowly, the water droplets were released from the cloud's cage. Like a ballerina, they danced across the perimeter as if marking their territory.

Simone stood outside in the backyard of the house in a damp cyan halter top. The wet soil from the garden squished beneath her, crawling between her toes. Looking into the skies, she saw the light shining through gaps in the clouds as what Money had said into the receiver of the cordless phone registered in her mind.

Simone walked over to the spacious, large, and wide oval cabana, painted in her favorite relaxing colors. She listened to the surreal built-in waterfall releasing a relaxing sound of water as she took a seat on the wooden furniture. To the far side of the waterfall was a hidden flat-screen television that would make any homeowner envious.

She held the phone to her ear, panting, saying nothing as she rocked back and forth. She thought about Aphtan and how the news she had just gotten would affect her. A tear fell from her half-closed eyes as the wind brought a slight sprinkle inside of the cabana. She put her head in her knees and exhaled wildly.

"Simone?" Money called through the phone. "Are you still there?"

"Yes." She stood up and peeked through the sheer covering of the cabana. "This isn't right."

"We can finally be together."

"You think I would want to be with you after you put my child's father in jail?" She paced back and forth. "The shit will never be accepted. Even if Boss goes to jail, the streets wouldn't accept any shit like that. The shit wouldn't end well. We would look too grimy, and he got too many niggas following him to let us live."

"I can protect us," Money pleaded.

"I have Aphtan to think about." Simone bit down on her index finger. "I can't betray my family. Not like this."

The silence on the other end of the phone told Simone that Money finally understood that she would never leave Boss for him. The love that they had for each other wasn't enough. The last thing she wanted to do was make Money feel like a fool, but she needed for him to let her go.

"They're on the way," Money spoke softly. "I love you, Simone. Remember that." He hung up the phone.

Simone pulled the phone from her ear and looked at it as the clicking noise attacked her eardrum. She paced toward the house, using the stone walkway as her guide. She burst through the glass double doors, leaving them open as her fast walk turned into a run.

Bumping into the grand piano, she stopped in her tracks to rub her knee. The phone call had left her speechless. Her heart hammered painfully in her chest as her breathing went from quick to next to nothing at all. In her state of numbness, the phone had dropped from her hand and clattered to the ground, and the next thing she knew, she was running again. Feet pounding against the Italian marble, only one thought raced through her mind: *How did this happen?*

Simone bit back on the need to curl up on the stairs and scream out her inner feelings. Instead, she settled on running faster. Panting, her eyes burned slowly; whether it was from holding her tears back or the air licking at them, she was unsure. The settling feeling of depression rankled her mind again as she took an immediate right to the bedroom.

Just a few more steps, she told herself, grinding her teeth together as she ran swiftly, then waited impatiently for the heavy door to open, which seemed to go slowly just to torment her. Rage flamed through her body like a fire mixed with gasoline, quickly spreading to create destruction.

She walked into the bedroom, which was as big as a school cafeteria. It had shiny, pure-white walls that seemed to emit an angelic glow. Boss lay asleep in the bed, which was larger than a king-sized bed and had a canopy of sheer drapes spread out gracefully above it. It was placed in the center of the room, just in front of two ceiling-high windows that looked out to the beautiful scenery just beyond.

On the right side of the room stood a very old, very large, beautiful mirror of pure gold. The light of the moon caught it at the perfect angle. On the other side of the room was a hot tub of sparkling white marble. When in use, the aroma from the bubbles of the water made the room smell of a rose garden. Overall, the room was of incomparable beauty. Any artist who could skillfully capture each corner of its fascinating uniqueness would have sold the painting for millions of dollars.

"Boss." She jumped into the bed and shook his upper body. "Boss, wake up."

"What's wrong?" His eyes opened.

"The feds are on their way here," she said, panicked. "They're coming, Boss."

"How do you know?" He threw the covers off himself and stood up.

"Money just told me." She shook her head as her eyes filled with tears. "I'm so sorry."

Boss walked over to the huge walk-in closet, the silk pajama pants he wore twisted at his waist. It had been only a matter of time until Money turned on him. The envy between them was crystal clear. The way Money looked at Simone gave it away. Boss was anything but stupid.

Boss went to the safe hidden behind hanging clothes and opened the door. He grabbed a folder and a pair of keys from the back of the hollow safe and closed it. Sobbing from the entrance of the closet, Simone watched his every move.

Simone didn't see a sign of worry on his face as he walked up to her and kissed her forehead. He handed her the keys and folder, then grabbed her face to look at her. She stood frozen as he walked by her, aware that her scent taunted his testosterone, his manhood.

"Boss?" She followed behind him as her hands shook like someone fighting Parkinson's disease. "Tell me what to do and I'll do it."

"It's simple." He sat on the side of the bed. "Take Aphtan and get out of here."

"What about you?" she asked between cries.

"I'm going to jail," he said calmly.

"Boss!" she screamed. "This is serious. Tell me what I need to do."

"Simone," his voice bounced off the walls. "Don't lose your head right now. It's information in that folder on all the legit accounts I have that not even Money knows about. Those keys are to an unmarked car in the back. Go."

"I'll call the lawyer that we have on retainer."

"I'll handle everything. It'll be okay." He stood up and walked toward her.

"We can't make it without you," she whispered as she rubbed the dimple that creased his cheek. "I need you. Your daughter needs you, too."

"Take care of my baby girl, Simone." He kissed her lips for the last time. "Promise me two things."

"Anything." She put her hand in his. The hand with the folder and keys hit together from her nerves going crazy.

"Get off that shit, Simone." He looked into her eyes. "It will destroy you eventually."

"What is the second thing?" she asked without denial.

"Be free." The coolness from his breath hit her nose. "Don't come visit me. Don't bring Aphtan to visit me. Y'all are free, and I don't want you to worry about me and be restricted on living."

"But—"

"Go," he cut her off.

"I never meant to fuck over on you with Money." She ran out of the room.

As she ran down the hallway with a determined look on her face, Simone's long, silky hair swished from side to side past her small shoulders. She burst through Aphtan's bedroom door. Her heartbeat pulsed throughout her body. The moonlight from the bay window teased her already red eyes as she walked over to the bed.

She grabbed Aphtan with her free hand as red-and-blue lights flashed in the window. Simone placed her hand over Aphtan's mouth to tell her to be quiet as her eyes opened with a stare of fright.

"When I take my hand away from your mouth, we're going to run. Don't talk. I'm serious, Aphtan. I need you to run as fast as you can."

Aphtan nodded her head as Simone lowered her hand. She grabbed her mother's hand as they dashed for the hallway. It seemed as if the eyes from the pictures lining the hallway were looking at them as they ran for dear life. It was if a killer from a scary movie was after them, and they were the ones who lived at the end.

They made their way to the back door as Simone hit the alarm on the set of keys in the palm of her hand. Lights flashed rapidly from outside of the private gate as they rushed toward the lights. Simone put Aphtan in the backseat, got inside, and drove off in the night.

"Where's Daddy?" Aphtan wiped her eyes. "Where are we going?"

"I'll tell you later." Simone looked through the rearview mirror so Aphtan could see her face. "Everything will be okay."

Simone cringed at the lie she told. Her mind raced the whole ride to the projects that she thought they had escaped from. She didn't want to go back. It was the last thing she wanted. She needed a plan, and this was part of it.

The tires screeched as she stopped and parked the car in front of the building next to the one they used to occupy. She grabbed the folder as she signaled for Aphtan to get out. They walked along the sidewalk, their bare feet stepping on a collage of rocks. They scurried up the stairs of the building, the breezeway darker than a country road at midnight. Simone knocked at the door unapologetically.

"Who is it?" a voice from the other side of the door asked.

"Simone and Aphtan." She knocked again.

The door swung open as Tammy Franklin stood with a smirk on her face. She moved to the side to let them in before she closed the door. She scratched underneath the hair wrap on her head as she cut the floor lamp on.

"Go in there and get in the bed with Jamila." Simone scooted Aphtan toward the hallway.

"Grab a blanket from the closet in the hallway," Tammy yelled as she sat on the couch.

Everything was closing in on Simone. She could feel her breath beginning to shake, and then grow rapid. Blood pounded in the back of her head.

She could feel the trembling. Her nails scratched the surface of the folder. Her hands clutched her sides. She was curling in on herself, her vision swimming. It was too much.

"What's wrong?" Tammy turned her head to the side. "You're barefooted and in a halter?" She pointed at her. "What in the hell is going on?"

"They got Boss." Simone sat next to her. "It was Money's doing."

"Are you still fucking with him, Simone?" Tammy whispered as if someone were listening.

"No." She looked at her. "He wanted me to leave Boss for him. I couldn't do it. This is all my fault."

"How are you going to get him out?"

"He sounded as if he wasn't getting out once he goes. I didn't stay to see any of it. He didn't have shit in the house. I know that for sure." She held the folder up. "He told me to take this and to get away."

Tammy grabbed her to hug her. "Hopefully, whatever's in that folder will be enough to get y'all by for a while."

"I hope so," she cried. "I just want things to go back to how they were."

Tammy stood up and walked into the kitchen. "Y'all are welcome to crash here for as long as you need. I'll talk to the landlord about the apartment across the breezeway. It's empty. Maybe you and Aphtan can move over there until you figure your next move out."

"Do that." Simone stood up and went into the kitchen. "Do you have something to drink?"

"There's soda in the icebox."

"No." Simone leaned against the stove. "I need something a little bit stronger."

"Under the cabinet." Tammy pointed.

Simone bent down to get the liquor. She opened up the top of the bottle and drank as much as she could in one gulp. Thoughts of how their life was about to change kept her brain busy. She had never struggled. She always had the best of everything, no matter what it was. She prayed that when she checked those accounts in the morning, there would be enough to hold them over. If not, she didn't have a clue as to how they would survive.

CHAPTER 5

Simone sat in the uncomfortable blue chair as she folded the paperwork open and closed in her hand. She looked at the large clock on the eggshell-white walls as the lines leading up to the bank tellers grew with each minute that passed. She clicked the bottom of her heel impatiently onto the lines of the cream floor tile.

She reclined back in the seat as her hair dangled freely over the top of it. She thought about what life was going to be like without Boss. It had only been half a night, but it felt like decades. She wanted to call his lawyer. She wanted to break into the jail and save him. He told her that he was going to handle it, so she decided to sit back and wait on him to contact her.

Trying to explain it to Aphtan when she got back to Tammy's was going to be hard. She didn't want to lie to her. She told herself that no matter what, she would tell her the truth at all cost. Years without her father would tear her up inside. She was a daddy's girl. She did everything with her daddy. The thought of him not being around would be enough to break her heart into pieces.

She felt naked without her jewelry. It was the first time in years that she had been caught in public without a ring on every finger. The material of the dress she borrowed from Tammy made her skin itch. All of her belongings were in the house. She didn't have a claim on Boss's illegal money, and everything would have been seized in the raid. One of the police officers' wives was going to get an early Christmas present on her dime.

"Mrs. Walker?" A lady stuck her head out of the clear glass office. "Please, come in."

Simone eased out of the seat and fought the urge to scratch at the itchy material. She held her head high with elegance. She wanted to be sure that this woman in charge of personal accounts wouldn't doubt that she could own whatever it was that was in them. She didn't want her to have any reason to question it.

She walked through the office, nodding at the woman to greet her. She sat down at one of the two chairs in front of the large, cherrywood desk. The woman ignored her, typing into a keyboard connected to her computer. Minutes went by while the woman's eyes were glued to the screen of the computer, not even acknowledging Simone.

"Excuse me?" Simone tapped on the desk. The woman stopped what she was doing to look at her. "Are you going to give me the information regarding these accounts?"

"I'm working on that now." The woman got up to close the door. "I know Boss very well. None of these accounts are in your name or his." The woman took off her glasses and set them on the desk. "Now,

Mrs. Walker, do you want the five hundred thousand in cash?" She winked at her, using the name on the accounts.

"Yes please." Simone closed her eyes and let out a sigh of relief.

The woman left out of the room as Simone sat patiently with her legs crossed. Boss wouldn't have left them without some financial security. She felt bad for doubting him. He always took care of her and Aphtan.

The woman returned with a steel briefcase in each hand. She set them beside the seat that Simone occupied before returning to her desk. She grabbed a piece of paper from the top of her printer and set it in front of Simone with a pen.

"Sign here." She pointed to a line.

"Is that it?" Simone set the pen on top of the piece of paper.

"That's it, Mrs. Walker. The money is exactly how your husband brought it in." She held out her hand.

"Thank you." Simone shook her hand, grabbed the briefcases, and left the small office.

The sun's rays beamed onto Simone's face as she exited the bank. She walked down the sidewalk with a briefcase in each hand. Her feet made a rhythmic note against the pavement. She sped up once she noticed a black Suburban trailing along the sidewalk matching her pace.

She stopped at the end of the street as cars reacted to the changing of the light. She looked over to her right as two men dressed in all black got out of the Suburban after it parked. They started to walk toward her at a fast pace.

Simone dashed between the cars, praying they

didn't hit her. She maneuvered with swiftness until she made it to the other side. The Suburban accelerated to catch up to her. The men ran between the cars with full force to get to her.

Her running slowed down as the Suburban blocked off the street in front of her while the men chasing her caught up to her and grabbed her. The window of the truck rolled down as Money's face appeared. "Come take a ride with me," he demanded, never looking at her.

"Can I come meet you after I go check on Aphtan?" Simone shook her arms to get the two men's hands off her.

"No." The window slowly rose. "Just get in," he ordered as the two men pushed her with force.

Simone entered the truck. The smoke inside irritated her eyes. She sat next to Money in the backseat and placed the briefcases on the floor. The men closed the door without getting in, and the truck accelerated into the traffic. She couldn't help but look at Money, then the driver, and then Money again.

She swallowed hard, her tongue almost going down her throat with the small amount of spit that formed in her mouth repeatedly. She looked forward to avoid eye contact with him. It felt like death, and she was breathing it in fully.

"How's the single life?" Money asked to break the ice.

"I'm still married," she snapped as she looked around the backseat of the SUV.

"That's just paper, sweetheart." He grabbed her thigh. "That nigga will never be free again."

"Don't touch me." She slapped his hand. "You ruined my fucking family."

"No, sucking and riding my dick every chance you could ruined your family."

"Fuck you." She slapped him as hard as she could. "How fucking dare you."

"Bitch,"—he grabbed her face and squeezed it roughly—"you better keep your hands to yourself."

"Loon." She pulled away from his grip. "You better think twice before you put your hands on me. I know it's been years, but don't forget what I used to do back in the day."

"Don't forget who used to hire you to do it." He softened his voice. "I just want you to reconsider my proposition."

"No." She shook her head. "Never."

"I love you, Simone," he said truthfully with a grin.

She barely heard the words he spoke next. His grin was enough to stop her entire world. All she could see at that moment was how attractive he was. His brown eyes that lit up as he said those words, eager to get a reaction out of her. His t-shirt was loose across his chest but still showed his toned body underneath. Even his imperfections—the small gap between his teeth, the scar on his chin, the small patch of gray hair—were enough to make her heart beat like crazy. All she could think was how badly she wanted him.

Unable to contain herself, Simone got on top of him, straddling him with her legs on either side of his body. Her sweet, slow kiss cut him off mid-sentence. She kissed him again, and again, until his soft, warm hand lifted her chin to stop her.

"What's this?" A smile formed on Money's lips.

Simone smiled back, but only answered with another kiss. Longer this time, hungrier.

Money was getting into it now, too. Each kiss was harder and more intense than the last. He ran his hands over her face and through her hair, and then worked his way downward. Simone felt a shiver run through her spine as he slipped his hands beneath her dress. He gently pulled it off, leaving her in only a blue lace bra and panty set. She had picked it out especially to impress him one day, but she knew now that it was silly; anything she wore would be sexy to him.

Simone's heart fluttered as Money reached back to unclasp her bra. She felt momentarily self-conscious at the exposure, until he pulled her up against his body and kissed her so sweetly. His strong arms wrapped around her. Never breaking the kiss, he sat up and flipped her around so that he was on top.

He kissed her mouth once again, then her neck, and then her breasts. He paused for a moment to take off his own shirt. She felt a rush of adrenaline as he ran his fingers beneath the elastic of her underwear before removing them as well.

Money's hands and mouth suddenly seemed to be everywhere at once, touching every inch of her naked body. She could feel his breath come hot and fast. She gasped as his fingers did their work below her waist, moving slowly at first, then faster. She squeezed her eyes shut, squirming under his relentless rhythm. The pulse between her legs grew stronger and stronger, unbearably strong, until he stopped.

"Don't stop," she moaned breathlessly. It felt

too good for him to stop now. He only kissed her forehead, and then rolled off her to open the lips of her pussy.

"Not yet," she said, grabbing his hand and pulling him back into the moment.

She rubbed her hands over the zipper of his jeans and pulled them down slowly. She reached down into his boxers to pull out his tool. It sprung up, eager for her touch. She ran her hands up and down, tentatively at first, until she gained confidence in her ability to touch him, pleasure him. She felt his body tense and leaned up to kiss him again. His erection felt hot on her stomach.

"How am I doing?" she whispered into his ear.

"As good as ever," he whispered back. "You know what you're doing."

She breathed in the scent of him, feeling herself melt at his words. He then once again reached toward her box, and this time she let him.

"Ready?" he asked after he positioned his face in front of her identity. She simply nodded in reply.

He pulled her legs apart and put his tongue in, moving in and out, slowly at first and then faster. She moaned with pleasure. Was there really anything better than feeling Money inside her? She grabbed the back of his head, pulling him closer, and wrapped her legs up around his head, wanting him to go deeper. He grunted with effort, panting and sweating, until finally he climaxed.

After it was done, they lay together in the spacious backseat of the truck, his arms wrapped around her. There was no greater feeling than sex with him. The closeness she'd never had with another human being, the safety of his arms, the knowledge that he loved her and wanted her. She could stay in the moment forever.

"I love you," she cooed.

"I did love you." He reached over her to open the door.

She stared at him, his dark eyes like daggers staring straight back in hers. "Wait," her voice came out as a squeak, "what are you doing?" A quick gasp of breath left her mouth.

"I'm opening the door for you." He sounded completely smooth, sincere. He didn't even seem disgusted by the insensitivity.

"I'll grab my shit and get out." Her voice was coming out in whimpers as she reached for her clothes slowly. Her eyes, haunted, still fixed on his darker ones.

His gaze pierced her like a knife. "I'll take those briefcases off of your hands."

"You trying to rob me, nigga?"

He took a threatening slide toward her. "I can't believe your stupidity. You really thought all that time that I meant it when I said I loved you? All those times I kissed you, you believed in those kisses?" He arched an eyebrow and smirked. "Oh, wait, of course you did, Simone. You were stupid then, and your ass is even dumber now. Get the fuck out of my whip."

Nervousness and bile wound up in Simone's stomach like a tightly coiled spring under pressure. She needed to throw up. No, she needed to get away. Her body was still frozen, only able to inch backward. Her gaze dropped from his to the briefcases on the floor between them. A cold shock ran through her as though she hadn't realized the meaning of his words until that moment.

"Come on." His smirk widened, and he put his hands around her neck, removing a gun from his pants with the other. "Don't worry," he teased her. "I'm not going to kill you," he said with trademark laziness. "I am going to take this money, though, as a parting gift."

"We need that money," Simone begged.

"What the fuck does that mean to me?"

Simone felt his cold hands land on her shoulders, pushing her backward. She stumbled, reacting fast. Everything around her spun and smeared, making her dizzy. All she could do was let out a deathly ringing scream. Lights blinded her vision as her arm got caught on something, stopping her fall.

Fear made her want to close her eyes, but the adrenaline flowing through her veins wouldn't allow her to do so. She could see the street through her half-opened eyes, and then it disappeared and everything was pitch black. Her eyes slowly blinked open to reveal the truth: Money had thrown her from a moving car, butt naked, and he had taken all of her money.

CHAPTER 6

Boss tapped the small gray table as the light from the lamp flashed on his face. He kept a straight face as the detective sat across from him, waiting on him to answer the questions he had just asked him. The detective glared at him with hate as his demeanor remained calm.

Boss knew the game. Silence was his best friend at the moment. Whatever they had on him wouldn't change. He refused to give them anything to hang him. They had enough rope on their own.

He thought about Aphtan and Simone as spit flew from the detective's mouth with each word that he spoke. He prayed they would be safe. He hoped that being in jail would be enough to satisfy Money. He didn't want him to go after his family. He wanted to get him first before he had a chance to.

He should've handled the situation when he learned about Simone and Money years ago. He blamed himself for the situation. He was weak, because of love. He wished that Simone would be only his one day, but that day never came.

"Lester?" The detective hit the table with the palm of his hand. "You may want to pay attention to me. I'm trying to be a good guy here. I'm trying to cut you a deal if you offer me information."

"You're trying to bury me under the ground." Boss put his hands together. "No, thank you. I thought I asked for my lawyer hours ago. Isn't it against the law to speak to me without one once I ask for him?"

"I want to make a deal with you," the detective spoke, his voice hitting the walls, causing it to echo through the room.

The room was dimly lit and Boss could barely see, and that was on his half of the room. On the other half it was dark, but the darkness looked as if it was moving. He had to focus to see. It looked like a solid black shadow, but then he could look again and see lighter grays mixed in. The shadows were where the detective was lurking.

"What kind of deal?" Boss asked out of curiosity.

"Are you willing to give up Money? I know you have some dirt on him."

"Y'all want his head, too?"

Anger pumped through his veins as he waited for the detective to respond. When he didn't, he started to shift from foot to foot and look into the shadows trying to see the man. Questions started to fill his head as he waited for him to respond. *Was he serious? Would it be a good deal?* He could feel his eyes on him, watching him intently.

"Of course," he finally spoke, his choice void of any emotion.

"I have nothing for you." Boss put his hands on the table. "I want my fucking lawyer. This shit is against the law." His voice rose.

"What's against the law is selling drugs." The detective spread pictures from a folder across the table.

"Is it?" Boss asked in a condescending tone.

"It is, and what we got on you, you'll be doing twenty, easy."

"I guess we will find out." Boss smiled at the detective as knocks from the door echoed throughout the room. "That'll be my lawyer."

The detective opened the door as a man in a midnight blue suit with a thin green windowpane pattern walked in. Single breasted, but with peaked lapels. This unusual detail, along with handmade buttonholes and functional cuff buttons, gave the garment away as bespoke. The shirt under it was white, with lavender stripes running up it. The tie was deep purple, solid and sleek. It was tied with an impeccable, effortless dimple. His pocket square was colorful and vibrant, yet tasteful.

The man took a seat next to Boss. His pecan colored skin glistened with oils. His hair was cut in the neatest fade around, and his face was clean-shaven like a baby's bottom. He was tall with a body to give the impression that he had played sports in high school. He fixed the glasses on his face after he set his briefcase onto the table.

"Can I have a moment with my client, detective?" the lawyer asked.

"Sure," the detective sneered before walking to the door and leaving.

"How does it look?" Boss leaned back in his chair.

"Eight years." The lawyer opened up the briefcase and took a stack of papers out. "Federal time."

"That's the best you could get?"

"With everything they have on you, yes."

"Fuck." Boss kicked the bottom of the table. "This plea is the best? What about my properties and my accounts?"

"Seized."

"Damn, Kevin." Boss stood up. The chair he had been in fell over from the sudden movement.

"Look, Boss,"—Kevin picked up the chair—"we've known each other since we were kids. I wouldn't steer you wrong. I called every favor I could just to get it this low. Trust me, take it."

Boss put his hands behind his head as he paced around the room. He wasn't naïve; he knew he was going to get some time. Hearing it out loud made it a reality, though. He didn't know if he could survive that long without seeing his family. That was his only concern.

"Okay." He sat down and looked over the paperwork.

"Sign." Kevin stood up. "We'll go stand before a judge soon, and he will present the plea information from the district attorney."

"How soon?" Boss signed the paper.

"It will be within the month. It'll be quick because you're agreeing to the plea." He closed the briefcase after putting the paperwork inside. "I'll keep you updated."

"Thank you." Boss gave him a handshake. "Tell Mariah I'm sorry to get you out of bed at this time of night."

"It's fine, Boss. Just keep your head up."

"Kevin?" Boss stopped him at the door. "Can you do something for me?"

"What do you need?"

"I need you to call one of my workers with a message." Boss rubbed his tamed beard.

"You know I don't do any illegal shit, Boss." Kevin stared at him.

"I just need you to say two words to him," Boss assured.

Boss gave him direct instructions on where to find Scooter. Boss had already paid him for the job. Killing Money had been on his mind for a while. After Kevin delivered his message to Scooter, Money would be six feet under before the sun set on the next day. That alone would help him sleep comfortably for the next eight years.

When she'd seen Money and his goons leave by his condo's rear gate, Simone ran inside and up to his home, threw all his possessions into her bags, and raced out of the condo. As she neared the top of the stairs, Scooter stepped to the bottom stair, bringing her to a near crashing halt.

"Who else is with you?" Scooter asked.

"Just me." Simone squeezed against the stairwell wall to let him pass.

Scooter didn't move. "What's in the bags?"

"My shit." Simone put her hands on top of the bags that hung from her shoulder.

Scooter ignored her as he slowly walked up the stairs almost like a tall, shadowy specter. His footsteps created a heavy, creaking noise below the nice vintage stairs. The sound grew more and more distinct as he got closer to the top.

Scooter could not be seen, but the sound of his footsteps slowly getting closer and closer sung in the darkness. He could hear her heart beating at a rapid pace. He could see the hair on her skin stand upright as she stood still with fright. Scooter ignored her as she ran down the stairs and past him.

Scooter looked ahead. He had received the instructions from Boss. He had a mission to complete. What Simone had going on wasn't his business as long as it didn't interfere with what he was sent to do. After he approached the door, he opened it up with force. He cut on the light; the apartment looked as if it hadn't been tampered with. If he hadn't seen Simone downstairs, he wouldn't have assumed someone had just robbed the place.

He sat on the couch and removed the gun from his person. He looked at the picture of him as a little boy on the oak end table. He grabbed the frame and remembered when Money took that picture of him. He finally saw what everybody saw; he really did look just like Money. He set the picture down as the front door opened.

Scooter didn't move an inch. He sat there as silent as a mouse. When Money and his goons saw him, they pointed their guns at him, but he didn't blink. He sat there and looked straight forward with no fear in his heart. He turned to look at them and pointed his gun in an instant.

"Lower your fucking guns." Money walked over to Scooter. "It's only my son, niggas."

"Can I speak to you?" Scooter lowered his gun after the goons did. "In private."

"Of course." Money waved the men off with his hand. "Why are you breaking into my shit, Scooter?"

"I saw Simone on the way up." He ignored his question. "She had a bag full of your shit."

"That bitch." Money hit the coffee table in front of them. "Did you stop her?"

"No." Scooter stood up as he looked at the picture of him. "I need you to get out of town for a little bit."

"Why?" Money's face squinted a little.

"I was sent by Boss to kill you," he said with no emotion.

Money smiled at his old friend. The rules of the streets were ruthless, because there were none; anything went. Sending his own son to kill him was a dirty thing to do, even for Boss. He stood up and held his arms wide open and faced Scooter. "Do it."

Scooter put his gun away. "You know I can't do that shit. I just need you to get away for some years. Lay low and stay under the radar. I'll tell Boss the deed is done."

"He's going to want proof." Money lowered his hands. "I know he's in jail, but if he finds out you didn't do what he asked, he will have you killed. He still has some power."

"I already know this." Scooter sat on the arm of the couch. "I'll take over and play my role here. When you return, I'll hand over the crown to you. No questions asked. We just need to let the power that he has fizzle."

It was if the proposition ran through Money's head as he sat back down on the couch. He wasn't a pussy. He never ran from a fight. However, he was a father first, before he married the streets. He would do anything to keep Scooter safe. Even if it meant going into hiding.

"I'll do it, Scooter. When I return, I want full control." He stood up and gave his son a hug. "Make me proud."

"Be safe," Scooter said before he walked toward the door and left.

Scooter walked down the stairs, about to be the youngest nigga in charge the streets had ever seen. He was eighteen going on thirty. He thought about his plan as he got inside of the foreign car that waited for him in front of the condominiums. His plan would go into motion as soon as he delivered the news to Boss. He just hoped that he believed him.

CHAPTER 7

A cold breeze brushed against the tree, making the leaves shiver under the too bright sun as Simone and Aphtan walked up the flight of stairs leading to the courthouse. Motes of dust danced through the air, glinting in the sun, like little wisps of life fading in and out of focus. They approached the solid wood doors as Simone thought, prayed, and pondered what-ifs.

Simone felt singled out, alone, and scared yet confident after talking to Boss's lawyer. Boss didn't want her or Aphtan there. He made that perfectly clear when he had called her over the past month. She didn't listen. She wanted Aphtan to see her father, no matter the circumstances. Simone couldn't live with herself if Aphtan didn't get to see him before he got shipped off.

Aphtan's face looked as if she had lost her best friend. Simone knew she could comprehend most of what was going on. Simone was aware that she understood what her father did for a living. She had been present when Aphtan saw it with her own eyes. It would have been preposterous for Simone to lie to her.

The room was huge, and all eyes were on them as they entered. Very silent, yet a single sniffle, cough, or clearing of the throat sounded as if they stood near their ear. They continued to walk in farther, and Simone started feeling a little more at ease when she saw Boss's face.

Simone thought she was at ease until she found her seat and sat down on the cold, solid wood bench. A chill shivered up her spine, to her shoulders, and down her arms and legs. She opened her eyes and tried to relax. She could never completely relax until it was all over. She wanted to run out the door and leave. A little choked up and sick to her stomach, she needed some fresh air.

Her face contorted into a terribly beautiful, yet heartbreaking expression as her eyes welled with tears. She wiped them quickly as Aphtan's face copied hers. She squeezed her baby girl's hand and leaned down to kiss her forehead. She touched her nose with her index finger like she always did when she became scared. It calmed her down instantly.

Thirty minutes passed before the judge called Boss's name. Simone watched him walk up to the judge with his lawyer next to him. His face looked normal, but she could tell from his wild facial hair that he was stressing. She cringed at the sight of the orange jumpsuit he wore as she stood up to represent her husband.

"That's the drug dealer," a woman whispered next to them.

"And this is my middle finger, bitch." Simone flipped the woman off as the woman gasped.

Simone's hands gripped the seat in front of her as her leg twitched with anticipation. She never thought Boss would get caught. He was always careful. He was as slick as oil. When he turned around and looked in her eyes, she couldn't help it; a tear had to fall.

"How do you plead?" the judge asked as the courtroom fell silent.

"Guilty," Boss answered as he kept his shackled hands out in front of him.

"I see you agreed to a plea offered by the district attorney's office for eight years to be served concurrently for all charges at a federal facility of my choice," the judge spoke loudly.

"Yes, sir," Boss said to him after Kevin nudged him.

"You will serve your time at Crosspoint in San Antonio, Texas. Since this is your first offense, I will make it easy for your family to visit you. I will not send you far. I hope you learn from this. Next," the judge screamed as he banged his gavel.

"Thank you." A cop grabbed Boss by the arm and led him to a door.

"Kevin." Simone scurried through the seats to get to him. "Can we see him? Please? We have to see him before he gets shipped off."

"Simone." Kevin closed his eyes. "I'll see what I can do, but no promises. I've run out of favors. Go out in the hallway, and I'll let you know what I can do."

Simone did as she was told, and she paced back and forth in front of the courtroom doors. Her heart fluttered with each minute that passed as families entered and left constantly. She watched

Aphtan looking with wonder from the two gray chairs next to the door as she twirled the ends of her hair.

"Simone?" Kevin called from a door next to the water fountain. "Come on." She grabbed Aphtan and rushed to the door. "We don't have much time."

"Thank you so much," Simone whimpered as the door closed behind them.

They stalked down a hallway. The lights from the narrow ceiling shined brightly on them until they approached a room. Kevin opened the door, causing anxiety to build within Simone. Smiles filled their faces when Boss appeared on the other side of the door.

"Daddy," Aphtan screamed as she ran into his arms.

"Baby girl." He picked her up and squeezed her with love. "I love you, Aphtan."

"I love you, too," she cried, her chest going in and out with each pant.

"Five minutes," Kevin said before leaving and closing the door behind him.

"Boss." Tears fell from Simone's eyes. The ability to touch him made her feet freeze. "I've missed you, baby."

"I've missed you, too." He walked up to her with Aphtan in his arms. "You have to be strong." He kissed her lips passionately as she wrapped her arms around his waist. "This is no time to fall apart."

"How are we supposed to make it out here without you?" She put her head in his chest as she wiped the tears from Aphtan's now red face.

"You'll be fine." He put his head on top of hers. "You got the bread back from Money. Just spend it wisely."

"I want to get out of the projects." She sighed.

"Stay there, Simone," he ordered. "Be smart about this. You don't have to worry about Money, either. I had him taken care of. Okay?"

"Okay," she answered.

"Baby girl." He put Aphtan down and kneeled so that she could see his face. "You have to be strong for your mama. Okay?"

"Okay." Aphtan nodded her head up and down.

"Don't become a product of your environment." He grabbed her face. "Always survive by any means, but be smarter than I was about it."

"I promise." Aphtan hugged his neck.

"Keep getting those straight A's."

"I will," Aphtan promised as the door opened.

"Time's up." Kevin stood at the door.

"I love y'all so much." Boss grabbed and kissed them one last time. "I'll be home before you know it." He stopped at the door. "Aphtan, be careful who you trust. The devil was once an angel."

Simone's eyes began to flow with water. It was not controllable. Her emotions had taken over her body. She quickly grabbed Aphtan's arm and walked out of the room and down the hallway, colliding shoulders with anyone who was near her. She went outside and strutted to her parked car on the street.

She grabbed a tissue from her purse to wipe away the tears as she put Aphtan in the backseat, then positioned herself in the driver's seat. B Angie B's hit song, "So Much Love," boomed from the radio as she accelerated off into traffic. She reached for her purse on the floor of the front seat as she came to a stop at a red light.

"Turn around." She looked in the backseat at Aphtan.

She eased the pipe out of her purse and kissed it. She needed one hit. One fix would make all of the pain go away for her. She looked in the backseat to make sure Aphtan's eyes were closed. She flicked the lighter underneath the pipe and hit it. The feeling took over her as she pulled over to enjoy it.

"Are you okay?" Aphtan asked from the backseat.

"Yes, sweetheart." Simone took another hit. "Just keep your eyes closed for mama."

Aphtan fought back tears as she looked in between her fingers at what her mother was doing. She was ten, but she had seen base heads on the street do the same thing; have the same hand gestures and movements. She closed her fingers together as her mother looked at her in the rearview mirror.

She didn't know it, but that day would be the day her mother lost herself to drugs forever. That was also the day that her life would change forever. Everything her father had instilled in her was about to be tested. The next few years of her life would be the hardest, and what she would have to endure would make her or break her.

Phase Two

TEENAGER

CHAPTER 8

The stifling heat smothered the atmosphere. Only a creaking, moaning floorboard under the teacher's shoe invaded the monastic silence. Seventeen-year-old Aphtan's eyes darted toward the window as she witnessed a bare tree branch silently dancing in the afternoon breeze. As the teacher resumed vigil seated at her desk, the creak of her chair invaded the classroom. She silently breathed the still present vapors of the custodian's pine-scented cleaner. Ahead of her, an empty much-scarred and faded desk sat in silent testimony, witness to countless generations of scholars.

Aphtan stared off into space as the teacher droned on about the food triangle. She had heard it a dozen times before and had better things to keep her mind occupied. She twirled her long, red quick-weave hairstyle around her finger and doodled on the paper in front of her.

The sound of the classroom door closing with a bang snapped her back to attention. Standing at the front of the classroom was a tall, good-looking boy with a Caesar fade, light brown eyes, and a smile that could make every girl in the room weak. The teacher introduced him as Cole Dixon, and Aphtan found it very difficult to take her eyes off of him.

He sauntered to a desk situated behind Aphtan, and as he passed, he winked at her and smiled. She felt a pang of annoyance at his cool, calm manner. He sat down, scribbled down something on a piece of paper, balled it up, and threw it so it landed in front of her. Looking around her to see that the teacher wasn't looking, Aphtan opened it. It read *"you have lipstick on your teeth."* She quickly rubbed her two front teeth and hid the note under her book.

She turned around. "That was rude as hell."

"I thought that you should know." He smiled at her, his neatly trimmed mustache shifting with the movement of his mouth. "What is your name?"

"Aphtan," she answered before she turned back around.

"Aphtan." He leaned forward so she could hear him. "You sure are pretty."

Red leaked into her cheeks as she nervously smiled and bit her lip. She looked away slowly, but she couldn't hide the red glow that came over her face. She tapped her hands on the desk gently as she batted her thick lashes.

"I'm serious." He leaned in further. "Do you have a boyfriend?"

"That's enough talking," the teacher yelled from her desk. "End all conversations, now!"

Cole leaned back in his chair and tugged at the polo he wore. It was if Aphtan would be his from the way that she blushed. She seemed like a good girl. Good girls were all he talked to. If he had to stay in a new city, he might as well pass time with a beautiful girl.

The sound of the bell ringing sent joy through the students as everyone stood to end their day. With her book in hand, Aphtan left the classroom and headed to her locker. She could feel Cole following her, and as she looked behind her, his smile was the only thing that she saw. She stopped when she made it to the royal blue locker. Before she could enter the combination on her lock, Cole was standing with his back to the locker next to hers.

"Can I help you with something?" Aphtan opened the locker.

"You can help me with your number." He smiled at her.

Cole, the six-foot-three God incarnate, had her lost for words. With a fresh fade and round eyes that you could swim in, he was a bit intimidating to her. His lips were full and plump, and his face—oh, his face—was just perfect. It was as if he were an angel that had fallen from Heaven, so perfect and sweet, and landed there, in that wretch of a city to grace her with his presence.

"You can't speak now?" He peaked around the locker door.

"Of course I can." Aphtan closed the locker. "It's just a matter of if I want to or not."

"Are you single?" He followed behind her as she walked away.

"You can say that."

"That's a good thing for the both of us."

"How do you figure that?" She maneuvered through other students in the packed hallway.

"That means that we can get what we want."

"What is that?" She stopped and leaned against a rusty old water fountain.

"Each other." He grabbed her hand.

"You're silly." She snatched her hand away from him quickly.

Aphtan looked past Cole and saw her best friend, Mila, walking toward them. A knockout, she strutted seductively, making everyone in the hallway look. Mila's skin was a rich shade of chocolate. She had long, brown hair and the silhouette of a goddess.

"Who is this?" Mila bit her lip. "I didn't know we had new meat at the school."

"This is Cole." Aphtan looped her arm inside of Mila's to walk away. "He ain't nobody." She pulled them in the opposite direction.

"He doesn't look like a nobody to me." Mila yanked away from her best friend's grip. "I'm Jamila, but everyone calls me Mila." She held her hand out for him to shake.

"What's up, Mila." He shook her hand as his eyes met Aphtan's. "So, I'm nobody," he asked with a smile, as two dimples on each side of his cheek appeared.

"I didn't mean it like that." Aphtan folded her arms into each other.

"I thought we went together," he joked as he walked toward her. "But seriously, Aphtan, whenever you ready, let me know."

Chills ran through Aphtan's body as Cole's skin touched her own as he walked by. Everything went into slow motion as they looked into each other's eyes as if it would be the last time. If someone were to tap her at that moment, she would have fallen

over. Her legs were noodles. She watched him walk
out of the door, her breathing retrieving its normal rhythm the farther away he was from her.

Aphtan smiled at his tenacity. She'd never had a
guy approach her like that. It was different to her,
so foreign. She couldn't tell if it was genuine, because where she was from, the approach was opposite. The magnetic connection between them
promised more conversations, and she couldn't
wait.

"Damn, he looked right through me." Mila shook
her head with disbelief. "It seem like he wants you."

"Is that so hard to believe?" They started walking through the now empty hallway.

"Well, over me, yes, very hard to believe." Mila
nudged her in a playful manner.

"Fuck you." Aphtan laughed as the rays of the
sun met them after they went through the double
doors. "Let's go. We can't miss the bus, even
though your ass missed it this morning."

"Girl, I'm over buses." Mila pulled a pair of keys
out of her purse and dangled them in Aphtan's
face.

"Who car you stole?" Aphtan laughed, thinking
her friend was talking shit like usual.

"It's mine." Mila hit the button on the keys, and
the lights on a brand new Lexus flashed twice. "It
was a gift."

Aphtan grabbed the keys out of Mila's hand and
hit the alarm for confirmation. As the lights
flashed at her command, she walked closer to
make sure the shiny new car with dealer tags was
really there and she wasn't imagining it. Other students looked on as she rubbed the cherry red
paint with the palm of her hand.

Aphtan looked back at Mila. The bus they normally rode zoomed by on the street behind them. Mila smiled as she ran over to the door to open it. She signaled for Aphtan to get inside as she rubbed her manicured nail around the rim of the steering wheel. She danced in the seat with excitement as Aphtan entered through the passenger door with hesitation.

Aphtan rubbed the leather seats that were underneath her as she closed the door behind her. She felt the new dashboard and tried to remember the last time she had been in a new car. The new car smell invaded her nostrils as she looked at Mila in disbelief. She tossed her the keys, the silent ignition started, and they were pulling off in an instant.

"This isn't bad for a bitch from the slums of Dallas, huh?" Mila tossed a small sack of weed onto Aphtan's lap.

"Spill." Aphtan started to break down the weed. "One day we're riding the bus and the next day you in a brand new fucking car. What's up?"

"I saved up for this." Mila cut down the radio. "I've been working this whole school year. This is my graduation gift to myself."

"Bitch, we stay in the projects. A fifty-thousand-dollar car is unheard of for girls like us. Are you in some illegal shit?"

"Aphtan, you know me better than that." Mila threw a lighter in her direction. "I've been working. Trust me."

"When the fuck did you get a job?" Aphtan emptied the guts of the cigar out of the window after she broke it down.

"You know how I been missing parties, football

games, basketball games, and other shit?" Mila raised her eyebrows.

"Yes," Aphtan answered.

"Well, I've been working at Pearl Tongue for the past eleven months."

Aphtan stopped putting the weed inside of the cigar as she looked at Mila. They had been friends since they were kids. They'd been staying next door to each other in the projects for years. The last thing that she wanted to see was her friend become a statistic. They had made a promise to each other to do better, so they could live better. All she wanted was for them to get out of the projects.

"Come on, Mila," Aphtan exhaled. "Are you fucking kidding me?"

"See, that's why I didn't want to tell you shit." Mila hit the brakes with full force. "Don't fucking judge me, Aphtan. I'm not playing."

"Shaking your ass to music for strangers for money, Mila? We are better than that, my nigga."

"No, you're better than that." Mila turned to look at Aphtan. "I don't have straight A's and acceptance letters from every college in America, Aphtan. You got the brains, and that's a beautiful thing, but I don't. This is how I'm going to have to make money. Either this or taking orders at fucking McDonalds."

"Mila, we promised to get the fuck out of this place; out of our situation."

"I'm going to keep that promise. We both gone get there. We just have to take different roads. It'll be the same destination, I promise." Mila grabbed her leg. "Anyways, let's change the topic. Do you like that Cole dude?"

"I don't even know him." Aphtan licked the

cigar to close it. "He's fine, though." She put the blunt in her mouth and lit it.

"Yes, he is." Mila bit her lips and started grinding in her seat.

"You're a yamp." Aphtan laughed as she passed the blunt to her.

"Sometimes." They both laughed. "You going to the party tonight?"

"I want to, but I got a lot of homework." Aphtan rubbed her fingers through her hair. "Besides, I don't have anything to wear." She grabbed the blunt from Mila's hand.

"Cole is probably going to be there."

"What the fuck does that mean?"

"It means that you should go. Let's go to the mall, peel some shit like we used to, and go have a good time."

"I don't know." Aphtan wrapped her lips around the blunt and inhaled.

"Aph, we have to go, it's Friday. You'll have all weekend to get your school work done."

"Okay." She rolled her eyes as Mila sped down the busy street.

They pulled up at North Park Mall as a light trickle of rain fell onto the dark tinted windows of the car. The sun still shone through the mist as they made their way into the clear double doors. They had a plan; they had been stealing at this mall since they were thirteen years old. They knew security guards by name and flirted with them on purpose. The map of the mall had been tattooed on their brains. They could maneuver through the whole establishment with closed eyes.

Store after store, they hit without a problem.

From the outside looking in, no one could tell that they had four full outfits apiece underneath their clothing. They didn't speak during the hits; they communicated with nods and facial gestures. They were professionals, and there wasn't anything from any store that they couldn't steal.

Thirty minutes had passed, which was their time limit to stay at the mall. They met each other at the escalator, their agreed place to meet up at a certain time. The escalators carried them slowly down as they noticed a group of cops going up on the opposite side. When the cops saw them and started to walk down the escalator that was going up, they understood they had been caught.

"Fuck," Mila said softly without panicking. "Aphtan, we got an issue." She nodded toward the cops. "Don't be stupid, bitch. Get away, don't hold on to shit."

"Oh, my God," Aphtan hyperventilated. "I can't go to jail. I can't fuck up my shit by having a record."

"You won't," Mila said as their feet hit the bottom level. "Run." She sprinted off.

The world passed Aphtan physically, sure, but her mind was racing as well, and that blurred disposition smearing by her line of vision was also all of the what-ifs and worries that she was thinking about. They dashed through the mall, hitting shoppers with no remorse as the cops ran after them.

"Split up," Mila yelled as she made a swift turn and Aphtan continued to run forward.

Aphtan trembled as she continued to run. Her slanted eyes filled up with tears, and for the first time in a while, tears were coming from her eyes.

She glanced back at the cops as the entrance to the mall got closer. She clenched her jaw and wiped the sweat from her brow.

All she could think about was her dresser full of college acceptance letters. All that crossed her mind was obtaining a college degree and making it. The last thing she needed was to have it all end before it even began. She had to get away.

Aphtan rushed through the entrance doors as she looked back to see the cops right on her tail. She looked forward, and before she could react, she had run into a man at full speed. They fell onto the ground as the cops surrounded them. She held up her hands with her eyes closed. Her head banged with pain from the collision.

"Lay flat on your stomach," one of the cops yelled as they drew their guns.

"Please," Aphtan yelled hysterically as she opened her eyes, "don't take me to jail."

"Shut the fuck up," another cop yelled as spit sprayed from his mouth.

Her intestines curled into her stomach, hands clawing up her throat and choking her, letting the words coming out of her mouth drag back down her throat and dissolve into the acid of her belly. Her heart throbbed violently like a fatigued wolf howling at the iridescent moon concealed in the black velvet sky. Laboriously, her hands began to perspire as the feeling of anxiety surged through her tender body like a waterfall cascading over granite boulders.

"Hey," the man that Aphtan had run into yelled as another man helped him off of the ground, "it's no need to be that rough with her."

"Sir, you need to shut the fuck up," another officer ordered.

Aphtan cried silently with her face pressed against the hot concrete pavement. Embarrassed, she tried to hide her face from the crowd of people who stopped to see the story end. The coolness from the handcuffs caused her to jump as the sound of them closing around her wrist made her sick to her stomach.

She rose from the smoldering ground with force from the arresting officer. Her jeans were stained with rocks and dirt from the ground. Her chest moved in and out animalistically, reacting to how hard she was crying. Her hair flowed loosely, a little bit of dirt showing at the ends.

"Who did you just tell to shut the fuck up?" The man walked toward the officer. "Were you talking to me?"

Aphtan opened her eyes, despite how she felt, and the first face that entered her view was the man that she had collided with. Aphtan's tears eased up as she noticed the Spartan-type figure in front of her. She couldn't help it; his appearance could brighten up the darkest nights.

"Sir, stand back," the officer ordered the man as he gulped loudly.

"How much did she steal?" The man looked at Aphtan up and down.

"From all of the stores, I would say about twelve thousand dollars' worth," the arrogant manager of one of the stores chimed in as the crowd gasped.

The man snapped his fingers at the dude that helped him up. "If I pay for everything that she stole, will you not press charges?"

"I suppose." The manager walked over to the clothes and collected them in her hand. "But who has that kind of money?"

"Here." The man walked over to the manager. "Pay all of the stores." He handed her a stack of crisp one-hundred-dollar bills.

"We still can take her in," the arresting cop spewed. "She still committed a crime."

The man walked over to the officer. "Since the theft was paid and the manager herself said she wouldn't press charges, you can let her go. If you don't, I promise you, you won't like what will happen."

"Are you threatening me?" The officer put his hand on his gun.

"I'm promising you this. Now, let her fucking go," the man snarled.

A relief eased over Aphtan as the handcuffs were removed from her wrists one by one. As soon as she could, she walked off slowly. Her slow walking turned into a slow-paced run. She had to get away. The shame she was feeling from it all was too much. She wanted to thank her knight in shining armor, but she would have to save that for another time.

She peeked over in the parking lot at Mila's new car, which was sparkling from the sun's glow, wondering if she had gotten away. She eased through the lot, the busy street to cross to get away from the mall right in front of her. Before her feet could hit the tar-lined surface, the screeching of a car gripped her attention. She turned around and saw through the open window the man who had helped her. He opened the door, got out, and started to walk toward her.

Upon his arrival, Aphtan felt her heart begin to race. Her eyes traced his tall, muscular figure, from his freshly cut waves down to the custom Nikes at his feet. The closer he got, the better she could view him. His eyes were warm, a range of soft colors, reminding her of sweet caramel. Lilac bags hung under them, aging him quite a bit, but he couldn't be much older than her nonetheless.

Seeing him stumble a bit, she relaxed. He was just as nervous as she was. Aphtan took a deep breath, inhaling his overly strong cologne. Naturally, she found herself lost in the powerful scent. However, his broad smile prevented that, and instead it transformed the scent into one she would not want to forget any time soon.

"You forgot your clothes." He paused as he held the clothes out in front of him for her to grab as he waited to hear her name.

"Aphtan," she whispered, still embarrassed as she grabbed the clothes.

"Aphtan," he said to himself as he smiled. "How old are you, Aphtan?"

"Seventeen." She tried not to make eye contact with him. "I don't want you to think I'm this hood ass girl who is a thief."

"No judgment." He held his hand up. "We all do shit that we aren't necessarily proud of. Did you need a ride?"

"No." Aphtan looked up at him. "I need to walk. I need to clear my head."

"Understandable." He walked toward the car. "Be careful and stay out of trouble, Aphtan."

"Hey?" She walked toward the car as he got inside. "Thank you for what you did. You have no idea what you just did for me. I'm forever grateful."

"No problem." He winked at her. "Just stay out of trouble."

"What is your name?" Aphtan asked as the car slowly accelerated.

"When you turn eighteen, I'll refresh your memory." The man smiled before the car zoomed off.

The atmosphere around her became so much more pleasant. The soothing sounds of the light rain pattering on the cars around took her to what felt like a world of only calmness; a place where all of the weight on her shoulders was lifted away. The fearful lightning was present, but through that, she could look up and see the baby-blue sky, so beautiful. A cheerful sun shone through the clouds and all that felt gloomy was gone. Aphtan felt almost enlightened.

The small drops of water attacked her body, making her awaken from the daydream that she was in. She ran across the grass that separated the parking lot from the street to make it to the bus stop. She rushed inside of the booth that protected the riders from different weather conditions and took a seat.

Aphtan leaned back in the connected gray seat with a heavy mind. Mila, Cole, and the mystery man she had just encountered hijacked her mind at full speed. She was worried about Mila and wondered if she had been as lucky as she was and got away. The last thing she wanted was for them to become a product of their environment. With the close encounter that they had just experienced, she wasn't so sure that she deserved more after all.

She stood up when she saw the bus, the thousands of dollars' worth of clothes in her hands. She joined the line and waited her turn to step onto the dark, musky-smelling bus. As the doors closed behind her, she found a seat and stared out of the windows while the rain poured effortlessly on the glass.

A very faint smell of the cleaner used to clean the floor lingered around. It was about the most positive smell on the bus, though. While moving, slight odors of diesel and exhaust distracted Aphtan from focusing upon more worthwhile scents: the career woman who wore that elusive fragrance, the bum's fetid breath and bad odor. The taco sauce that the two boys played with and one stomped on it, spraying its contents across to the wall of the other side of the bus about an inch from the floor.

As the man who had to stand adjusted his stance, she detected the hint of Aqua Velva, or Old Spice. Then the world seemed to get close, too close, when the bus stopped for passengers, and two young urbanites bound up the bus steps and shoved their change into the fare machine. One smelled of beer and cigarettes, the other of gasoline and grease.

Aphtan blew out a sigh of relief from her mouth when her projects came into view. She pulled on the string to let the driver know that it was her stop as she stood up. She eased through the aisle when the bus stopped and paced down the steps to get off. The doors closed behind her as she stepped onto the sidewalk.

"Aphtan," one of the little boys from the neighborhood called out as he ran up to her.

"What's up?" She looked at the little boy.

"Can you help me with my homework again? Please," the little boy begged. "I really want to make a good grade."

"Tyrone." She leaned down so her face could be in his. "Of course I'll help you. You have to promise me something, though."

"What?" Tyrone smiled.

"That you'll make it out of this place."

"I promise." He ran off. "I'll come over as soon as I grab my homework."

"Okay." She continued walking.

"That was close," Mila screamed from the open window of her car as music blasted for all to hear when she pulled up next to Aphtan.

"Too fucking close." Aphtan walked up to the car. "I'm glad you got away." She tossed the clothes in the window. "I know you dumped everything. Take one of these outfits and meet me later at my house before we head out."

"You good?" Mila cut the music down.

"Hell, no." Aphtan stood straight up. "I will be, though."

"The nail shop?"

"I would, but I have to help Tyrone with his homework."

"Still trying to save the hood?" Mila shook her head.

"Just meet me at my house in a couple of hours." Aphtan flipped the bird before walking away.

"Look at all of that ass back there." Mila laughed, messing with her friend. "Make sure your ass is ready. Don't be playing tutor all night."

Aphtan waved her friend off as she heard the

tires screeching. She spoke to different people as she made her way to her apartment building. She opened up the large brown door and walked up the tan stairs. She opened the door as Mila's mother came out of the door across the hall.

"Aphtan, have you seen Mila's ass?" She put her hands on her hips.

"No, ma'am," Aphtan lied, shaking her head.

Aphtan looked at Ms. Franklin up and down. From the banana peels on her head, to the jelly slippers on her feet, she defined the word *ghetto*. The colorful matching warm-up suit she had on proved that. She was a pretty woman, but she had become too comfortable in her situation. She looked exactly like Mila but with age on her.

"If you do, please tell her ass that I'm looking for her." She rolled her eyes.

"I got it." Aphtan closed the door after she went into her apartment.

Aphtan walked into the somewhat shabby, down-at-the-heels apartment in among others just the same. Peeling paint, sagging wallpaper, threadbare rugs. It had obviously seen better days, but she could if she took the time to look carefully see glimpses of what could almost be opulence in the faded silk drapes and the dim, dusty lampshades.

Echoes of grander times and decadent parties when fashionable, beautiful laughing girls danced and sang, and athletic, handsome men laughed back and ensured their glasses were never empty. But now, it was just a project apartment.

"Mama?" Aphtan knocked on her door. "Are you here?"

As she walked into the bedroom, she saw her mother lying facedown, with clothes all around her. To her right was a pipe, still hot to the touch. Aphtan walked over to her side and checked her pulse. She closed her eyes and blew as a heartbeat danced around her fingertips.

She pulled the cover off of the bed and covered her mother's tiny frame. She reached down and gave her a kiss on her forehead. She grabbed the necklace around her neck, admiring the locket. It was the only thing that her mother wouldn't sell for rocks, and she respected that. It was a family heirloom passed down from generation to generation. No matter how hard times got, it was the only thing her mother held onto.

She left out of the room, closing the door behind her. She walked to the living room as memories of her life as a child hit her. Thoughts of her mother, before the drugs controlled her actions, brought tears to her eyes. She wiped them as she remembered the promise that she made herself. That she would do whatever it took to get them out of the projects. And that she would do everything to get her clean once and for all.

CHAPTER 9

"I don't know, Aphtan." Tyrone poked the side of his head with the eraser end of the pencil.

"Think." Aphtan pulled her chair closer to him. "You know this."

"Is it,"—he paused—"seven?"

"See." She grabbed his face. "You're smarter than you think."

"You really think so?" He smiled.

"Absolutely." Aphtan stood up as someone started to knock on the door. "Your brain is like your body, Tyrone. You have to train it constantly if you want results."

"Simone, I know you're in there," the manager of the projects screamed through the door as she approached it. "You're two months behind. You have to pay the rent."

Aphtan swung the door open. "My mother is asleep."

"I don't give a damn if she is on the moon." The small Latino man tried to force himself inside. "I need to talk to her, face to face."

"Aphtan put her hand up to block his attempts. "She's not available right now. Come back tomorrow."

"You always tell me that, Aphtan." He put his finger up and shook it. "I'm tired of the same fucking excuses from you two. If she can buy—"

"It's no need to go there." Mila walked up the stairs as the small red dress she had on hugged her body like it was her skin. "How much are they behind?"

"Two months." He moved out of the way to let Mila walk inside.

Mila dug around inside of her purse. "That's fifty dollars, right?"

"Exactly," he agreed.

"Here, motherfucker." She handed him a one-hundred-dollar bill. "That's for the two late months and for the two months coming up. Don't come around here fucking with them anymore."

"That's all I needed." The man walked down the stairs.

Aphtan closed the door after Mila walked inside. "You didn't have to do that."

"That's what family is for." Mila sat down at the table with Tyrone. "What's up, little punk?"

"Shut up, Mila." He got up and put his papers inside his backpack.

"Are you leaving?" Aphtan asked him.

"Yes." He gave her a hug after putting his backpack on his back. "If Mila is here, you know no one in the room can focus."

"Ain't that a bitch." Mila laughed.

"Smart kid." Aphtan walked him to the door and opened it. "I'm here anytime for you, Tyrone."

"Thanks." He ran down the stairs.

"What's the plan for tonight?" Aphtan closed the door then sat back down at the table.

"First, we do something with that hair of yours. This isn't any ordinary party. Everyone from the hood is going to be there and most people from school. We may even run into Cole." She started blowing kisses.

"Bitch, you're childish." Aphtan stood up and ran her fingers through her hair. "What did you do with the other fits?"

"I sold them." Mila handed her some money. "You know how we do it."

"What am I going to wear?" Aphtan put the money inside of her bra.

"Of course, I didn't forget about you." Mila pulled a dress out of her gigantic purse. "Let's go get you ready."

An hour and a half later, they found themselves in front of the hottest nightclub in the city, Jaguar. Aphtan walked past the crowd with Mila following, knowing that the hottest of the hot got in; no matter if the club was full or not. Side by side, they strutted down the sidewalk until they were in front of the bouncer. He eyed them up and down, smiled, and lifted the rope to let them inside. That let Aphtan know that they were on point.

A whiff of unpleasant and repulsive body odor filled the atmosphere while the stench of cigarettes wafted from the hallway that led inside. A large, corpulent, and hideous being struggled his way by them as the lights from inside finally hit their eyes. Music becoming the loudest thing in the room, it was damn near impossible to hear each other.

Aphtan eased through the crowd, Mila on her

tail as they made their way to the bar. She looked up
at the VIP section as the see-through glass showed
her everyone who was up there. Strobe lights continued to flash in her face as she checked her surroundings. Everyone she knew from the city was
present. It was possibly the hottest party of the
year.

Aphtan shoved away from hands of men trying
to get at her. It was constant, but she was used to it.
She looked back and noticed that Mila was getting
the same treatment. They were beautiful. It was
nothing new to them. They approached the bar
and eyed the circular stand to see who was going
to be responsible for their tab that night.

"Him." Mila nodded toward a man with his back
turned to them.

He was the kind of man that Aphtan knew
looked good, even from behind. She didn't need to
see his face. The suit that he wore was confirmation
enough that he was a man with money and power.
Aphtan looked at her best friend to let her know
that she had it before she walked over to the man.

She fixed the expensive gold dress that she wore
to make sure that it rested on her curves perfectly.
She swung her hair side to side and walked with
the poise of a model. The heels on her feet barely
touched the floor she was walking so smoothly.
She was in predator mode, and he was her prey.

"Excuse me?" Aphtan tapped the man's back.

The man turned around with a scolded expression. Aphtan watched a smile spread across his
face once they locked eyes. It was the man who
saved her earlier. She turned red immediately and
smiled softly. She looked down at the floor. He
made her feel like a little girl, and she couldn't

face him. Not with the embarrassing scenario from earlier still being so fresh.

"Aphtan?" He leaned in so that she could hear him over the music.

"That's my name." She looked up at him.

"What are you doing here?" He grabbed the glass of Hennessy from the bartender behind Aphtan.

"The same thing as you." She pulled her dress down a little more.

"Is that so?" He looked her up and down and shook his head.

"What?" She looked back at the ground.

"You're too fucking tempting, Aphtan. You're embarrassing every woman in here." He walked around her so he could get a better look.

"Stop playing." She rubbed her hands together.

"I'm serious." He sipped the chilled brown drink in his hand. "I never play with a beautiful woman."

"Thank you."

He leaned in so close that she could smell the fresh drink on his lips. "I'm in the VIP tonight. Whoever you're with, grab them, and come fuck with me."

"You remember that I'm seventeen, right," she screamed over the music.

He bit his bottom lip. "Tonight you're however old I want you to be."

Aphtan watched him walk through the crowd as the lights flashed wildly in her eyes. She stood there, observing his movements. Watching him walk up the stairs and going through the VIP entrance was all the confirmation that she needed. She walked back over to where Mila was in a flash.

"Bitch." Aphtan tapped Mila, who was conversing with a neighborhood roughneck. "Mila?" She shoved her body.

"What?" Mila turned around with an attitude.

"We just got invited up to VIP."

"You lying." She shooed the man she was talking to away. "By whom?"

"I don't know his name," Aphtan admitted. "But he helped me out earlier at the mall when I got caught."

"You got caught earlier, bitch, and you didn't tell me?" Mila changed the subject.

"It was nothing to tell. I got caught, he paid for the clothes, and they let me go." Aphtan shrugged one of her shoulders.

"Let's go, then." Mila grabbed her hand and led them through the crowd.

Aphtan went willingly. She had never been into a VIP section before. She had been going to clubs since she was sixteen, and not once had she seen how it looked in VIP with her own eyes. Having men gawk over her was normal, but to have a man invite her to VIP was a different level.

She looked at the women that were dancing around the rope that separated the rest of the club from the VIP and wondered if what the man had said was true about how she looked. The women around the entrance were the hottest of the hot. They were the women that got into VIP every week, yet she was passing them up to go in without even trying.

The man securing the VIP lifted the rope when they got close enough. Aphtan looked back as the rope was put back into place within a second. She sniffed as the smell changed while they walked up the stairs. The lighting was different, and the music that played in the room was different as well.

"Which one was it?" Mila asked as she eyed the room.

"Him." Aphtan nodded toward the man as he engaged in conversation with other men in suits.

"The one with the maroon gaiters on?" Mila's eyes opened with excitement.

"Yes," Aphtan answered and then waved at the man. "That's him."

"Aphtan, do you not remember who the fuck that is?" Mila grabbed her and turned her around with her. "That's Scooter."

"Who?" Aphtan held her hands out in front of her.

"He used to work for your father. He used to be around a lot when we were growing up, but he disappeared after your old man got locked up. He is the youngest nigga with the most power in the drug game since your father." Mila licked her lips. "Introduce me to him, Aphtan. This is a different level, girl. This is the big leagues. That nigga comes to Pearl Tongue and spends a hundred stacks like it's nothing. He's that nigga right now."

Aphtan thought back to when she was a kid as memories of Scooter came back to her like a Frisbee thrown into the sky. He looked different as a grown man. She hadn't seen him in years. There was no wonder she didn't recognize him. He grew up to look how she expected him to. He was dapper and intelligent. A younger version of her father.

"I'm glad you accepted my invitation." Scooter approached them, interrupting their conversation.

Mila turned around first. "It was our pleasure."

"What she said." Aphtan turned around to face him.

"Come take a seat with us." He grabbed Aphtan's hand and led her. "If you want something to eat or drink, just say it."

"I am a little parched," Mila chimed in.

"And you are?" Scooter looked at her with squinted eyes.

"I'm Aphtan's best friend, Mila."

"Nice to meet you." Scooter nodded at her as they all sat on the plush, long, white couch. "Aphtan, do you want something to drink also?"

"A Coke is fine." She crossed her legs.

"I want something a little bit stronger than that." Mila crossed her legs the same way.

"Something like what?" Scooter signaled for the waitress to come over.

"Whatever is in your glass that you're drinking." Mila smiled.

"Two Hennessys straight up and a Coke," Scooter told the waitress.

"I'm confused." Aphtan looked at him. "If you have someone to go get your drinks, why were you downstairs?"

"It's simple." He stood up as a group of men walked toward them. "Sometimes I like to see the surroundings with my own eyes."

"Scooter, how you living, baby?" one of the men asked as he shook his hand.

"I'm good, Levi. How are you living?" Scooter stepped back to look at the man. "I see that's a high thread count on that suit, my nigga."

"I'm trying." Levi looked past him at Mila. "Don't you work at Pearl Tongue?"

"That's her business," Aphtan answered for her. "We're not at Pearl Tongue, so whether she works there or not doesn't matter at this moment."

"My bad, damn." Levi held his hands up. "I didn't mean anything by it."

"It's cool." Scooter looked at Aphtan with a smirk. "It's all love."

"I'll get at you a little later, cousin." Levi shook his hand as his eyes stayed on Mila.

"Bet," Scooter said as the waitress set the drinks on the table in front of the couch.

"What a fucking creep." Aphtan grabbed the Coke and sipped it.

"He didn't mean any harm." Scooter passed Mila her drink after sitting down. "I'm always in Pearl Tongue, and I thought you looked familiar as well."

Mila took the Hennessy to the head. "I definitely see you in there a lot."

"A lot?" Aphtan laughed. "So you love the strippers, huh?"

"What man doesn't like the strip club?" He leaned back into the couch. "Besides, I don't have someone who looks like you waiting for me at home."

"That's shocking." Aphtan set her glass down. "I can't believe a man like you is single."

"I never said I was single, Aphtan." He smiled. "You have to pay closer attention to what I say."

"I do?" Aphtan rolled her eyes slowly.

"Yes, you do. I said, I don't have someone who looks like you. I have someone there. She's just not you, Aphtan," he confessed.

"Why would she ever let you leave the house by yourself?"

"Let?" He looked at her with a serious face. "Nobody can let me do anything. I do what I want, when I want. I'm a grown ass man."

"I'll be right back." Mila stood up and walked toward Levi.

"I see someone has a fan." Scooter pulled a blunt out of his pocket and lit it. "Do you smoke?"

Aphtan reached over, grabbed the blunt from his lips, and hit it. "I don't know. Maybe."

"You're not as innocent as your face says." He grabbed her thigh, his eyes playing tag with hers. "You grew up to look exactly how I thought you would."

"Now you want to admit that we know each other." She exhaled.

"You finally figured it out?" He grabbed the blunt back from her.

"With Mila's help, I did. I haven't seen you since I was ten years old. It seems like when my father went to jail, everybody disappeared."

"That's the game." He shrugged his shoulders. "Loyalty is rare in these streets."

"I see." She leaned back into the couch. "Whatever happened to that one girl I had a fight with back then?"

"The one who checked you for crushing on me." He laughed.

"No, the one I beat up for thinking that I was crushing on you." She laughed, too.

"I don't know." He held his hands up and puffed from the blunt, holding it with his mouth. "She around, I guess."

Time flew as they sat and conversed. Countless people came in and out of the VIP section; however, all they saw was each other. Seconds turned into minutes, and minutes turned into hours. Before they realized it, the club was closing, and all of the lights turned on in an instant. They stood up to leave as everyone else did the same.

"Here." Mila handed her keys to Aphtan after she approached her and Scooter. "Drive my car home. I have a ride home." She looked back at Levi.

"Mila, you're drunk." Aphtan grabbed her arm. "Do you really think you need to leave with a nigga that we don't know?"

"He's good people," Scooter assured.

"It's cool," Mila slurred. "I'll see you tomorrow."

"Be careful, Mila." Aphtan released her grip on her and watched her walk into Levi's arm. "He better be good people." She looked at Scooter with a raised eyebrow. "Or that's your ass along with his."

"So you threatening me," he asked as they made their way down the stairs.

"It's a promise. She's like blood to me."

"I promise you, he's cool, Aphtan."

The crowd split and made a walkway whenever they saw Scooter coming. Aphtan grinned at the pull that he had. She had never talked to a man with so much power. Hell, she had never talked to a man, period. Every guy she had ever talked to was a boy. This was all new to her. It intrigued her, and that was a first.

Her focus had always been on school. For as long as she could remember that was the only thing that mattered. It had always been her main priority. She saw too many girls with potential who gave it all up for a man, and all they got out of it was a baby and no future. She refused to be one of those girls.

"How can I get in touch with you whenever I want to hear your voice?" he asked as they walked through the entrance, the night air brushing against the skin that showed on their bodies.

"I thought you had someone at home who has a voice that you should love to hear." Aphtan folded her arms together. "Besides, I don't have a phone."

"Mind your business." He waved at one of his men as they continued to walk. "You have on a two-thousand-dollar dress, but no phone?"

"Don't forget that you paid for this two-thousand-dollar dress," she said as her teeth chattered.

"It was a good decision. Especially since I get to see how it looks on you."

"What kind of game are you playing with me?" Aphtan hit the button on the key ring to unlock the door to Mila's Lexus.

"No game." He looked at the car. "Whose whip is that?"

"Mila's," she answered before walking to the door of the car.

Scooter put his hand out to grab a phone from his man who had walked up on them. "This is so I can reach you." He handed her the phone. "It's brand new. Just cut it on and use it."

"I can't accept this." Aphtan reached for the door.

"Yes, you can." He reached quicker to open the door for her. "My future wife doesn't open doors when I'm around."

"Now I'm your future wife?" Aphtan sat down in the seat. "That's funny, because you never even told me your name. All of these years and all I know you by is Scooter."

"You know my name." He smiled. "Everyone knows my name."

"I want you to tell me." She started the car.

"Christopher Wayne Dixon."

"I got it." Aphtan waved the phone at him before closing the door.

"You better use it, girl," he called out as she pulled off.

Aphtan tossed the phone onto the passenger seat when she came to the red light at the end of the street. She cut on the heat and let the radiant feeling warm her body. She looked through the rearview mirror and saw Scooter crossing the street to go back inside the club. Familiar with his line of work, she could only assume that he had some unfinished business to take care of in the club.

At the change of the light, she accelerated, half her focus still on the man in the rearview mirror. She reached over with a free hand and powered the phone on, as the night she had just had felt like a dream. She had bagged the hottest nigga in the whole city. That night, he only had eyes for her, and it made her feel special.

The sound of the phone ringing startled her. She grabbed it and looked at the number that was flashing on the screen. It was local. Without a doubt it was Scooter calling. Aphtan pulled over to a corner store and parked. She hit the button to answer as she laid her head back on the headrest.

"What took you so long to answer?"

"What took you so long to call?" She looked through Mila's purse, which was on the floor, for some money.

"That had to be one, two minutes, tops," he bellowed through the receiver.

"One or two minutes too late," she teased as she got out of the car.

"I want to see you."

"When?" She went inside of the store.

"Is tomorrow good for you?"

"I have some studying to do." She pointed out the pack of cigarillos she wanted to the clerk.

"You really are as innocent as you look."

"I'm just trying to get out the hood." Aphtan nodded her head at the clerk and handed him the money as he held up a box.

"I feel you."

"After I get done, I can call you. We can set something up."

"Whew," he sighed. "I thought you were going to blow a nigga off."

"I should." She grabbed the box and change from the clerk. "But I'm interested."

"Aphtan," a voice called out as she walked out of the store.

"I'll call you tomorrow," Aphtan whispered into the phone as she saw Cole waving from afar and walking toward her. "Is that cool?"

"Yeah, that's cool." He hung up the phone.

"Damn, you are wearing that dress." Cole walked up on her. "Where are you coming from looking like that?"

"Jaguar," she said coldly.

"Me, too." He leaned on Mila's car. "I didn't see you in there."

"You weren't looking hard enough." Aphtan opened up the door to the car.

"This you?" he asked as he pushed himself off of the car.

"No, this is Mila." She started the car.

"When we gone make that happen?" He fixed the fitted cap on his head.

"Make what happen?" Aphtan put her seat belt on.

"Us getting to know each other." He pulled at his beard.

"I don't know."

"Hand me your phone." He reached out until she put the phone that Scooter had given her not even ten minutes prior in his hand. "I'm putting my number in here. Use it." He handed her back the phone.

"I'll think about it." She closed the door.

"That's all I can ask for, beautiful."

Aphtan reversed, zoomed through the parking lot, and headed home. She couldn't believe that she had two guys sweating her. She was always approached, just never like this. She didn't know what to expect. She didn't know which one of them to talk to. What was certain was that she couldn't wait to wake up and use both of the numbers that had been given to her. She wanted to get to know both of them, no matter the cost.

CHAPTER 10

It wasn't completely dark in the dingy hotel room; it was that in between day and night dimness when Mila awakened. The light from sunrise gleamed gently through the outdated orange curtains. They were embellished boldly with a garish yellow pattern. It reminded her of the summer dresses she wore to church as a little girl. They were hideous.

Time moved slowly as she took in every detail of the hotel room while the hangover headache hit her full force. The cheap off-white ceiling tiles made of polystyrene; the damp coming in through the sky light; the various mismatched furnishings; and the smell of tacky sweet peach air freshener. There wasn't a stir, just the murmur of the television from the room below.

Mila crawled to the end of the bed to put some clothes on as she looked at a sleeping Levi underneath the covers. She was cold, her hairs stood on end, as a draft seeped in through the skylight. The smell of his cologne still clung to her body as she put her panties on. The scent made her stomach even more upset.

"Did he use a rubber?" she asked herself aloud as she slid the dress up her shivering frame.

She tiptoed over to the window and peeped through the curtains, letting a glimmer of light shine through the room. The view was raw and beautiful. She could see the city's high-rises, a concrete jungle, but the morning sky contrasted with it. The bright orange, pink, and indigo colors ran through the clouds like a painting.

She slid the patio door open after much difficulty. The handle was rusty and stiff to move. The hinges complained as they let out a screech when she finally got the door free. She walked carefully on the balcony, minding the shattered glass, trying to be as quiet as possible. She breathed in the cold morning air and took in the extraordinary view. The scene was beautiful, yet chaotic at the same time. Although there was an air of ugliness about the hotel, her view told a different story.

Mila had never seen that side of the city. She was from the slums. She couldn't remember staying at a hotel room that didn't come with bedbugs and roaches. Although the room wasn't as nice as she wanted it to be, it was nicer than the many she had seen before. For that, she was humbled.

The silence was broken by yawning from inside of the room. Mila smiled, knowing that she would be accompanied by Levi at any moment. She faced the door that led to the patio and waited for it to open. When the other side faded with darkness, she knew the door was about to open.

"Did I wake you?" She walked up to him as he stood in the door way fully naked.

"I can't sleep if you're not next to me." He leaned down to give her a kiss.

She smiled as she closed her eyes.

"Are you okay?" He wrapped his arms around her.

"I have a horrible headache."

"It's that dark liquor." He kissed her forehead. "You weren't playing last night." He laughed.

"I need some medicine." She put her head against his chest. "Can you go get me some?"

"I got you." He smacked her on the booty before walking through the door.

"Thank you." She walked in after him. "Did we use a condom last night?"

"Nope." He put on a shirt.

"Fuck." She sat on the edge of the bed.

"It's cool. I'll grab one of them morning-after pills."

"Good thinking." She lay back onto the sheets.

"Do you need anything else?" He walked to the door to leave.

"No, I'm good." She heard the door close behind him.

Memories of trips to the abortion clinic and health department had Mila on edge. She didn't have any more names to make up to use at the clinics. She rubbed her stomach and prayed that whatever pill Levi brought back would work. She didn't want any kids, mainly with a dude that she didn't know.

* * *

It wasn't love at first sight for Aphtan. It wasn't infatuation at first sight, either. It was a slow and growing fondness for Scooter, a surprising discovery of little quirks and twists. It all caught her eye like finding little seashells on the sandy shore and feeling bound to each and every one of them. You stick them in your pocket and examine them later in the solitude of the four walls of your room. Exactly like how she later examined the notions of the night before in the space occupied by her still wandering mind.

Yet, no matter how sharp the human mind, the aftermath stays a recollection of events seen in false light. This beam is of a rather fickle nature. It is constantly altered by the state life unwillingly throws us in until the next tide washes another wave your way.

And in the state she was in, was for once a lonely one, craving a companion, a feeling Aphtan was not all familiar with or never complained about.

However, that morning as Aphtan lay in bed with the corners of her lips slightly slipping into a tipsy resemblance of a grin, she magnified last night to an extravaganza of fun affairs and heart-bounding first encounters. Before long her excited mind started slipping into a lulled state of altered universes. Thoughts distorted into exaggerated stories bound to escape her consciousness the next time she opened her eyes.

"Aphtan," her mother's voice echoed throughout the apartment. "Aphtan, get your ass up," she screamed.

Aphtan removed the covers from her head as she checked the phone at her side to see if she had missed any calls. She sat up in the bed and stretched, letting out a long yawn. She walked out of the room to find her mother. She could feel an argument brewing. Her mother was confrontational, and by the screech of her voice, she was craving crack. That was when she was the meanest.

"Yes, Mama?" Aphtan sat down on the couch.

"I need some money, Aphtan. Rent is due." Simone ran her fingers through her wild hair and paced back and forth in front of the faded coffee table.

"It's paid, Mama."

"I don't need you to pay shit for me," she screamed. "You give me the money and I'll pay it. How it looks for my sixteen-year-old daughter paying rent?"

"I'm seventeen, Mama." Aphtan stood up. "It's paid; it's nothing to worry about."

"I need the food stamp card."

"It's food in there, Mama." Aphtan pointed to the kitchen. "It's fully stocked. Tell me what you want and I'll fix it for you."

"I can go to the store and buy my own shit." Simone turned her head to the side. "You think I'm going to sell the food stamps for a rock? You think you better than me, Aphtan? It's not my fault we in this situation. It's your sorry ass daddy's fault. His ass is the one locked up for God knows how long. Give me the food stamp card."

"I'm going to sleep." Aphtan walked out of the room.

"Aphtan." She grabbed her arm. "Please," she started to cry, "I just need the card for a little bit. I'll bring it back, I swear."

Tears filled her eyes. "I'm not giving you the card."

"Fuck you," Simone screamed as she pushed her. "Fuck you, Aphtan. You think you better than me. You are smelling yourself. I'm *your* mama. I'll beat your ass."

Aphtan closed the door to her room and slid down it until her body met the floor. This routine was common. Her mother would break the door down and start a fistfight if she didn't make it so she couldn't get in. She was tired of it. She didn't want to fight with her mama. She only wanted to help her.

"I'm leaving." Simone banged against the door. "Don't come looking for me, either."

Aphtan rushed to the phone on her bed as soon as she heard the front door close. She wiped her eyes as she went through the call log and found Scooter's number. It was early. She understood that he was probably with his woman. She needed to get away. She needed a fresh pair of ears to vent to, and his was the newest pair that she knew.

"Hello," he answered in a slur.

"Did I wake you?" Aphtan walked to her closet and grabbed some clothes to put on.

"Yes," he coughed into the phone, "you okay?"

"Yes." She sat on the bed. "No," she whimpered softly. "I just really need to get away."

"Where are you?"

"The projects." She walked to the bathroom and cut the shower on.

"I'm on my way."

"Okay." Aphtan hit the end button on the phone and set it on the sink.

The response was immediate. The metallic head that hung loosely above her spread water onto her body. The sudden shock made her tense her muscles. The water slowly warmed her, soothing the ache that clawed at her heart. She wished her day had started off better.

A tear tickled her cheek and mixed with the clean water as she poured gentle soap into her hands. Her fingers met her long red hair, dancing into the mess it was, ridding it of the knots sleep had given. She never wanted this to have happened. She never wanted to lose her mother, and sure enough, this only made her confidence crumble that she would one day.

Aphtan dragged the soap over her body. The action soothed her skin. It reminded her of brighter days. The soap caressed her neck like kisses, running along her body like gentle hands. More tears escaped her eyes, followed by her fist meeting the wall. She hated how she had to keep stuff bottled in. Now, she could let it all out.

Somewhere, above the surface, a young girl dropped to the floor, letting the water caress her skin as she broke down and wept. She needed to cry. She had been holding all of her feelings in since she was ten. It was time to let it all go emotionally.

She cut the water off and grabbed the lavender towel that hung from the shower rod. She wrapped it around her body, grabbed the phone from the sink, and went into her room. She dried her body roughly, letting the prickly towel run along her body. She felt numb.

"Aphtan," Mila yelled from the front door as she walked in.

"I'm in here," Aphtan yelled as she applied lotion to her body.

"I just need my car keys." Mila walked through the bedroom door. "What did Mama Simone do?" She sat on the bed after examining her face.

"She is just being her." Aphtan put her bra on.

"It's gone get better, Aph." She put her hand around her neck. "She will get clean one day."

"I hope so." Aphtan put the phone to her ear after it started to ring. "Hello?"

"Who phone is that?" Mila pointed to the phone.

"I'm downstairs," Scooter said into the phone.

"Here I come," Aphtan said before hanging up the phone.

"Bitch?" Mila stood up. "Who was that?"

"Scooter." Aphtan put her clothes on one piece at a time. "I need to clear my mind."

"What did y'all do last night for him to give you a phone?" Mila grilled.

"Nothing at all." Aphtan walked to her closet to get a pair of shoes. "We just talked. When we left the club, I came home. I don't know where he went. What about you?"

"Girl." Mila put her lips together and posed. "Levi fucked the shit out of me. To think all that dick was down there was mind blowing. Bitch, I cummed over and over."

"Did you make that nigga wrap it up?" Aphtan tied the laces on her Kool-Aid red Jordan's.

"I handled that, Aphtan." Mila rolled her eyes as they walked to the front door.

"Cool," Aphtan said as she opened the door and they walked out of it. "I'll get at you when I get back."

"You better, and don't do anything I wouldn't do," Mila called down the stairs.

Aphtan rushed down the stairs, her small blue-jean shorts hugging her thighs. The red tank top clung to her body, making her breasts look fuller than what they were. Her hair, still damp, hung curly on her back as she made her way through the doors of her building.

The sun grazed her pupils while she held her hand over them to see through the rays. She scanned the parking lot for any unfamiliar cars as she started walking toward it. A black-on-black Escalade pulled up to the curb, the music disturbing every home on the premises.

She walked up to the car and was met at the door by Scooter, who held it open for her. She fought back a smile when Scooter's body came into view. She hopped inside of the car. He handed her a freshly rolled blunt when he got back inside and drove off.

She couldn't help but look at him. It was a magnetic pull. Something about him enticed her, and she could tell it was the same for him. She wanted to laugh because he could barely focus on the road from looking at her so much. The chemistry in the car would have left a science professor confused.

Aphtan admired his handsomeness. She never seen a man so close to perfection in her life. His full lips looked soft. The muscles in his arm that showed from his grip on the steering wheel turned her on. Even the basketball shorts, tank top, and fitted cap had her wanting him. It wasn't the outfit, but how he wore it that was so sexy to her.

Aphtan sat back in the seat and lit the blunt. The silence in the car would have suggested that they were lovers in a quarrel. His presence alone calmed her down. No words needed to be exchanged, and she loved it. The music blasting, mixing with the weed entering her lungs, was enough for her.

They pulled up to an IHOP and parked. He smiled at her, showing the bottom grill in his mouth before he hopped out of the car. Seconds later he was at the passenger side door, opening it, telling her with his eyes to get out. She obliged, following his instructions while she tossed the end of the blunt on the ground.

He put his arm around her neck. The smell of her hair flowed up into his nose. The sun was hot, but her touch was warming him up more. It had been a long time since he had had that kind of attraction for a woman. It felt like they had known each other for a lifetime.

"How many?" the hostess asked as they walked inside.

"Two." He held up two fingers.

They followed the hostess to a booth and slid into one side. Menus were placed in front of them as chatter from other customers danced around the restaurant. The waitresses walking by in a frenzy never caught their attention; they only saw each other.

"I'm Kelly." The waitress approached the table with a pad and pencil. "What can I get you two to drink today?"

"I'll have an orange juice." Aphtan smiled at her.

"Coffee, black." Scooter slid the menu away from him.

"That is so nasty." Aphtan turned the pages of the menu.

"I can't have it any other way." He put a piece of her hair around his finger. "What's on your mind, Aphtan?"

"Too fucking much," she confessed.

"Watch your mouth." He shook his head. "You don't always have to curse to make your point, Aphtan. That shows a sign of ignorance. You're a lady, so speak like one."

She looked at him as the waitress sat their drinks in front of them. "I have shit . . . I mean stuff at home going on. Graduation is in a week. I'm having money issues. You just wouldn't understand my problems."

"I doubt that." He took a sip of the coffee. "Otherwise, why would you call me?"

"I needed someone to talk to." She opened up a straw and put it in the orange juice. "I don't want to annoy you with my problems."

"If I felt annoyed, I wouldn't have picked you up. Trust me." He grabbed her face so she would look at him. "I wanted to see you."

"I wanted to see you, too." She turned a pinkish red.

"Red face, red clothes, red hair." He laughed. "Man, I'm just going to start calling your little ass Red."

"It's my favorite color."

"No shit."

"Are you two ready to order?" the waitress asked.

"I don't eat breakfast." Scooter looked at Aphtan. "Order whatever you want."

"I just want some pancakes." Aphtan handed the waitress the menu.

"I'll have them right out." The waitress nodded before she walked away.

"Are you going to tell me what's on your mind?" Scooter asked.

The sun peeked in the window of the booth, lighting Aphtan's hair like a fiery halo as they engaged in deep conversation. Deep family stories were discussed. Neither of them left out anything. They both put everything on the table with no judgments.

Scooter couldn't believe he was telling her some of the things that he was. He was a thug. Some things had to be taken to the grave. However, there was something about Aphtan that was safe to him, and real. It was easy to trust her. She was different from any other female he had ever met.

Aphtan didn't trust men. After her father got locked up and left her and her mother on their own, she despised them. That alone had stopped her from being in a relationship before; from giving herself fully to a man. All of that was changing with each minute that passed in Scooter's presence. He was a bad boy and probably no good for her. It felt right to her, though.

Walking out of the restaurant, Aphtan knew the seeds they were planting; yet she didn't care. As they got into the car, their hearts beating like they had just run a marathon, she understood that there was no going back. She was feeling him deeply and had no doubts that he felt the same way. They were smitten, and being together now was inevitable.

"What do you have planned for the day?" Scooter asked as they pulled up to Aphtan's apartment building.

"Studying for my last final," she huffed.

"You gon' ace it?"

"I'm going to try." She looked at him.

Scooter leaned in and pressed his warm mouth over hers, doing it ever so gently. His perfect, lush lips were sending an indescribable but happy feeling into the pit of her stomach. When she began to realize that she hadn't pulled away, she melted into his embrace, letting him cup her face as she kissed him back. The heated moment was so intense that she hadn't noticed he unhooked her bra and had his hands under her shirt.

When his firm lips crashed around her nipples through her shirt, she froze. But after feeling the effects that he had on her, she couldn't help but close her eyes. She kissed the top of his head knowing she wanted it. To say that there were butterflies in her stomach would be an understatement, because what she felt was a zoo. Scooter pulling her breast out the side of the tank top was almost enough to let her moan in pleasure. She wrapped her arms around him, and his tongue begged for an entrance, which she allowed.

He bit at her nipple. One of his hands unfastened the button to her shorts. Scooter went back up and kissed her lips. His eyes looked directly into hers as he unzipped her shorts. She cooed at the touch of his fingers around her love bowl. He felt around, slowly flicking her pearl tongue repeatedly. She gasped for air as he slowly put a finger inside of her.

His manhood jumped through his shorts from how tight she was. It was clear that she hadn't been touched. The way it sucked his finger up was a clear sign that she was a virgin, and he had to have her. He removed his finger and slowly put it inside of her mouth, still kissing her lips as she tasted herself.

"You better stop me," he whispered between kisses. "You deserve your first time to be somewhere better than inside of a car, outside of an apartment building."

"First time?" Aphtan pulled away from him.

"Everything's intact." Scooter licked his lips. "It's nothing to be embarrassed about. That's wifey shit right there." He pointed to the area of her pussy.

"Come open my door for me." Aphtan fastened her shorts back up and fixed her shirt.

"I got you." Scooter got out of the car.

"Don't think I'm fast." Aphtan hopped out of the car as the door opened. "I usually don't do this."

"I know." Scooter kissed her lips. "I believe you."

"What is this?" She leaned back on the passenger door pointing to him and then herself.

"I want you to be mines."

"What about your girl at home?"

"What about her?" He shrugged his shoulder. "There are no feelings there. It's just pussy, and that shit is old. She's gone as of right now."

"You call me the minute you get single, and we will talk more about labels." Aphtan shoved past him.

"All right." Scooter licked his lips. "I'll call you within the hour."

CHAPTER 11

"This is the start of the beginning," Aphtan spoke clearly into the microphone, ending her speech. "As your valedictorian, I promise that we all have very bright futures. Let's go out and show the world what the class of 2006 is made of." She held her hands up as the rest of the graduating class yelled and cheered in unison.

Aphtan smiled at the crowd as she made her way back to the seat on the stage aside the rest of the top ten percent. She looked up at the circular structure of the auditorium with a heavy heart. It was the proudest moment of her life, and her mother was nowhere to be found. She looked throughout the crowd countless times and didn't see her face once.

She sat and fidgeted with the manicured nails on her hands. Although Mila was in the crowd, draped in a cap and gown, she felt alone. She was the only student there without family in the audience for her. Everyone else had somebody, and she was alone, all over again.

She fought back tears as the principal called out the names to hand out the diplomas. She walked across the stage with a smile on her face when she heard her name. No one would have guessed that the smartest girl in the school was also the saddest. She couldn't let that part of her show.

Her body tensed up. The sadness melted away as her eyes locked in on Scooter's. The past week with him felt like a fairy tale. Spending all of her free time with him brought her spirits up. It took her mind off the fact that her mother was doing one of her disappearing acts. Having him around freed her mind from the problems that she couldn't control.

Aphtan moved the tassel on her hat to the side before throwing the hat in the air with the rest of the class as the graduation came to an end. She removed the gown, revealing the elegant black dress that complemented her frame. She made her way down the stairs of the stage, congratulations coming from every mouth as she passed. She held the degree that she had worked hard for tightly in her hands.

"Your mama is wrong for not showing up." Ms. Franklin smacked her lips as she hugged Aphtan. "Well, I'm proud of you. A black girl from the projects number one? All these white kids and you smarter than everybody. Gon' on with your bad ass."

"Mama, shut up." Mila hugged Aphtan. "You deserve this, girl. No matter who here and who not."

"Thank y'all." Aphtan blew kisses at them. "I need some fresh air. I'll see y'all at home a little later."

Aphtan slowly made her way through the auditorium; through the crowds of people like waves on a vast ocean. She wasn't quite awkward through the small talk, but something seemed off about her. The building was full of people, engaging in cheerful conversation. Everyone's bodies touched, like a silent dance of a mosh pit.

"Congratulations." Cole stopped her, his gown folded on his arm.

"Same to you." Aphtan looked past him.

"Are you looking for someone?" Cole waved his hand in her face to get her attention.

"Yes," she answered softly.

"Is it a guy?" He raised his eyebrow.

"Why do you ask that?"

"I gave you my number a week ago." He leaned back on one of the connected seats. "You still haven't called me."

"I've been busy. There's been a lot on my plate," Aphtan defended.

"I get it." Cole stood up straight. "No pressure. I see my brother coming. Would you like to meet him?"

"Sure." Aphtan turned around to greet his brother, and Scooter's face met hers.

"Congratulations, baby." Scooter kissed her lips.

"Thank you, boo." She hugged him. "I'm glad you made it."

"I had to come see my baby and my little brother walk across the stage." He reached over her to grab Cole's head.

"Really, Aphtan?" Cole shook his head as his nostrils flared. "How did you get mixed up with Chris?"

"Brothers?" Aphtan looked at them one by one. "Damn, y'all do favor."

"Y'all know each other?" Scooter hugged her from behind.

"This is the chick I told you I was feeling." Cole's eyes stayed on Aphtan's.

"She needs a man, baby brother," Scooter suggested.

"Trust me, I'm definitely a man," Cole spat. "Of all the girls in this city, how did you cross paths with her?"

"We go way back." Scooter put his fist to his chest. "She's your sister-in-law now, so get those nasty thoughts out of your mind."

Cole opened his eyes as wide as he could and gave them a death stare. His face was glazed for a split second, and then he frowned. His lips pursed and his eyes were unblinking. At that moment, if his eyes were a weapon, the piercing look in them could have caused serious destruction. He was a lion, and Scooter had just gone into his territory and he was about to attack.

"This shit is crazy." Cole took a step back in shock. His voice was so loud, so thunderous, that they couldn't concentrate on what he had said, only the tone in which he had said it. He had become a whole different person. His shining, golden brown eyes had turned into a dark and gloomy black. His eyes narrowed and his teeth clenched together. His hands fisted in rage.

"Can I speak to you for a moment?" Aphtan grabbed Cole's arm. "I'll be right back," she told Scooter as she looked back at him.

Aphtan pulled Cole by his arm through the busy crowd. The last thing she wanted was for brothers to be at odds over her. She didn't have a lot of family; however, it was still important to her.

"What's up?" Cole shoved away from her when they made it outside.

"I know we don't know each other that well, Cole." She looked serious. "I don't want you and Scooter at each other's necks. I'm with him, and you have to accept that."

"You don't know him at all." He put his hand on her cheek. "He's bad news. I know I don't know you that well. I do know that you're smart. You're number one in our class. You're destined to be a lawyer, a doctor, or something equivalent to that. I know you not supposed to be the wife of a drug dealer."

"I know what I'm supposed to be." Aphtan moved out of the way for an old woman who was walking by. "I just want to live better, by any means. I'm tired of roaches." Her eyes teared up. "I'm tired of the projects and stealing to get by."

"I understand what you're saying. Get out the right way, though. Don't get sucked up in that shit. Once you get in, you can't get out."

"You ready?" Scooter walked up on them.

"Yes, let's go." Aphtan looped her arm into Scooter's.

"Are y'all coming to my graduation dinner?" Cole called out to their backs after they walked toward the parking lot.

"We'll be there." Scooter threw up the deuces.

Aphtan thought about what Cole said as she sat in the plush seat of the car. She couldn't shake his words the entire way to her house. Life with Scooter would be so much better. She wouldn't have to worry about a thing. All of her needs and wants would be taken care of. It was an easy way out, and nothing ever came easy for her.

She didn't want to take that way out. It was exactly what her mother had done. Simone had given her all to Aphtan's father and ended up with nothing. She wanted her own stability. She didn't want to become dependent upon a man. She wanted to find her own way.

Aphtan looked around the foreign car that she was in as they stopped in front of her building. She could only imagine the kind of life she would have if she gave her all to Scooter. She kissed him before going up the stairs, her diploma still in her hand, to change before the dinner.

She opened the door to her apartment. The smell of Raid tainted the air. She looked around the apartment for her mother, but she wasn't there. She went to her room and set her diploma on top of her dresser next to all of the acceptance letters from colleges all around the globe.

As she passed the coffee table full of bills on the way out of the door, she decided that college wasn't for her right now. After the dinner, she planned to talk to Mila about working at Pearl Tongue.

CHAPTER 12

Water poured endlessly from the gray sky. Lightning illuminated the day occasionally followed by the deep roar of thunder. Aphtan leaned closer to the glass, her nose pressing against it. The grass seemed to drown in the low flood of the storm. Eerily, yet not unexpectedly, a popping sound floated through the air. More than likely a tree was getting knocked down nearby.

The cold rain pelted the window of the car, drumming a hypnotizing beat that thrummed painfully in Aphtan's skull. The lightning flashed spookily and the wild wind shook the stark, leafless trees. Every now and again thunder would boom, shocking her heart and making her cringe involuntarily. Icy wind stole through the cracks in the windows and doors and snaked delicately around her skin, raising goose bumps. The day, only sunny and bright some minutes ago, was now dark and shadowed.

"You sure you want to do this?" Mila looked at

the large tongue with a pearl in the middle of it on top of the building in front of them.

"I need this money." Aphtan sat up in the seat. "Do you think your boss will hire me?"

"Who? Crisco? Hell, yeah, he will hire you. But will Scooter be okay with you stripping?"

"It isn't about if he will be okay with it." Aphtan opened the door. "It's about survival."

"Well, let's go." Mila got out of the car with her.

Aphtan glanced wearily at the dull white building, knowing it was her prison today and for a while. The flowers were growing slowly and weakly around the sidewalk as if they were feeling her pain. Her heels galloped down the walkway as she pulled the halter she wore down some.

They walked through the double doors. The inside of the building was dark as night. The smell of cheap perfume owned the hallway as they made their way through the establishment. Mila held up her hand as they made it to a red door. She knocked as hard as she could and waited for an answer.

"Who is it?" a voice asked through the door.

"Black," Mila answered.

"Black?" Aphtan whispered.

"My stripping name," Mila replied as the red door opened. "You will get one, too."

Crisco sat behind the office desk as the door closed behind them, twiddling his thumbs and gazing around the darkly lit room, with only a lamp producing little light. He never looked at them as he leaned back in the chair, the tie around his neck hanging loosely. His Egyptian-like skin glistened under the scarce light. His face wasn't so easy to see.

He took a sip from a glass full of chilled Hennessy, which by now had gone a little warm, as his eyes inattentively gave focus on the money piled neatly next to his free hand. He scanned the money from the night before, then the two women who were now sitting in front of him.

"Black,"—Crisco looked at them—"the only thing you better have for me is an explanation as to why you weren't at work last night."

"It was my graduation." Mila dug in her purse and took a stack of money out. "I told you I wouldn't be here, but this should cover what I owe." She tossed the money on the desk.

"You're lucky you make me so much money." He snapped his fingers to order the man guarding the door to remove the money from the desk. "Who is this?"

"My home girl." Mila made her finger go up and down to signal Aphtan to stand up. "She wants to work."

"She does?" Crisco looked at Aphtan's small body as she spun around. "How old is your friend, Black?"

"Seventeen," Aphtan chimed in and answered as Mila gave her a scolding look.

Mila shook her head. "What she meant to say is that she's a fresh eighteen."

Crisco poured a line of cocaine on the desk and snorted it through his nose. "I really don't give a fuck about her age." He wiped some powder from the tip of his nose. "Can you dance is the money-making question."

"She can dance," Mila answered.

"Let's see, then." He snorted another line.

Crisco stood up. The light from the single lamp

flashed on him just enough to show his face. He was short but stout. His skin had the brown tone of a Reese's and scars covered his handsome face. His demeanor was calm, yet strong.

The man guarding the door opened it as Crisco, Mila, and Aphtan approached it. They walked down the long hallway. Aphtan's stomach felt like it would fall out of her anal cavity at any moment. The smell of rum and sweat was prevalent as they entered the main room of the business.

"I'll go cut on some music." Crisco headed to the DJ booth. "I need to see what you can do."

"You ready?" Mila grabbed Aphtan's purse from her.

"I guess I don't have a choice." Aphtan gulped loudly as she eyed the stage.

The lights beamed throughout the room at Crisco's demand. The long stage lit up as smoke rose from the bottom of the pole. Aphtan bumped into tables as she made her way to the stage. She approached the stairs leading up to the stage as her back filled with sweat.

"Next up to the stage it our new booty here at Pearl Tongue," Crisco screamed into the microphone. "Y'all open y'all hearts, and wallets, to our new dancer, Lotus!"

"Don't Make," 8Ball and MJG's hit song, came blasting through the speakers at full force. Aphtan walked up the stairs as her tongue rubbed the roof of her mouth. She swallowed hard as one large light shone down on her. She closed her eyes as she held her head back and let out a big sigh.

"Make me want to hire you," Crisco yelled into the microphone. "Dance, girl."

"Clean that pole," Mila yelled as she pointed to

a bottle filled with clear liquid that had a towel on the top of it. "Dance while you cleaning the pole. These hoes are nasty in here, Aphtan. Always clean the pole before you touch it."

A feeling of dread crept up from the pit of her stomach. A cold wave embalmed her as the hairs rose on the back of her neck and her mouth ran dry. She was paralyzed to the spot, the menacing aura holding her in a tightening grip.

Aphtan blinked for a minute, wishing she could be as graceful as Mila. She imagined how it must feel to have the world spin around her while she twirled on the pole. Or how it felt to climb to the top. Or even how to just have a general rhythm to the movement of her hips. She found herself drifting out of her clothes. She wasn't even conscious of it.

Before she knew what was happening, she was twirling around to the beat the music gave her, grinding around on the pole as if she always belonged on it. Even though she was unsure of when her daydream had crossed into reality, she knew she was doing the dance right, and she could feel that the music emphasized her every move.

Aphtan grabbed the pole and climbed to the top. Her ass bounced to the bass in the song as she slowly turned around while she held on for dear life. She did a split in the air, using every ounce of the upper body strength she had. She slid all the way down until she was flat on the surface of the stage, her legs still in a split.

"Yes, bitch." Mila stood up and walked over to the stage. "You killed that shit. You gon' get paid."

Aphtan put her clothes back on as Crisco walked up to the stage. She could see a look of satisfaction

on his face. The way he grinned let Aphtan know
that she had gotten the job. He held his hand out
to help her off the stage.

"You can definitely dance." He stepped back to
get another good look at her. "You can start whenever you want."

"We gone be the most wanted in this bitch."
Mila handed Aphtan her purse.

"I've got to go." Crisco walked off. "Black, fill
her in on the rules."

"I got it." Mila leaned back on the foundation of
the stage as Crisco disappeared through the hallway. "Let's do this run-down."

"Cool." Aphtan sat down on the edge of the
stage.

"I already told you about cleaning the pole."

"I got that."

Mila looked at her phone to read a text message. "Second, always give Crisco his cut off top.
The requirement is five hundred a night. It goes
up by how popular you are and the more you
make."

"Five hundred dollars?" Aphtan crossed her
legs. "Damn, that's a lot."

"Maybe for these ugly hoes in here, but for pretty
bitches like us, that ain't shit. Third, never tell these
niggas or bitches your government name. Crisco
names every stripper that works here, and he called
you Lotus, so get used to it."

"I don't like that name. I'm not feeling it."

"You think I like Black? Hell no. It's all about
the money. Fuck a name."

"What else?" Aphtan eyed the room again.

"Set boundaries off top. That's with these niggas

and these hoes that work here. Don't let these nig-gas touch you any way they want to. Be known for being a bitch for not letting them touch. Don't let these hoes in here lie to you and pretend to be your friend. There are no friends here."

"You know I already know that." Aphtan put a piece of hair behind her ear.

"That's about it, though. Leave your pride at the door and think about the money."

"You're a trainer now, Black," a woman asked as she walked up on them.

"Lotus,"—Mila pointed at the woman—"this is Tsunami. Tsunami, this is my girl Lotus."

"Hey," Tsunami said with force.

Tsunami's hair was the color of melted gold with natural butterscotch highlights that brought out the bronze flecks in her golden eyes. They cas-caded down to her curvy hips, smooth and soft as silk. Her eyes flickered under the strobe lights, lush long lashes brushing against her delicate brow bones. Her skin was clearer than the glitter-ing ocean. Her full, pink rosebud lips were shaped in a glossy, puffy O.

She was taller than average and thick, with ample creamy breasts. She was fully nude, except for a thin gold body chain that accentuated her pink nipples, and made her thin arm look as if it would snap under the weight of it. She was all gold and endless legs, too beautiful for words.

"This is one of the bitches you definitely shouldn't trust." Mila laughed.

"You should work on that jealous thing." Tsunami walked up the stairs to the stage to practice. "It's not a good look for you."

"Bitch, please." Mila rolled her eyes. "Lotus, let's go. We need to go get you some outfits anyway."

"What was that about?" Aphtan nodded her head toward the stage after she jumped down and followed behind Mila.

"Nothing," Mila lied. "That bitch is garbage."

Boss inhaled the fresh air deep inside of his nose as the gates to the federal prison closed behind him. He looked up at the sky with a squint, his eyes trying to get use to the beautiful light the sun produced. He tugged at the pajama pants he had been arrested in eight years prior as a pearl-white foreign car pulled up in front of him.

He walked toward the car. The muscles in his arms flexed from the weight of the bag he was carrying. He opened the door to the car and got inside. He threw the bag in the back as the car accelerated forward with ease. He was finally free, and he planned to remain that way.

"Welcome to the free world." The woman driving the car grabbed his hand and held it. "I'm so happy you're free."

"Me too." He reached over and kissed her lips. "Have you been watching my daughter like I asked you to?"

"Baby, you know I've been on it." She tossed him a bag full of jewelry. "She graduated number one in her class a couple of months ago."

"That's my girl." Boss put the jewelry on piece by piece. "What about Simone?"

"She's in them streets. She's strung out, and I

don't think there's no coming back. She's a full blown crack—"

"Watch your mouth," Boss snarled as he cut her off and grabbed her mouth, causing her to swerve into the next lane. "That's still my wife and the mother of my child."

"I'm sorry." The woman stopped the car in the middle of traffic as Boss released his grip on her. "I shouldn't have said that."

"No, you fucking shouldn't have." Boss signaled for her to accelerate the car. "Is Scooter still running shit?"

"Yes." The woman rubbed her face. "I've been looking for years, and no one has spotted Money. Do you think Scooter really let his father go?"

"I know he did." Boss put his hands together. "Let's go to the bank, and then let's go pay Scooter a visit."

"You don't want to go see Aphtan first?"

"I will, right after I handle a couple things." He held up his hand to let her know he was done talking about it.

Boss leaned back in the seat and wondered how he had let five years go by without talking to his wife and child. It wasn't as if he didn't want to. He wanted them to be free and live free. He had a lot of time to make up for. The birthdays and holidays he missed enraged him just thinking about it. The last time he saw Aphtan, she was a girl, and now she was all grown up.

Thoughts of how he was going to take over the streets again haunted him as well. He didn't want to go to jail again, but hustling was all that he knew. He was willing to take the chance. It was in his blood. All he had was time to think and come up with plans, so that he would never have to see the inside of a jail cell again.

He abated those thoughts as the car accelerated onto the highway. He couldn't wait to hold his baby girl in his arms. Nothing else was as important. Of course he wanted to take over the game, but first he wanted to get his family straight.

CHAPTER 13

Scooter grabbed Tsunami and pulled her toward him. The warmth between them was pleasant and felt cozy. His hands wandered around her bare skin and made their way inside her clothes. Her body was a freeway, and he was GPS trying to get to her G spot, which was the destination.

Kissing wildly, Scooter removed her top with ease. Her perfect breasts tempted him, begging him to suck and bite them. He removed his t-shirt as she arched her back gently to welcome his lips as they caressed her skin. Her body felt so soft to him. He picked her up and carried her up the stairs as their tongues danced in sync.

The remainder of Tsunami's clothes slithered off her wet body. Scooter slowly raised his hands, massaging her shoulders. He turned the water on. They faced each other. Her hands gripped his chest, pulling him so close that their noses were touching. He moved his hands lower, to her breasts, and felt them with hunger. Hunger for her.

Her hands gracefully moved to below his waist,

feeling his naked body. They were yearning for each other. He opened his mouth and inserted his tongue in her mouth. They kissed so passionately that her opening vibrated with excitement. She stood on the precipice of life, her heart at variance with her mind.

His lips slammed against hers with full force, catching her off guard. He kissed with a ferocity that made her burst into flames. Scooter licked her lower lip, asking for entrance, which she eagerly granted. All of Tsunami's thoughts went out the window. She could think of nothing but his lips on hers. She wrapped her arms around his neck and pulled him closer to her, and he moaned in satisfaction. She kissed back with everything she had in her, all the passion and love that she could muster. They broke apart gasping for breath, but he didn't say a word, just kissed the path down her neck, making her ache with wanting.

"Grab a condom," Scooter ordered.

"We don't need one." Tsunami kissed him and bit his lip.

"Get one." He pulled away from her. "We're not even about to get into this all over again."

"Get into what?" She got up from on top of him. "You want us to fuck like we're married, but we can't even think about kids?"

"Here we go." Scooter stepped out of the shower and walked into the bedroom. "I'm not about to argue with you."

"You'll never have to again." She followed him and sat on the bed to put her clothes on. "I hope this new bitch that got you tripping with me sticks around. I'm so through with you."

"You always say that," Scooter assured her. "You will come back."

"Don't count on it." She walked toward the door fully clothed. "I promise you, I'm not fucking with you ever again."

"Yeah, yeah." Scooter lay back on the bed.

Scooter lay there deep in thought as Tsunami left his mind the second she left his view. Aphtan was the only thing that he thought about. A beautiful woman was just in his presence; kissing him and sucking him, yet all he could do was think about Aphtan.

He'd never felt like this about anyone. It scared him a little, because he didn't know how far he would go for her. In his heart, he felt like he would do any and everything for her. He had fallen in love with her, and as he looked back on when he knew her from his childhood, he figured the feelings had always been there.

He got up as her face flashed in his head repeatedly. He felt bad for having Tsunami at his crib. Aphtan was a good girl, and he wanted to treat her like one. He didn't want to lose what he loved for something that he liked. He grabbed the keys to his car. He had to see her. He wouldn't be able to sleep until he had.

The glow of the moon lit the stairs through the vertical window as he walked down them. He cringed as he exited the door, hoping Tsunami had driven off into the night. When he saw that only his vehicles sat in his parking area, he sighed with relief and he entered his car. He started the car, cut the music up as loud as it would go, and put the car in drive.

"Hey." Knocks hit the driver-side window. "You got something for me?"

Scooter pulled the gun from under his seat as he shook his head at the crack head scratching at her arms outside his window. He opened the door with force, causing it to hit the woman. She wailed from the pain as he got out of the car.

The woman got on her knees. The ripped shirt she wore was blowing from the breeze that the night offered. "I know you the head man in charge, and all I need is a favor for a favor. I'll do anything. Just help me."

"How the fuck you find out where I live?" Scooter pressed the gun to her head. "Tell me who sent you."

"Crack," the woman screamed as she grabbed his leg and rubbed it softly. "Let me take care of you."

"Lady,"—Scooter shook his leg to make her grip fail—"get the fuck off of me."

"I'm sorry." The woman started to cry. "I didn't mean to disrespect you. I got food stamps. I got . . . I got . . . I got this necklace." She took the necklace from around her neck as the pure gold locket sparkled. "It's vintage. It was my great, great, great grandmother's. I told myself I would never sell it, but I need this fix."

"Get the fuck out of here." He opened the door to the car. "I don't know what you're asking. I'm not affiliated with drugs."

"Don't fucking lie to me." Anger filled her face. "I know who the fuck you are. Don't lie to me. Just help me."

Scooter ignored her as he got into the car. She banged on the window, spit spewing from her mouth onto the glass. She kicked at the car as Scooter's threats fell on deaf ears. The woman disappeared behind the car, and just when he thought she had left, the tire pressure light on his dashboard lit up in a golden color.

"Hell, naw." He got out of the car and checked out his tires.

"I just needed a little help." The woman held the knife out in front of her.

"Bitch." He walked toward her. "Those were custom tires."

"I don't give a fuck," she screamed as she dashed toward him. "Fuck you!"

The gunshot rang out, momentarily deafening both of them. The bullet erupted from the barrel and pirouetted into the damp night air on its mission of death. As it tore through the humidity, the accompanying crack was muted in the cool, sodden air.

The woman jerked suddenly before collapsing to the concrete pavement. For a moment a look of wonder took over her face. It was if her body had gotten hot, because she stared down at where the bullet carved a hole inside of her. She saw blood. Then reality set in.

She slumped forward, the earlier desperation dissipating as she surrendered to the inevitable. In a few minutes it would be over, and she lay still, accepting her fate in the knowledge that in a short time, her life would end and there would be no more pain. There would be no more want for the drug. The addiction would no longer be a burden.

Suddenly the grimace on her countenance changed, now to a smile and then, inexplicably, the insane cackling laughter of one who knew that her time had finally come and that soon her heart will stop beating forever. She thought about her life until this point; the good, the bad, and the ugly situation that she was in now.

Thoughts of Boss caused her to smile bigger. Thoughts of her only child, Aphtan, brought about an even bigger smile as numbness overtook her. Guilt ate at Simone for leaving Aphtan alone in this cold world. As if the past few years hadn't been hard enough for her. It was a relief, in a sense, to her; now she wouldn't be a burden on Aphtan. She would now have the ability to move forward in life without anything holding her back.

"Fuck." Scooter put the palm of his hand on the side of his head. "I don't need this shit."

"Aph . . ." Simone tried to speak, but the name wouldn't come out.

Scooter stood over her; her face looked vaguely familiar to him. He had met her before and possibly knew her, but he couldn't put it together as to from where. He watched as she took her last breath, unaware that he had taken the life of the mother of the girl he had recently fallen in love with. He reached down, yanked the necklace off of her neck, and then got inside of his car.

"I need a body picked up and the scene cleaned." He drove off as he held the phone to his ear. "It's outside of my crib."

CHAPTER 14

"Lotus." One of the strippers stuck her head into the dressing room door. "There's someone asking for you in room three that wants a private dance."

"I'll be right there." Aphtan put the blunt to her mouth before standing up to look at herself in the mirror.

It had been a couple of months since she started working at Pearl Tongue, and the money was everything Mila told her it was going to be. She found her groove in the club. The boundaries were set, and it was understood that she wouldn't do more than dance. There was no touching allowed at all. It was for her, but mainly for the respect she had for the relationship she shared with Scooter.

The word had spread around town that a new girl was working who was bad, and that alone brought tons of money. All she had to do was show her breast, and the rest she left up to the imagination, making them come back for more, hoping to see it one day. She was making more money than the seasoned strippers and they hated her for it.

Aphtan flicked the end of the blunt onto the ground and stepped on it with her red stiletto heels. She checked herself in the mirror one last time as she fixed the black thong resting in between her ass cheeks. She gathered her thoughts as best she could and walked out the door to head to the private room area.

"Good luck," Tsunami shouted with envy in her voice as she left the room.

"I don't need it," Aphtan called back to her.

She walked through the tables as men grabbed at her arm for dances. She smiled softly while pulling away from them as she focused on the entrance to the private rooms. That was where the money was. Those rooms cost a minimum of a thousand dollars to get a dance. Not every stripper was requested, but she started getting the invitation her first night working.

Stopping at the third curtain, Aphtan cut the outside world out of her mind. She had gotten used to it, but she would never be comfortable with it. It was easy money for her. She would make more money there than she would if she graduated college. It was business to her; nothing more or less.

"Somebody asked for me?" She opened up the thick curtain and walked inside.

"Cover your fucking body up," Boss ordered as the darkness of the room hid his face.

Aphtan used her hands to cover her body. She couldn't see him, but she knew that it was her father. She didn't know whether to be mad or happy. It had been years since she'd seen him, yet she didn't feel the urge to run into his arms like she thought she would the day he was free.

A full dose of embarrassment filled her being. It was like a hand had wrapped around her windpipe and squeezed until she couldn't breathe properly. She felt like her heart was about to burst through her chest. Her mind drew a blank to the point she couldn't remember her thoughts from only moments earlier. She shook her head, and her vision blurred just a little while a ball of lead formed in her stomach.

"Aphtan, why are you doing this to yourself?" Boss leaned into the light, his face full of scars.

"It's good to see you too, Daddy." Aphtan sat next to him. "Welcome home."

"Give me a hug, baby girl." He put his arms around her and squeezed tightly. "I haven't held you in my arms in years. I've missed you, Aphtan. I've missed you so much."

Aphtan didn't want to, but she couldn't hold back her tears. For years, she wished she could talk to her father, to hear his voice. No matter how mad she was at him for leaving, she was like a little girl on Christmas after getting an Easy-Bake Oven, when it came to his touch.

"I've missed you, too." She hugged him back. "It's been rough without you," she cried harder onto his shoulder. "It's been too much to deal with."

"I'm here now." Boss wiped the tears from her eyes softly. "I fucked up and got caught. I'm sorry I left you with so much responsibility. I'm sorry I left you to fend for yourself. It was my responsibility as a man to take care of you, and I failed. I'm sorry, Aphtan."

Aphtan reached for him again in disbelief. She could feel him, yet it felt like a dream. She had spent many nights praying for this moment, and she couldn't believe it had finally come. She was still collecting her thoughts, little by little.

Boss pulled away from her. "I'm about to be back on top, and I can't have my daughter dancing at Pearl Tongue."

"Back on top?" Aphtan held her hands up. "Shouldn't you be trying to lay low for a little bit?"

"I have to make my move now," Boss stressed as a waitress walked through the curtains with a bottle of Hennessy and two glasses. "I got a plan."

"Your plan got you in jail last time," Aphtan protested. "Just relax and lay low for a little while."

"Aphtan, I got this." He poured one of the glasses full of chilled liquor. "I got this." He looked at her as if he were reading her mind. "Are you scared I'm going to hurt your boyfriend, Scooter, to take the crown back?"

"That didn't cross my mind," Aphtan lied.

"It should have." Boss took a long sip from the glass. "His life depends on how he reacts to my plan."

"Daddy." Aphtan shook her head. "This is going to turn into a war."

"If it does, so be it." He shrugged his shoulders. "I knew you two would be together one day. I just can't believe that he would let you work here." Boss cringed. "No man wants another man to see his woman this way."

"Let me?" Aphtan crossed her legs. "I'm with him, but he doesn't own me. He can't tell me what to do."

"Lotus," Crisco screamed from the hallway. "I know you're not still doing that private dance when there's niggas out here ready to spend money. Do you hear me?" He stuck his head inside of the curtain.

"Crisco." Boss walked toward him. "I know you're not letting my daughter work in this fucking dump when I own a third of this raggedy motherfucker. If I own a part of it, so do she."

"Boss." Crisco eased inside of the room. "I didn't know you were out, mayne. Welcome home." He held out his hand.

"Get your fucking hand out of my face." Boss removed his gun from his waist and pressed it to Crisco's now sweating head. "I don't take kindly to disrespect. Good night." He pulled the trigger.

Aphtan sat up as two buff men entered the room dressed all in black. Boss didn't say a word, but the men knew exactly what to do. They carried Crisco's lifeless body out of the room without muttering a word. Boss took a seat back on the couch as he put the gun back inside of his waist.

"I'm sorry you had to see that, baby girl." Boss picked up his glass and took a sip.

"It's fine." Aphtan stood up. "I'll go put on some clothes so that we can properly catch up."

"Agreed." Boss fixed the button on his suit after setting the glass down.

"Daddy,"—Aphtan stopped at the curtain and looked back at him—"I haven't seen mama in months. Do you think you can get someone to find her?"

"I'll get right on it," he lied, smiling in a comforting way.

Boss watched Aphtan walk out of the room with a look of concern plastered on his face. Aphtan would never see her mother again, dead or alive. He had received the call prior to driving to Pearl

Tongue that Scooter had ordered the same men who cleaned up Crisco's body to clean up Simone's. He couldn't tell her that her mother was dead. It would break her heart. It would be better if she thought Simone was missing.

CHAPTER 15

The fan blew hot air on Levi; luckily, it was supposed to rain that night. As he was walking downstairs to get something to drink, the doorbell rang. Grabbing the knob and the gun under his shirt at the same time, he turned the knob; he was greeted by Mila in her work getup. She was standing there in front of him. Her posture was slumped a bit, and she was looking at him with a funny expression on her face.

"Levi?" Suddenly he felt his back against the floor. She was warm weight on him. She felt so soft. "I have some news to tell you," she said before she laughed.

"Mila,"—he softly pushed her off of him—"you're drunk."

"Just a little." She giggled as he helped her off the ground after he got up. "What I have to tell you is important." She put her finger over his lips.

"Let's go upstairs, and you can tell me when you wake up, baby." He wrapped his arm around her.

"I just thought you may want to know that Boss is out."

"What did you just say?" Levi grabbed her face as his expression changed to a serious one. "Boss is out? The man that used to run shit is out? The Boss from Oakcliff?"

"Yes." She kissed at him through the air. "I heard him talking to his daughter, who is my best friend." She pointed at herself.

"All right, baby." He walked her to the stairs and watched her walk slowly up them. "I'll be right up." He pulled out his phone and dialed a number. "We got a problem." He paced to the kitchen.

"What kind of problem?" Scooter's voice came through the receiver.

"Boss is out of jail."

"Who told you this?"

"Mila just showed up drunk." Levi sat at his dining table. "She told me he was at the club talking to Aphtan."

"Aphtan knows about this?" Scooter asked as he turned at a red light.

"That's what Mila said."

"I'll test her loyalty and see if she tells me."

"What if she doesn't?" Levi put the blunt in his mouth and let it hang loosely as he talked. "It's blood over mud in these streets, cousin."

"I'll handle it either way."

"If he's out, he's coming for you."

"I got it. Good looking out." Scooter hung up the phone.

Scooter parked in front of his house as his heart raced just a little. He had an uneasy feeling come over him after hearing the news. He didn't fear Boss, but he knew the power he had in the streets before he left. The magnitude of respect was still unreachable to him.

He sat inside his car as he played a game of chess in his mind about what his next move should be. Aphtan couldn't get involved. That was the only thing he was sure about. No matter what, he wanted her to remain safe, no matter the cost.

Scooter shuddered from the cold as he got out of the car. He walked across the parking area. He quickly noticed it was deserted; no one was around. It was almost eerie, for it was beginning to darken; the warm light from the better part of the day was long gone. He bit against the gut feeling that something was wrong and continued to walk.

The rain pouring down on him gave the pavement a shimmer, almost like black water. Wind whistled against the trees that lined the lot. He sucked in a quick breath as he saw a dark shadow dart in front of him. But then it was gone, just as fast as it had appeared.

The urge to get his gun out became strong, and before he could reach for it, a bag was shoved over his head. He fought as his hands were held. His body was lifted into the air, and he could feel the men who grabbed him walking. The sound of tires screeching played in Scooter's ears after his body was thrown into the back of a van.

Ropes were tied around his hands and feet as the bag was loosened around his neck. He could feel hands searching his body, and all of his belongings were taken out of his pockets. He could hear the doors close, and the feeling of motion was present. He had been kidnapped, and there was nothing he could do about it.

As Scooter's eyelids fluttered open, the thick smell of must filled his nostrils. He tried to open his mouth to exhale and take a bigger breath, but something was slapped across his mouth that was sticky and tight. He tried sitting up and bumped his head on a metal roof. Using his hand, he grappled around. No door. He was definitely in a trunk. The lid of the trunk lifted rapidly, and he was pulled out.

Scooter's white sneakers hit the ground, and dust flew up as the bag was lifted off his head. He could see trees, and a large white building, but the world was still shaking way too much for him to focus enough to tell what it was. He closed his eyes and squeezed them tight. He heard a car door shut, and for a moment he wondered where Aphtan was. It hurt his head, though, so he stopped.

His hands were being held behind his back, and he was being pushed forward. He tried looking at his white sneakers so he could walk straight. His entire body felt way too heavy.

"Fuck y'all," he said. It sounded like water in his ears more than words. "I can't walk," he tried to say, but he couldn't understand the words. His hands were suddenly let go of, and he fell to the dirt. He tasted it on his tongue and gagged.

Scooter tried to get up, but all he could manage with his hands bound as they were was to turn on his back. The sunlight hit his eyes, and he tried to think why it was wrong that the sun was shining. He could finally see the blue of the sky, and that seemed even more wrong.

He heard a second pair of footsteps approach. *Calm down*, a tiny voice inside him whispered. He tried to obey, but all that came out was a small croak, something like a tiny frog trying to sing. He heard the sound of two sets of feet behind him, followed by laughter.

Scooter recognized one of the voices, and he could understand them, but he couldn't focus on the conversation long enough to give it any meaning. "Too much drug" and "soldier" were the two phrases he caught before the world began to tilt again. He turned his head to the right and retched out his guts.

The men, or at least the manly voices, stopped laughing. He felt a foot turn him over to the left, and a giant hand picked him up by the ropes on his wrist. He heard a popping in his shoulders and knew it should have hurt, but he couldn't remember how it felt not to hurt. He couldn't tell the difference.

His feet dragged along the ground, and one of his shoes fell off. His toes hit the gravel, and he was literally thrown onto the steps of the building. He managed to turn over as Boss hovered over him with a smile on his face. He sat down next to him, giving his men a look that demanded that they walk away.

"My young bull." Boss looked up at the sky. "You've looked better."

"You didn't have to do it like this." Scooter struggled to sit up. "I would have met with you if you would have asked me to."

"I know." Boss looked at him. "I like it better this way." He stood up. "I have a few bones to pick with you, Christopher."

"I've always been loyal to you, Boss."

"Loyalty." He leaned down and pulled a picture out of the front pocket of his blazer. "You call this loyalty?" He held the picture up to his eyes. "I know this is your father, but you know this game."

"I couldn't kill my father." Scooter looked into his eyes. "Anything else you've asked of me, I've done it."

"The only thing you've done for me is let my daughter work at Pearl Tongue, showing her ass." Boss pulled a gun out, pointed it at his foot, and shot. "And kill my wife." He shot a bullet into the other foot as Scooter screamed out in pain.

"I didn't know that was Simone. I didn't know Aphtan was working there, either. I promise you that." His teeth ground against each other as the pain became unbearable. "If you're going to kill me, then do it."

"Don't tempt me." Boss put his gun away. "The only thing saving you is the love my daughter has for you." He grabbed his face. "I won't tell her that you killed her mother. However, effective immediately, I run these streets. You got it?"

"I got . . ." He paused and closed his eyes as his feet burned with pain. "I got it."

"We are at the back of a small clinic." Boss walked off. "Crawl to a door and get someone to look at those wounds. Open flesh and the sun don't mix well."

Scooter sweated heavily as he saw Boss get in the back of a Suburban before it drove off. He panted while he watched the blood slowly rush out of his feet onto the hot pavement. His vision blurred, and before a thought could cross his mind, he fainted.

CHAPTER 16

Tears fell from Aphtan's eyes as she threw the phone into the vacant passenger seat. She made a U-turn and sped in the direction of the hospital. Her hands shook so bad that she couldn't get a firm grip on the steering wheel.

Her stomach did somersaults as the hospital came into view. She parked at the entrance and jolted through the large double doors as they opened for her. Bumping into strangers, trying to find the information desk, the tears kept running away from her eyes.

"Excuse me?" She waved her hand in the face of a security guard. "How can I find out what room a patient is in?"

"Over there." The woman pointed.

Aphtan walked as fast as she could to the desk. Quickly, she gave the name of who she was looking for, tapping her foot impatiently as she bit back the sadness that was swimming through her veins. The woman behind the desk was typing, and Aphtan was waiting, grinding her teeth together, unclenching and clenching her fist too many times. Her nails dug into her palms.

After what seemed to be an eternity, the woman gave her the room number, and she muttered a thank you, dashing past people who only gave her curious looks, and toward the large set of stairs, seeing as she had no time for the elevators. The stairs glistened in mocking with their shiny tiles and she sped up them, the muscles in her body aching ferociously as each step took forever for her to reach her destination.

Taking a deep, shaky breath, she took a moment to collect herself before walking up to the door. She gathered her thoughts and slowly opened it as darkness met her at the entrance. She peeked around the room as Cole, Levi, and Mila all stared at her from where they stood around Scooter while he lay in the bed asleep. Their eyes made her feel even more uncomfortable as she walked up to the bed.

"What the fuck is she doing here?" Levi spat.

"I called her." Mila shoved him. "She deserved to know."

"Who did this?" Aphtan softly rubbed Scooter's leg through the covers.

"Boss," Scooter whispered.

"I told him to relax." Aphtan walked to the top of the bed and ran her finger across his cheek. "I'm sorry, Scooter."

"Let's give them a minute." Cole blew out his mouth. "They need to talk."

"Find out her loyalty, cousin." Levi walked to the door behind Cole.

"I'll be right outside." Mila gave her a hug before she walked out of the door.

Aphtan grabbed Scooter's hand. "I didn't know he was going to do this. I didn't even know he was out until yesterday."

"I know." Scooter made room next to him as he patted the rough, hospital sheets. "I believe you."

"You not mad at me?" She climbed into the bed.

"Your father is responsible for his own actions." Scooter eased his arm around her. "I love you, and that's all that matters. Besides, I was looking for a reason to get out of the game. I have enough money to take care of us for the rest of our lives."

Aphtan laid her head on his shoulder as she thought about how life would be with Scooter. With him out of the game, things would be better for them. There would be no choosing. There would be no beef between the man whom she was in love with and the first man she had ever loved.

"I heard about that dancing shit." He forced her to look at him. "That shit ends now. I can't have my future wife dancing at no fucking strip club. I can take care of you."

"It's over with."

"That's what I needed to hear." He kissed her forehead. "You need to move in with me, and we can go through this thing called life together."

"Are you serious?" Aphtan kissed him softly as the door opened.

"Dead ass serious." Scooter kissed her back as his eyes went to the small, dark hallway to see who the visitor was.

"Son?" Money walked deep enough into the room that he could be seen. "How are you doing?" He took a seat in one of the hard wooden chairs in front of the bed as he cuffed the jacket of his tuxedo under his arm.

Scooter leaned up in the bed. "Pop, what are you doing here?"

"Uncle Money?" Aphtan squinted as if she had seen a ghost.

"Romeo and Juliet." Money turned his ring straight on his finger. "I guess it was inevitable. I used to tell Boss to keep you two away from each other."

"You shouldn't have showed yourself." Scooter shook his head. "It's not safe."

"I'm sick of hiding like some bitch." Money stood up and placed his jacket on the chair. "Boss knows I'm alive. The compound I was living at was shot up. One thing about my dear old friend Boss is, he'll find you, if he wants you."

"You really did betray him?" Aphtan jumped off of the bed.

"It's business, little girl."

"Pop, what do you think is going to happen? I don't want to start a war. I just want to grow old with Aphtan." Scooter grabbed Aphtan by the arm to make her sit back down.

"The war started before either of you were born. This rivalry between me and Boss has been around since we were kids."

"Y'all need to let that shit go." Aphtan's voice began to rise.

"In this game"—Money pulled out a gun and pointed it at Aphtan's foot—"it's an eye for an eye."

Scooter blocked Aphtan's body with his own.

"You can't shoot her. She doesn't have anything to do with this."

"Sometimes people are guilty by association, Scooter." He put the gun away. Money grabbed his jacket and walked toward the door. "There will be no neutral in this war. Pick a side, and soon."

Scooter grabbed Aphtan's hand to let her know everything would be all right. They didn't exchange words; they just lay there, stuck in each other's presence. They weren't getting in the middle of the war. That was something that was for certain. They were going to be together, and nothing would stop them.

"Are you all right, Aphtan?" Cole parked in front of her apartment building. "You look a little worried."

"I am," she admitted as she opened the door and got out. "Wouldn't you be?"

"No," he replied as he got out of the car. "Whatever is going to happen is going to happen."

Aphtan walked into the breezeway of her building with Cole following her every move. She crept up the stairs slowly. She was excited to grab her stuff and move in with Scooter, but she hoped that her mother would be okay if she returned and she wasn't there. It was a bittersweet moment.

The soft scent of lilac and roach spray took over her senses as she opened the door and walked inside. It bothered her that everything was exactly the same as the last time she was there. That meant her mother hadn't been there, and she was still missing.

Aphtan grabbed everything she needed before sitting on the couch to get one last look at where she had spent the last eight years of her life. She wanted to leave all those memories in the past. Everything bad started happening then, and the apartment was the start of it all.

"You were born into this life." Cole leaned back on the couch. "You didn't choose it."

"I know that." Aphtan snapped out of her daydream.

"Being with my brother is a choice." He looked down at his phone. "You know what comes in this lifestyle."

She stood up. "I'm well aware. I know all too well."

"I'm just reminding you." He reached down and picked up the box of the belongings she had packed. "I just want you to make sure this is what you want. I would hate to see you get hurt behind this decision."

"Thank you." Aphtan held the door open and let him walk through. "But I got this, Cole."

"I know." He walked up on her as she closed the door behind them. "I just think that you deserve better."

"What is better to you?"

"Us," he replied. The box in his hand was the only thing separating them from each other as Aphtan's back hit the door.

"Stop playing." She eased by him. "We're not talking about this."

The only thing Aphtan heard was the box hitting the floor as she felt Cole's hands spin her around. He looked into her eyes; deeply, passionately. There was not a fragment of falsity in those hazel orbs, but rather they held the dreams of their future. How so little could reveal so much, she wasn't certain. But, as he moved his face nearer to hers, she let out a shaky, nervous breath.

As those pink colored lips hit her own, she felt a burst of emotion fly forth from every inch of herself, overtaking her very person. Wrapping her arms around his neck, she felt more secure and safe than she had in longer than she could remember.

It was as though in his arms nothing could hurt her; nothing. His lips seemed to cascade over hers in glorious feeling. She felt his mind meet hers, and suddenly she could hear him. Hear his thoughts, his emotions.

As he pulled back, she winced. It had only been a few seconds that had lasted minutes. "Scooter" managed to escape her lips as her eyes remained closed in awe.

"What about him?" Cole grabbed the rail along the wall. "He doesn't have to know."

Aphtan opened her eyes as reality hit her. She eased down the stairs. She needed some fresh air. Everything was happening too fast, and there was too much on her mind. She needed to scream, and she didn't care who was around.

"My bad." Cole caught up to her with the box in his hand.

"Please." She held her hand up as she walked away. "Just give me a minute."

Her attention was easily on Cole. It didn't surprise her that the whole projects were paying attention to them. They were practically dying of questions, in hysterics over the altercation. And, even if you hadn't met Cole before, you could tell he was a mystery.

She stumbled around, fanning her face, trying to decipher what it was she was thinking. She squeaked when the air tickled her nose, teetering over into a parked car. She leaned against it as her eyes met Cole's as he stood by the entrance to her building with her box in his hand.

Aphtan looked up at the clear, crisp, blue sky with a few fluffy white clouds scattered intermittently throughout the firmament. A bright, warm sun shined on her as she tried to figure out how to handle the situation with Cole.

The sound of a car coming to a halt caught her attention as she turned around. A black Suburban with dark tinted windows came into view and parked right behind her as she held her hand over her eyes to block out the sun. The window slowly rolled down, and her father's voice hit her ears.

"Take a ride with me," Boss ordered as the door opened in front of her.

"It's cool," Aphtan called out to Cole, who was running toward the truck. "It's my father. I'll call you later." She got inside the car, and it drove off.

"Cole sure has grown up." Boss fixed the cufflink to his shirt.

"I thought Cole just moved here."

"He's still Money's son. His mother just took him away for a while." He held his hand up to the driver. "Are you moving in with Scooter?"

"Who told you that?"

"I know everything." He looked at her. "I'm not here to try to change your mind. You'll be eighteen in a couple of days, and you can make up your own mind. I just want you to be able to protect yourself."

"Daddy, we're not doing that." She turned red.

"Baby girl." He tossed a gun in her lap. "I'm talking about life or death."

She picked the gun up and felt it. "Why would I need this?"

"You're about to be with a gangster, and that's all the reason you'll ever need."

"We are not going to be in that life anymore." Aphtan held the gun out for him to grab it.

"Believe me." Boss pushed the gun away from himself and put his hand on her knee. "Sometimes it's not about you. I run these streets, and if a nigga can't get to me, then he will try to get to you, to get to me."

"What are you saying?"

"You need to stay ready to keep from getting ready. I'm not telling you to live in fear."

"I have Scooter to protect me."

Boss laughed. "You'll be safer if you learn how to handle a gun. You need to keep one on you at all times."

"I understand." Aphtan looked out the window. "Where are we going?"

"The shooting range," Boss answered dryly. "You need to practice."

"Right now?" Aphtan sat back in the seat.

"There's no time like the present."

The chill of the gun ran through Aphtan's hand with an intensity she'd never known before. She felt one with the gun. It was as if she was meant to hold it; meant to shoot it. It felt like home to her, and she'd never felt safer.

She pointed the gun out in front of her as best she could, being confined to a backseat. Learning how to use it, she was okay with. It was the using it part that she had a problem with. She dreaded the day she would have to use it. Knowing her life, it would be sooner than she anticipated.

PHASE THREE

ADULTHOOD

CHAPTER 17

"Keep your eyes closed, baby." Scooter covered Aphtan's eyes with his hand as they walked through a door.

"What do you have planned?" Aphtan tried to remove his hands from in front of her eyes.

"You'll see." He pulled his hands away from her eyes.

"Happy anniversary!" the room shouted as they clapped and cheered.

Aphtan smiled as her eyes scanned the room and she saw all of her friends. "I love you." She turned around and kissed his lips.

"I love you more." He held her as tight as he could. "Happy fifth anniversary."

"Happy fifth anniversary." She kissed his chest through his tuxedo as her girlfriends surrounded them.

"We'll bring her back," Mila called out as she pulled Aphtan by the arm in the opposite direction.

"Y'all have fun." Scooter waved her off as Levi approached him.

"You sure have molded her into a goddess." Levi admired Aphtan's beauty from afar. "Who would have thought the last six years would be so good to her."

"I did." Scooter grabbed a drink from a silver tray as the girl holding it passed by. "That's why I married her."

"Smart decision." Levi hit his glass against Scooter's. "Happy anniversary, cousin."

"Thank you." He sipped from the glass as Aphtan's eyes locked on him. "I love you," he mouthed to her.

"I love you back," she mouthed.

Aphtan played with the tennis bracelet around her wrist and began walking through the crowd. She knew once she sat down, all eyes would turn to her. They always did. Then they would look away again, pretending they didn't see her. People in their circle were like this. They always wanted to make themselves look as good as they could. It was all about dresses and gentlemen, or the horse racing and women. They didn't stop to look at the world, and she resented them for it.

Her shoes made tiny clicking noises as she took the last few steps. As predicted, every face immediately turned to her as she sat down. She could see her own face reflected in the eyes closest. Then they hastily looked away again, gossiping, laughing, and dancing.

All the women were shallow, and all that the men were interested in were the other women. Not that she wanted their attention. Even though she loathed them all, she saw every opportunity for photographs. She tossed her short hair in a nonexistent breeze, mouth pouting slightly as she talked to her girls. Women waltzed with their men; couples stared into each other's eyes so intensely they almost melted. The dark ballroom glowed with elegant candlelight, dark enough to hide anyone's flaws. It was the perfect scene.

Aphtan couldn't stop smiling as she thought about the last six years. Life had been perfect and peaceful. With the exception of her mother still being missing, everything else was blissful. She couldn't have asked for a better life.

She tugged at the Alexander McQueen dress as she crossed her legs and rubbed her belly softly. She was late, and giving Scooter his first child would be the cherry on top of their happy lives.

Eyeing the room one last time, Aphtan looked for her father's face. She saw him in spells and was hoping he would be in attendance. Seeing as he hadn't attended her wedding, it didn't surprise her at all that he wasn't there.

"Aphtan." Mila snapped her fingers in her face. "Do you hear me talking to you?"

"Yes, girl." Aphtan looked at her. "I hear you. Who's watching my godbaby, heifer?"

"My mama." Mila rubbed on her breast. "Girl, if I would have known breast-feeding would hurt this bad, his little ass would have started on formula."

"Leave auntie's baby alone." Aphtan pushed her playfully.

"Well, auntie needs to come get her baby when his ass cries at night." Mila rolled her eyes. "If Levi thinks I'm popping any more out anytime soon, he's as crazy as he looks."

"Hopefully, I'm the next to push one out." Aphtan smiled, making the small dimple in her cheek show. "I'm late."

"How late?" one of the women at the table asked.

"A month." Aphtan smiled as the women all gasped in excitement. "I don't want to get Scooter's hopes up again."

"Go to the doctor," Mila suggested.

"The appointment is tomorrow." Aphtan looked down at her platinum wedding ring with a diamond the size of a large hailstone. "I want to give him a baby."

"You're pregnant." Mila reached in to give her a hug. "These weird cravings that I've been having belong to you."

"Let's hope so." The sound of someone hitting a microphone caught their attention.

"I would like to make a toast to my beautiful wife, who has made the last six years of my life the best years of my life." Scooter held up a champagne glass as he talked into the microphone. "Would y'all please help me get my beautiful wife up here?"

Aphtan's dress cascaded flawlessly as she stood up. The dress kissed the shiny, pearl-white floor as she walked to the center of the room to stand next to her husband. The lights shined elegantly on her as the chandeliers seemed to brighten more as she passed underneath them. Her short black pixie cut sat beautifully in place as the red-bottomed heels on her feet thudded against the floor.

"I love you so much." Scooter pulled a box from

the inside pocket of his blazer. "I couldn't have asked for a better wife. Happy anniversary." He kissed her passionately before handing her the black jewelry box.

Aphtan smiled as she held the jewelry box up to the crowd. They all looked on as she opened it, the big smile plastered on her face changing into a look of confusion as a necklace with a small locket stared at her. She took the necklace out of the box before throwing it to the ground. She turned the locket around to see if it had her great grandmother's initials engraved in it—and it did.

Her forehead crinkled in confusion. She looked bewildered and wide-eyed, and really didn't look like she knew where she was or what she was doing. She kept looking around, and her eyes kept darting back and forth very fast. She looked like she didn't trust anyone there.

"Where did you get this from?" She turned to look at Scooter as she held up the necklace.

"What?" he asked, the claps, cheers, and music making it hard for him to hear her.

Aphtan grabbed his hand and pulled him toward the large glass door to go outside. The cool air attacked their skin as the ushers held the door open for them. She waited for the doors to close before she continued with her rant.

"Where did you get this necklace?" She held it up again in his face.

"I don't remember." He scratched his head as he tried to think. "It was in my safe, baby. Why?"

"It belonged to my fucking mother." She bit her lip and walked off.

Scooter stood frozen as that night came to him

and knocked the wind out of his stomach. Small beads of sweat formed on his forehead as he tried to speak, but nothing would come out. His legs wouldn't allow him to move. The only thing he could do at that moment was tell Aphtan the truth. He prayed it wouldn't end them.

"This shit isn't adding up." She paced back and forth in front of him. "My mama is missing, and all of a sudden you have the one thing that she always wore."

"Aphtan," he called out, but it fell on deaf ears.

"You have to remember something." She continued to pace back and forth.

"Aphtan,"—he grabbed her to make her stop walking—"she's dead."

Aphtan never felt a pain so strong, so demanding in her life. Every pore in her skin dripped a little bit of sweat as she tried to register what Scooter had just told her. She didn't know how to react to it. It was too much to deal with. She felt like Bambi in that moment, and he was the hunter that took her mother's life.

She told herself to move, but her body wouldn't listen to her commands. She was in a world of hurt, and her emotions were at an all-time high. She touched her throat to make sure she could feel a pulse as she caught her breath that she wasn't even losing. She was seeing things, hearing things, and everything around her started to spin.

She was going to fall at any moment. She caught her balance as her heart fluttered when she thought about life without her mother. She had concluded she was dead a long time ago. Speculation and the truth were two very different things, and now that it was confirmed, she had to feel the pain behind that truth. There was no escaping it.

The tears flowed effortlessly. She stood still, hunched over as the tears ran down her face like rain falling onto the window of a parked car. She didn't want to wipe them. They were a testament to how much she loved her mother. They were falling, each one a piece of her heart leaving her body.

"How did it happen?" Aphtan asked between sobs.

"It was before we moved in together." Scooter talked with his hands. "She came to my crib for some rock, and she tried to attack me. I didn't know it was your mother. Had I known, I wouldn't have pulled the trigger."

"Oh, my God." She tilted her head back as she kneeled down slowly. "Oh, my God."

"Aphtan?" He put his hand on her shoulder.

"Get the fuck off of me," she screamed. "I can't believe you let me spend the last six years searching for her, and you knew she was dead."

"I'm sorry," he said honestly. "I didn't know it was your mother, baby."

"Did my father know?" She rocked back and forth.

"Yes."

"Go get my fucking car," Aphtan screamed at the valet who was watching from the front of the street.

"Where are you going? The party is still going on."

"I don't give a fuck about this party." Her hands began to shake. "It's best that I get away from you right now before I do something I'll regret." She walked toward the street to wait for her car. "Do not follow me, Christopher."

Aphtan snatched the keys from the valet before getting inside of the ruby-red Mercedes. She took her heels off and tossed them in the backseat. She put the car in drive, smashed her foot against the gas pedal, and sped off as fast as the engine would allow her. She didn't know where she was going, but she had to be alone. She needed to mourn.

CHAPTER 18

The four gentlemen that were dressed warmly instantly took off their coats when they entered the cozy restaurant. The air smelled of pepper, and the hostess glared at them as if they were the reason why she had to be there. One man arched a brow and smiled at his brother beside him. His brother was not paying attention, but he did snort at the hostess's rude behavior. The third man did not really care about his surroundings, because he was debating with himself. He tended to look angry when he was thinking.

"You are upsetting the waitress," Money said. His eyes were extremely brown, like honey resting in a jar. But the third man did not hear him. Instead, his face became darker.

"I'm sorry, Pop." Scooter sat down at the table. "I got a lot of shit on my mind."

"Hey, what do you want?" the waitress said defensively.

"Well, aren't we unhappy today? Four scotches," Danny ordered.

Danny was six-foot-eight in height, with a neat fade, dark skin, and dark brown eyes. He had a scar from his left pectoral to the right of his hip, which some people said he received from the streets, yet his abdominal muscles were gained through manual labor. He had a slight five o'clock shadow, visible but not overgrown. On his right shoulder there was inscribed a tribal wolf tattoo, perhaps a hint at his true identity.

"I don't drink no fucking scotch," Buggy interjected.

Buggy had blue eyes, the color of a shallow pond in the middle of the day, that rested above his curved nose. A smile stretched across his face, his perfect white teeth almost shining against his pale pink lips. His slightest bit of stubble matched his dark chocolate, barely waved hair that grazed his forehead ever so slightly. His black shirt, unbuttoned at the top, contrasted his fair skin, making him stand out, which made tearing your eyes away difficult.

"Three scotches and a beer," Danny corrected his order.

Money waited until the waitress left and said, "So, is it time yet?"

"I don't think so." Scooter shook his head. "Aphtan and I are already going through enough bullshit." He looked down at his phone. "The last thing we need is her father coming up dead. She doesn't even know I'm back in the game."

Money sat up in the chair. "Son, this isn't about your marriage woes. This is business. You know some of the decisions you have to make when you're in this business."

Danny pulled a cigar out of his blazer pocket. "Nonetheless, Boss isn't an easy man to get to. After he did that bid, his security got airtight."

"That's true," Buggy agreed. "We worked for the nigga in the beginning. We know how he operates."

"He's touchable." Money looked around the table. "Trust me, he can be touched. Anyone can."

The table grew silent as the waitress set the three oval glasses and the beer in front of them. They ordered food and drinks for the future before the waitress took the menus and left. They all sat for a moment, to let what Money said marinate.

Scooter felt uneasy as he took a sip of the dry scotch. Aphtan wasn't answering his calls, and it had been well over three days since the night of the party. No one had seen or heard from her. His first priority was fixing his marriage, and plotting Boss's death wouldn't help his case any.

"Scooter can get to him," Money tossed the idea out there.

"I'm not doing it." Scooter set his glass down. "I'm not killing that man, Pop."

"I agree with you, Money." Buggy sipped from the cold beer. "Scooter is the only one who can get to Boss."

"Boss doesn't trust Scooter." Danny dipped his cigar in his drink. "I know that for a fact."

"Exactly." Scooter took the scotch to the head and waved for the waitress to bring him another one. "I can't get any closer to Boss than anyone here."

"Scooter,"—Money held the oval glass firmly in his hand—"I'm not asking you to do shit."

"You're not telling me, either." The waitress set another glass in front of Scooter and left with the empty one. "I'm not a kid anymore, Pop. If I don't want to do something, I don't have to dance around it. I'm just going to tell you no."

"Is that so." Money laughed. "Son, your nuts will never be bigger than mine."

"Listen." Danny stopped the argument that was about to happen. "If there's any other options, let's go over them."

"I don't trust you two yet." Buggy pointed at Money and Scooter simultaneously. "If you want me on board, one hundred percent, Scooter has to kill Boss. I want to know you two are loyal."

"Y'all niggas can't hear or something?" Scooter stood up. "I don't give a fuck what you want, Buggy. I don't trust anybody at this table. Either we're going to handle this business or not."

Scooter's face was beyond just red as he threw the oval glass as hard as he could. He was turning different shades of crimson and even a tinge purple, while a sort of an unearthly, demonic look over came him. His breathing became strange, sort of ragged. The men around the table noticed as he tried in vain to control himself, but his anger still sparked through the air, giving them a cold jolt of fear.

All they saw was rage, but he saw everything else. Memories of him and Aphtan were replaying over and over in his head, and it just wouldn't stop. So, he killed her mother, he had a moment of weakness, and now she was getting her revenge unknowingly, torturing him with those ignored calls.

Though he could see they were shocked and afraid, they had no reason to be. He was angry at himself, his stupidity, and his weakness. He deserved every minute of her ignoring him. Every tear that fell from her eyes that night was like a dagger, and inside he deserved it all. The self-loathing and rage was so intense. He had been holding his breath. He exhaled, breaking the tense silence between them; his sighs shook with emotion, and cold bullets of sweat trickled down his face.

"What the fuck are y'all looking at?" Scooter screamed at the onlookers before he sat back down.

"Are you done with your temper tantrum?" Money asked.

"I'm just going through some shit." Scooter wiped his forehead.

"You can't let your personal mix in with the business."

"I know, Pop."

"The fact remains that Boss has to die." Buggy took a sip from the new beer that the waitress had set in front of him.

"I'll handle it," Scooter assured the table. "I'll get it done."

Aphtan yawned as she looked around the guest bedroom, which was furnished in rich Persian jewel tones. She squirmed around the king-size bed draped in a luxurious satin bed skirt with flowing cherry reds, burnt oranges and golds, with splashes of midnight blue. Solid blue silk sheets carried through the blue splash, and an oversize comforter shimmering with paisleys that reflected the colors of the bed skirt rested underneath her.

Dancing against the west wall were flames from a crackling fire in a fireplace studded with historic tiles. Flanking the fireplace were two Victorian-era crystal sconces. Aphtan wiped the morning out of her eyes as the sun greeted her face with its rays. She got out of the bed and dragged herself into the bathroom.

She cut on the light and stared at herself in the huge mirror above the sink. Bags had found a home underneath her eyes. Her skin was pale and breaking out. Her hair was untamed, which was rare for her. She was depressed, and as she grabbed the toothbrush to brush her teeth, it finally hit her.

"Aphtan?" Mila called from the door of the room.

"I'm in the bathroom," she called out as she cut on the faucet.

"Look who wanted to see their auntie this morning." Mila entered the bathroom as she held her son up so that he could face Aphtan.

"Look at my fat man." She put the toothbrush on the sink and grabbed him. "You're getting so big, aren't you?" She gave him kisses on the forehead as he smiled from hearing her voice. "You will never hurt auntie, will you?"

"I still can't believe Scooter killed Simone." Mila cut off the faucet and leaned against the counter. "I know your head has to be fucked up right now."

"It is,"—she cradled the baby in her arms—"look at me."

"I see." Mila ran her fingers through Aphtan's hair. "I haven't seen your hair like this in years."

"Tell me about it." Aphtan walked past her to go to the bed. "My heart is broken. How can I love my husband after something like that? How can I trust him again after he kept something like that from me? This is my mama we're talking about. The woman who gave me life, and he killed her." Tears began to form in her eyes.

Mila grabbed her son and sat next to her on the bed. "You're going to hurt. That's normal. Simone is gone, but Scooter is still here. I don't know what I'd do in a situation like this. I just know that Scooter is in love with you. If Levi treated me half as good as the way Scooter treats you, I would have a football field full of kids."

Aphtan thought about how she felt about Scooter. She started to question whether she could live without him. She tried to remember anything else that he had done to make her question him. There was nothing else. When she couldn't answer the one question that she asked herself over and over, she realized that she needed to talk to him.

"I still love him." Aphtan fell back onto the bed. "I'm still in love with him."

"Then go talk to your husband." Mila got up as the baby started to go to sleep. "I'm going to go put him down for his nap. You should definitely call Scooter. You need to go home."

"I know," she agreed as Mila walked out of the door.

Aphtan let Mila's words run through her mind like a marathon runner. She needed to talk to

Scooter. Forgiving him wouldn't be easy, but she had to try; she owed him that. Crashing at Mila's wouldn't solve anything. She gathered her things and left with hopes that whatever was broken could be fixed in her marriage.

CHAPTER 19

Tsunami stood on the porch with her hands behind her back. Her eyes dazzled with the amber glow of the porch light as it reflected against her gray eyes. She peered into the darkness surrounding the brightness of the light and smiled.

Emerging from the darkness was Scooter, one hand in the pocket of his jeans and with chiseled features that looked as if they were shaped by the sculptor Michelangelo. He ambled up the stairs and towered over Tsunami.

"Hey," he said gently.

Tsunami's inner soul was infiltrated with warmth that made her feel alive. His voice was sufficient to make her feel comfortable. Hiding on the outskirts of town made her feel anything but safe. With Scooter, she felt safe, secure, and loved.

"Scooter." She looked up and gazed into his eyes. "What took you so long?"

He put his hand underneath her chin and looked into her eyes. "I'm sorry. You know I had to handle business."

Her eyes watered as she put her arms around his waist. "I'm just happy that you're here."

"I know." He wiped the tears from her eyes. "I'll make some moves to get you two out of hiding as soon as I can."

Scooter leaned forward with closed eyes and placed his rosy lips on Tsunami's. A strong surge of electricity commenced and loosened the tightness of her muscles. Her doubt was suddenly consumed in an instant.

"I know, baby," she said, withdrawing from his face.

"Where's little man?" He looked through the open front door.

"Inside playing." She kissed him again.

"Chris," Scooter yelled as he put his hands to his mouth, "your daddy is here."

Scooter stepped closer to the door to see his son sitting on the floor. Chubby and pale, he sat on the marble floor playing with his trucks. His light gray eyes and thick shaggy hair reflected the light in the room. He was enjoying the loneliness as he made "vroom" and "chooo" noises. Scooter giggled, and his head snapped up. He looked at his father with happy eyes as he stood up to run toward him.

As he ran with full passion and speed, joy spread across his face with every step. As he leaped in the air into Scooter's arms, a look of pure happiness crossed his face. As he landed with a soft thud, shrieks of laughter filled the air.

"Hi, Daddy," he said as he grabbed his neck.

"Hi, son." Scooter kissed him on the forehead. "Have you been good for your mama?"

"Yes," the little boy answered, then giggled.

"You sure?" He kissed him again.

Scooter looked at his son as the moon's beauty lit his face. It was his seed; there was no denying it. They were identical. He hadn't been happy when he first found out about Tsunami being pregnant. It was right before he and Aphtan got married, and the last thing he needed was a child from his side piece ruining them before they started.

He didn't want the child at first. He gave Tsunami a slew of options for getting rid of the child. But, when he was born, and he looked into his eyes, it was a feeling he had never felt before. He promised Tsunami that he would always take care of them, under one condition: that she disappeared. She obliged.

No one from around the way had seen Tsunami in years. Rumor had it she had moved up north. Little did anyone know, she had been closer than they thought. With designer everything and unlimited money available at her whim, she didn't mind being the side piece. Scooter would never leave Aphtan. She had come to terms with that. As long as she had given him something Aphtan couldn't, she was happy.

"Do you love me, Scooter?" Tsunami laid her head on his shoulder as she tickled their son.

"I care about you," he answered honestly.

Tsunami watched the man that she loved, the man she had given a child to, look at her with regretful eyes. He didn't regret their son; however, he did regret having him with her, and she could feel it. She went in the house to let them spend some time together. When Scooter left, there was no telling when he would be around again.

                        *   *   *

Boss removed the bags from Danny's and Buggy's heads as one of his lieutenants threw water on their faces to wake them up. They tried to move, but their bodies were bound to the chairs that they were in. Their faces were wounded, and it was apparent that someone used them for punching bags.

Boss slid a chair in front of them before he took a seat. One of his workers handed him a glass of Hennessy as he leaned back to look at the two men he had grown up with. He shook his head at the way they had betrayed him as their mumbles echoed throughout the abandoned warehouse.

"Snakes." Boss took a sip from the glass. "There's nothing I hate more than a motherfucking snake."

"Boss—" Danny tried to explain.

"Save it." Boss held up his hand, cutting him off. "I already know everything. We were like family." He shook his head. "I can't believe y'all would do me like this."

"You didn't give us a choice." Buggy coughed as blood spewed from his mouth.

"Life is about choices." Boss stood up. "Y'all just made the wrong one."

Bullets flew into their bodies at the command of Boss. They took their last breaths as the bonds they once shared severed and they left the earth. Their bodies slumped over, lifeless. He simply drank from his glass without a hint of remorse on his face.

"I knew these niggas all of my life." Boss eyed the room. "Take a good look at them. Loyalty is loyalty, and if you're disloyal, this is what will happen to you. I won't lose any sleep over it."

Boss tossed his empty glass to one of the workers

as Cole walked through the door. He signaled for him to come over to where he was standing. Cole approached him as the Timberlands on his feet pattered calmly. He unbuttoned the top button to his polo as he observed the dead bodies bound to the chairs in front of him. He looked at Boss. "Why am I here?"

"You're here to see this." Boss put a blunt to his lip.

"I see it." Cole put his hands inside of his pockets.

"You see what happens when you're disloyal?" Boss asked.

"Boss,"—Cole's shoulders tensed—"what is the moral behind this?"

"I need to know you're loyal. Your father and brother are coming for me. How do I know you're not in on what they are planning?"

"I haven't talked to them in years," Cole protested. "I don't give a fuck what they do."

"I believe you." Boss lit the blunt. "Just keep running the projects, and I'll let you know when I need you."

"All right." Cole walked out of the warehouse, and the man guarding the door handed him his guns back.

He put the guns back on his body as he walked to his Range Rover. He opened the door. The leather seats felt perfect against his skin as he got inside. He started the car and drove off as he thought about how his life got so off track.

He drove through the city, imagining how different his life would have been if he had gone to college and never got in the game. Thoughts of Aphtan invaded his mind as he came to a red light.

It had been years since she had seen him. He'd
seen her, all of the time, but he made sure to keep
his distance. She didn't know if he was alive or
dead, and probably didn't care, yet he still thought
about her every day. Those few months he had
spent around her were special to him. It infuriated
him that she ended up with Scooter.

The relationship between him and his brother
stopped the moment Scooter and Aphtan moved
in together. He didn't want to seem like a sore
loser, but he couldn't deny he was bitter. Scooter
would bring her nothing but pain and misery. He
hated that Scooter was going to ruin her life.

Cole parked in front of his condo as he shook
the thoughts of Aphtan from his mind. He got out
of the car and walked up the sidewalk as a small
breeze hit him in the face. Staying loyal to Boss
meant that he would always be on the side that
protected Aphtan. That was all the confirmation he
needed. Money and Scooter were blood, but he
would do anything for her. Even if she didn't know it.

CHAPTER 20

Aphtan pulled into the circular parking area in front of her home. The size of it was breathtaking. It was an older mansion with renovations that would make it on par with any newly built one. It shined in different shades of brown with canary yellow offsets to complement the style. The home was of high value. It was simply gorgeous.

She got out of the car as her maid, Madeline, met her before the door could close behind her. Aphtan walked into the house with Madeline following. Everything looked opulent, from the gleaming wood floors covered in lovely throw rugs, to the sheer curtains billowing like mist on the walls.

The furnishings were old, but had a story to tell, so they had to be antiques with what looked like hand-carved workmanship. Each area of the room melted into the beauty of the next with some delicate settees next to more heavy bookcases and fireplaces that mated with the walls.

Aphtan walked into the kitchen as light gleamed through the window onto the shiny utensils in the kitchen. High-tech appliances strangely fit in with the traditional feel of the old house. She sat down at the island as Madeline poured her a drink.

"Where have you been, Mrs. Dixon?" Madeline set a wineglass down in front of her. "You haven't been home in days. Is everything okay with you and Mr. Dixon?"

A florid, corpulent woman, Madeline stood in front of her with heavy breasts and an ample bottom. Her chest mocked her stout frame. One's eyes wavered around the bosom as they followed the contours of her body that curved pleasantly inward, lightly cinched at the waist, before moving outward as the invisible line caressed the thickness of her thighs and the large, rounded derriere.

"No." Aphtan put her elbow on the top of the island and rested her head on her hand. "I'm really angry with him right now, Madeline."

She poured some more chilled red wine into the tall glass. "Whatever it is, it will be okay. You two were meant to be together. After working for you for all of these years, I know that for sure."

"Are you two talking about me?" Scooter walked into the kitchen and stood on the other side of the island.

"*Sí*," Madeline replied as she put the wine away. "I'll let you two talk," she said before she left the room.

Aphtan sipped on the wine as she and Scooter stared at each other. He played with his beard, waiting for her to break the ice that they had both formed. She set the glass down and twirled her wedding ring around her finger. She held it out in front of her to see if she still got butterflies just from looking at it.

"Aphtan—" Scooter walked around the island.

"I know," she cut him off and stood up to hug him. "I know you didn't mean for it to happen."

"I didn't know it was Simone." He wrapped his arms around her. She could tell from his body language that her smell drove him as crazy as it always had.

"I believe you." She kissed his lips over and over again. "I know you wouldn't do anything like that to me."

"Never." He reached down and put his hand inside of hers. "We in this thing for life."

"Until the casket drops." She hugged him with passion. "I've missed you."

"What did you miss about me?" He bit his lip and slowly felt on her pussy through her jeans.

"Everything." She rubbed on his manhood, and it began to grow in her hand.

Her body begged for his touch as the air that allowed her to be conscious exited her mouth at his presence. Aphtan couldn't picture anywhere better to be at that moment. She was enjoying every second of his hands on her body and vice versa. The passion between them was so raw, so real, that they almost couldn't contain themselves.

Scooter picked her up, turned her around, and sat her on top of the island. He kissed her as his hands slowly trailed down to the buttons of her pants. He sucked on her tongue as he used one hand to unfasten her jeans and the other to fondle her breast. He rose up her shirt and whirled his tongue around her erect nipples one by one.

"Scooter," Aphtan moaned as she tried to lift his head, "stop it."

"Why?" He continued to taste her flesh.

"Because we have three maids." She tilted her head back in ecstasy.

"Don't worry about them." He pulled her pants down. "This is our house."

Scooter pulled his shirt off with an urgency he had never known before as Aphtan groped his member and fumbled with his pants. He kissed the lips of her identity, sucking slowly on her pearl. She moaned and grabbed at his head with pleasure, begging him to continue. His tongue played peekaboo with her opening as he went in and out. Sucking and slurping constantly, it wasn't long before she had creamed inside of his mouth.

She took his hands and placed them on her breast while kissing his face and neck. Upon disrobing in the commotion, there was a pause filled with peace only, to be broken with the pain of entry. Their bodies collided and danced in the motions of delectation while reaching for the unattainable, only to fall in the abyss over again.

She glided her hands over his smooth skin and tasted the salt of his sweat on her lips. The movement of his hips, thrusting against hers, drove her to ecstasy. She lost her breath a little with each stroke, but the feeling was worth it. Aphtan felt like she was an addict, and she was getting her drug of choice in the midst of an overdose.

Scooter stroked faster with each cry that left Aphtan's mouth. She couldn't imagine anywhere else she would rather be at that moment. Inside of her was home to him, and she loved every second of it.

His body tensed up as she tightened the grip on his dick with her pussy muscles. She couldn't resist; she would climax any second. He kissed her as her nails dug in his back like a lion ripping open a gazelle after a hunt. Their bodies shook in unison as they shared their happy endings together. They gasped to catch their breath as sweat fell from their bodies onto the top of the island.

"I needed that." Scooter took his manhood out of her.

"We both did." Aphtan bit his neck gently.

"I'm about to go shower and handle some business." He put his clothes on as she hopped off the island.

"That's fine, love." Aphtan kissed him as she slid her pants up her legs.

The butterflies almost flew out of her stomach as she watched Scooter walk out of the kitchen. She was still madly in love with him. The way she had an urge to write his name on any piece of paper nearby like she was a little girl assured her of it. She couldn't imagine life without him in it.

She collected the rest of her clothes and walked out of the kitchen as she played with her wedding ring with her thumb. Forgiving him for murdering her mother was going to take some time. There was no way that he could change it. As she walked up the beautiful staircase, she prayed that she would be able to fully forgive him one day.

Cole stood in total awe outside the main offices of Epps Enterprises. It made him feel so tiny and insignificant. The base of the building occupied an entire city block. Looking up, he saw it went on and on; the top literally vanishing in the distance. He didn't falter, although it was his first time going to see Boss where he worked. He walked through the double doors as if he had been there countless times before.

"How may I help you?" the cheerful blond receptionist asked him as he approached the large, circular wooden desk in the middle of the floor.

"I'm here to see Lester Epps." Cole looked around the first floor as people scurried by.

"Do you have an appointment?" she asked as she fixed the headset on her head.

"Yes." Cole leaned against the desk.

"What is your name?"

"Cole Dixon."

"One moment." She turned around and spoke into the microphone at her mouth. She turned back around. "Go all the way up to the top floor. He's expecting you."

Cole pushed the metal button outside the steel elevator door, waiting for the digital reader to display the floor. Anxiety began to build in his stomach as he waited. He didn't enjoy being inside of an enclosed space.

Ding! The elevator arrived. He wiped his sweaty palms on his slacks, took a deep breath, and dug his loafers against the threshold. Thankfully, other people joined in his elevator ride.

"What floor?" a voice asked through the intercom inside of the elevator. His mouth opened but words couldn't find their way out. The pounding of his heart over took his reality. He looked left. Then right. Beads of sweet began falling down his forehead. He didn't care. He was frozen. Unable to speak or move, he put his back against the back of the moving box.

Both hands gripped the rails inside the elevator car. White-knuckling his way past twenty floors, he wished he had taken the stairs, but he was running late for his appointment. As he began fearing the worst, the elevator stopped. It was his floor. At the topmost floor, the city became a mere map beneath Cole.

In his uncomfortable moment, he must have uttered the floor he desired to go to. He collected himself. He tightened his polo button up, ran his hands over the waves in his head, and walked out of the elevator smoothly.

He found himself in a large lobby. The floors were made of colored tiles arranged in beautiful patterns, and the walls were made of glass, revealing additional views of the city. A frosted glass partition separated the lobby from a large, private office. Silk banners hung from the ceiling. Polished stone pedestals held golden and silver statues portraying nude men and women. Everything in the room was rich and lavish.

"Mr. Dixon?" the woman at the desk directly in front of the elevator asked as he stepped off.

"Yes." Cole wiped the sweat from his forehead.

"Right this way, sir." The woman got up as she directed him to follow her.

Cole admired the paintings along the hallway as they made their way down the trail. Small statues aligned the tile they walked on. Golden lights hung vertically from the ceiling, showing any and every imperfection on the visitors' faces.

They stopped at a large oak door as the lady knocked softly against it. She hit the button for the intercom on the side of the door before crossing her arms into each other. She looked back at Cole and smiled as the red button on the intercom lit up.

"I have a Mr. Dixon here for you, Mr. Epps," she said cheerfully into the microphone.

The door opened as the lady signaled for him to go inside. Cole walked into the room, the large exotic-fish tank by the entrance catching his attention. He watched wild fish swim freely as he walked deeper into the office. A strong smell of a man's cologne filled the room like a potent candle.

Cole approached the large desk as Boss sat behind it, draped in a business suit. He took a seat in one of the large chairs in front of the desk as large windows on the wall allowed him to see the city from a view he hadn't before. Boss held his finger up to let him know it would be a minute as he held the receiver of the phone to his ear.

Cole continued to observe the office. A flat-screen television took up the wall directly behind him with a picture showed so crisp that it felt like you were a part of whatever program being watched. Directly in front of the television were off-white Italian leather sofas with burnt orange pillows. A table with every popular magazine on top of it separated the two.

"I'm glad you could make it." Boss put the phone on the hook. "How do you like my corporation?"

"Kind of hard to believe a man like you would run a company this big." Cole sat back in the plush seat. "I guess doing that bid made you smarter."

"I've always been smart." He stood up, hit a button on a small white remote, and the blinds started to cover the window. "See, I went to jail, that is true. However, while I was in there, I had businesses all over that no one knew about. Of course I had to let other people run them because Aphtan's mother was strung out. Nonetheless, my bank account ain't never looked so good."

"I'm guessing you didn't ask me to come all the way here to tell me your life story."

"Of course not." Boss sat back down. "You know it's strictly business."

"Then what do you need?"

"Are you thirsty?"

"Somewhat." Cole swiveled a little in his seat.

Boss hit the intercom on his desk. "Rachel, bring me two glasses of anything brown."

"I don't drink."

"It's a first time for everything."

The woman from the front desk scurried inside of the office with a glass in each hand. She set one in front of Boss and then one in front of Cole. She asked them if they needed anything else before she paced out of the office and closed the door behind her. Boss took a sip from the glass as Cole watched his drink.

"You should taste it." He nodded toward the drink.

"I don't drink." Cole slid the drink from in front of him. "Nothing has changed in the matter of minutes it took your secretary to pour it and bring it."

"I see." Boss sat his glass down. "I've asked you here today, Cole, because I need a problem eliminated."

"What kind of problem?"

"Your brother." Boss waited for Cole's facial expression to change, but it didn't. "I need him to disappear. He's the brains of the operation. That is a fact. Whatever your father is planning will just be a plan that Scooter comes up with that he will take credit for. Scooter is the thinker between those two."

"When do you need this done by?" Cole stood up.

"I'll let you decide that." Boss grinned as Cole started to walk toward the door. "You have nothing to say about this?"

Cole stopped, never looking back. "There's nothing to say."

Cole's body language didn't make it clear whether he would be able to go along with the order he was just given. It was an order even Scooter couldn't follow, and he was more ruthless than Cole. His life was based upon whether he could do something like this. It was sink or swim for Cole, and sinking meant death.

CHAPTER 21

Aphtan's hands jumped wildly as she tugged at the pale blue hospital gown. The parceling paper underneath her crumbled with every movement that she made. The sound of little drips of water falling from the head of the faucet next to her drove her insane as her stomach whimpered with emotion.

She looked down at the Band-aid on her arm that the nurse had put on after taking her blood. She had been there so many times that the excitement she used to feel turned into fear. Every time she had thought she was pregnant in the past, it always turned out to be just a thought. She wanted to give Scooter a baby more than anything in the world.

She made a beat with her hand against the metal of the bed as she waited for the doctor to come and give her a yes or no. Her heart fluttered. She couldn't move. She wanted to get up and put her clothes back on, but her body wouldn't allow her that luxury.

Her throat became dryer than it already was as the eggshell-white door opened. Her physician, Verna Coffee, came into the room and sat down in the chair in front of the bed. She watched her look through her folder as she crossed her legs. Minutes passed as Aphtan sat there about to faint. The anticipation was too much.

"Just give it to me." Aphtan blew air out of her mouth.

"Well,"—Verna put her hand on Aphtan's leg—"you're not pregnant."

"Are you sure?" She squelched across the paper underneath her. "I thought I was this time for sure. Why do I keep missing my period like this?"

"Are you stressing?"

"That's an understatement."

"Aphtan." Verna stood up and put her arm around her. "Whatever it is you're stressing about, you have to let go. Stress isn't good. Especially for us black women."

"I know, Verna," she agreed, addressing her by her first name. "It's hard not to stress."

"That's for everybody," Verna said as she sat on the teal bed next to her. "We all stress, that's life. But what separates some from others is the ability to dissect the stress and cope with whatever's wrong."

"I think you're right." Aphtan wiped her eyes and eased off of the bed. "Let me get my clothes on and get out of here."

"Hey," Verna called out after she walked to the door, "you'll get pregnant when God says it's time. Remember that." She left the room.

Aphtan put on her clothes with a heavy heart. The only good thing about the news was that she hadn't gotten Scooter's hopes up. She walked into the waiting area to leave. She was happy she hadn't told him this time.

"What happened?" Mila stood up to greet her.

"I'm not pregnant." Aphtan shook her head as she fought back tears.

"I'm sorry, best friend." Mila hugged her tightly. "It will happen. When you least expect it, that's when it'll happen."

"I'm tired of waiting."

"Anything worth having is worth waiting on." Mila hugged her as they walked out of the doctor's office. "Let's go get some food, my treat."

A cold breeze brushed against the tree that hung over the parking lot, making the leaves shiver under the too bright sun as they got inside the car. Aphtan laid her head on the window as if it were a pillow and enjoyed the ride.

Aphtan had weighed her options before the appointment. She understood the chances, yet she couldn't help but to feel down. She felt like she was failing as a wife. Scooter wanted a child. It was all he had talked about for years. It was the one thing that she couldn't give him.

They parked at a restaurant and got out of the car. As they walked through the doors, the smell of soul food made their stomachs thump. They waited in the long line in silence. Aphtan wasn't in a talking mood, and Mila knew how she had acted last time, so she let her be.

"Tsunami?" Mila turned her head to the side so she could see the front of the line. "Is that you?" she asked as Aphtan looked with her.

Tsunami pretended she didn't hear Mila as she grabbed her bags off the counter. A look of worry took over her face as she turned around, her hand in her son's. There was no other way to leave. She had to walk by them.

Tsunami walked slowly to the door, changing her expression to a happy one. The pearl necklace around her neck felt as if it was going to choke her the closer she got to them. Her nerves were getting the best of her, and she hadn't even reached them yet.

"Black? Lotus? It's been years. How are y'all?" Tsunami stood in front of her son to block him.

Aphtan looked down at the little boy and smiled. He reminded her of someone, but she could not put her finger on it. His eyes were familiar. The shape of his head, the way he stood, and his dimples seemed so familiar. Everything about the little boy reminded her of her husband.

Aphtan had always heard rumors about Tsunami and Scooter, but she never entertained them. She even went as far as to ask Scooter if he had ever had a fling with Tsunami, and he denied it. The way that her stomach grew sour, she realized that he had lied all those years ago. Her woman's intuition was telling her that she was looking at Scooter's son.

She opened her eyes and gave Tsunami a death stare. She was waiting for an explanation. If Tsunami said anything out of the way to her in that second, she would have slapped the eyelashes off of her face. Aphtan was furious. Another betrayal at the hands of her husband.

"Girl, we just been living." Mila looked at Aphtan's face, wondering if she had the same thought as her. "You had a baby, too?"

"Girl, yes I did." Tsunami tried to stop the little boy from moving around so much. "That's why I haven't been around. I'm just a full-time mom now."

"I see." Mila looked at Aphtan, whose eyes remained on the little boy's.

"Well, it was good seeing you two. Y'all take care." Tsunami tried to make an exit before Aphtan grabbed her arm. "Let me go." She tried to pull away.

Aphtan got close enough to her so the child couldn't hear. "I know that's my husband's child, bitch. I'm not going to cause a scene, because I know that fact already. What I want you to know is that I think you're dumb as fuck. Obviously this was a mistake, because I haven't heard shit about this. He won't even mention either of you."

"You're the dumb one, bitch," Tsunami snarled. "I gave him something you are having such a hard time giving him. He loves *our* son. Take a good look at what caused you to never catch up to me. I will always have Scooter. That's the fact you should be worrying about." She pulled her arm away from Aphtan's grip.

"See you around," Aphtan called out the door as she pulled out her phone and dialed Scooter's number.

"Tell me she didn't just say that." Mila shook her head as she watched the door close behind Tsunami.

"Scooter, get the fuck home, now," Aphtan screamed into the phone as she walked out of the building with tears in the eyes.

She was broken. There was nothing Scooter could say to save them. She could forgive him for a lot of things, but getting a woman pregnant and not telling her was a betrayal that she could never come back from. She didn't know how she was going to look at him. As the tears fell, she knew that she could never lie next to him again. She could never kiss him again. She could never make love to him again. Their marriage was over.

CHAPTER 22

"Aphtan, calm down." Scooter spoke calmly into the phone as he sat in his parked car on the street directly across from the private lake.

Watching Boss for the majority of the morning, he was finally ready to make his move. Today was the day he was going to kill Boss. The last thing he needed to hear was Aphtan finding out about his son with Tsunami. It was a distraction to him. It was something he would have to address, but now wasn't the time. He needed to remain focused to be as sharp as a knife.

"Baby," he blew out of his mouth in aggravation. "Let's talk about this face-to-face. Let's talk about this when I make it home."

"You don't have a fucking home," Aphtan screamed through the phone.

"You don't mean that, love." His attention remained on Boss.

"Get here now," she screamed again before hanging up the phone.

A plopping sound echoed as a fish broke the surface of the water and ripples widened out. Boss was at the edge of the lake now, the pebbles under foot. A moorhen was disturbed and ran off along the bank, distracting him from its nest. A kestrel, attracted by the disturbance, hovered above the next field. The smell of water was calming. Ever since he was little, being around water took his mind off whatever it was stuck on.

Boss lay down on the edge of the water and peered into its depths as a bottle of Hennessey rested in his hand. Pondweed and small insects were the first thing to be seen. As he remained still, layers of water somehow became apparent: the open light layer with minnows darting about; the next, darker layer, where a large carp was sitting, watching him as he watched it. Then the dark bottom of the pond, where the brown silt moved with life.

The dragonflies caught his attention, landing on a bulrush nearby. Boss lifted his gaze for a moment to see them in their metallic blue finery. From the corner of his eye, he saw a shape move in the water. He looked back and realized there were loads of fish he never noticed before. He saw their black shapes, but did not recognize them as fish.

A sailboat rode slowly between Boss's small rowboat and the opposite shore, heading for the public landing at the park near the south end of the tranquil body of water. About ten feet from the shore where he was were lily pads and some water lilies coming up about three inches from the top of the water. In the midst of the lily pads was a log where a turtle was sitting, aware of his presence, but not alarmed.

It was evening, and the tall cedar and oak trees cast their reflections on the water on the west side of the lake, making a dark silhouette against the blue. When the wind blew, the sun's reflection made the ripples glimmer. Boss looked out at the street, wondering when Scooter would make his move. He had seen him the moment he pulled up.

Boss closed his eyes as shade cascaded over him. He didn't have to look; it was Scooter. He opened one of his eyes to let Scooter know that he saw him. He closed it back, his heartbeat remaining normal. It was obvious what was going to happen next.

"You must have promised my security something that I never would, to make them turn their back on me so quickly." Boss put his hands on his stomach.

"Loyalty is hard to find these days." Scooter pointed the gun at him. "You know that."

"I do know that." Boss sat up and took a sip from the bottle of Hennessy in his hand. "You're going to take the lives of both of your wife's parents?"

"I don't want to," Scooter said with honesty. "I've hurt her enough, but sometimes you don't have a choice. Sometimes your decisions are made for you. Sometimes you're dealt a shitty hand."

"Tell me about it." Boss looked at the gun in Scooter's hand. "Is that the gun that I gave you all those years ago?"

"It is." Scooter hit a bug that landed on his face. "I thought it would be fitting to use this gun to take your life."

"What are you waiting on?"

"For you to smoke your last blunt."

"A thoughtful murderer," Boss said and then laughed.

"I had a lot of respect for you. Enjoy your last blunt."

Boss took the small blunt off of the ground next to where he was sitting and lit it. He put it to his lips. It was his last blunt. He had only a few minutes to live. Scooter was going to kill him. The only thing left for him to do was ask God for forgiveness for all of the things he had ever done wrong. His life was about to end.

Boss stood up as he tossed the end of the blunt onto the grass. Scooter and he stared each other down as Boss held his arms open in the air, welcoming his end. He didn't flinch at all. It was bound to end this way one day.

"I'm ready, young blood."

"I'll make it quick." Scooter stepped closer to him.

"Make it whatever you like. I'm not begging for an easy death. It is what the fuck it is."

"Anything you want me to tell Aphtan?" Scooter cocked the gun.

"No." Boss shook his head as he hit his chest. "Stop stalling, Scooter. Do it, motherfucker."

Scooter pulled the trigger hesitantly, the bullet flying at full speed at Boss's head. It pierced through him with an unwelcome force, killing him instantly. Blood flowed into the stream of water as Boss lay halfway in the lake.

Scooter let out a sigh as he looked at the body. It

was stiff and taunting him. A man was dead, yet all Scooter saw was another problem in his household. If Aphtan ever found out, it would be hell to pay.

He pulled Boss out of the lake in fear that he would float away. He closed his eyes. He thought about how Boss had looked out for him when he was growing up. He had been more of a father figure than Money. He felt guilty. It was faint, but he still felt it.

"I didn't think you would do it." Money walked up to him. Scooter had noticed him a long time ago. Scooter knew he was watching. He always knew.

"Business is business." Scooter looked around the lake. "You didn't give me much of choice."

"You had one; you just chose this particular choice."

"Whatever you say." Scooter walked past him, brushing his shoulder with him. "You can tell Danny and Buggy that it's done."

"No need to." Money followed behind them. "They are dead."

Scooter laughed as he looked back at Boss's body. "That motherfucker moved quickly."

"He did," Money said as they walked onto the street. "I guess we are in this by ourselves."

"I guess so," Scooter agreed as a black Yukon pulled up in front of them.

"I'll let you know the next move." Money got inside of the truck. "Be ready."

"I stay ready," Scooter said as the door of the Yukon closed and the truck drove off.

Scooter walked to his car as he checked his surroundings one more time. He got in the car and tossed his phone, which was ringing nonstop. Both Aphtan and Tsunami were calling back to back. He didn't want to talk to either of them. As he zoomed down the empty street, he knew he would have to face the situation before the night was up.

CHAPTER 23

Aphtan paced back and forth in her large living room as her heart beat so fast that it hurt. All she could see was Tsunami and Scooter's son's face flashing over and over again in her head. She stopped in her steps and tried different breathing exercises to calm herself down, which was in vain. She was mad, sad, confused, and a slew of other emotions all in one.

It piqued her curiosity as to how many times Scooter had stepped out on her. When did he do it? Was he still doing it? Questions danced around her head like a choreographer. She needed answers, and as she sat on the couch and hit a button on her phone, she realized that she wouldn't wait another minute.

"Are you about to call him again?" Mila asked from the other sofa.

"You damn right." Aphtan held the phone to her ear. "He needs to get his ass here." She hung up the phone as the beep from the alarm rung to let her know the front door had opened.

Aphtan hopped up, her adrenaline rushing beyond her control. She paced to the hallway. The built-up emotion enraged her. Her insides boiled as her eyes looked at a calm Scooter, who trailed down the hallway at a normal speed.

"It took your ass long enough." Aphtan folded her arms into each other as Scooter passed her. "You got some fucking explaining to do, Christopher."

"You need to calm down first." Scooter turned to go into the kitchen. "I'm not talking to you while your neck rolling and shit."

"How the fuck am I supposed to feel?" Aphtan followed close behind him. "You had a baby on me." She pushed the back of his head. "How could you do that to me?"

"Keep your hands to yourself, Aphtan." Scooter stopped at the refrigerator to turn around and look at her. "We can talk, but keep your hands to yourself."

"If I want to put my hands on you, then I will." Aphtan pushed him in the forehead. She wiped the tears that were beginning to fall from her eyes. "Don't tell me what I can or can't do when you have been fucking off on me and had a baby on me."

Scooter's grip tightened around the handle of the stainless steel icebox as Aphtan stood in front of him heaving, trying to fight back tears. His heart ached for her. He loved her more than anything. Her heart breaking before his eyes pulled at his soft spot.

Aphtan was shaking. She was furious. Imagining him and Tsunami in that light made her sick to her stomach. She pushed him away after he repeatedly tried to grab her. With no energy left, she submitted to his urge to grab her as she cried into his chest as hard as she could.

"It's okay, Aphtan." Mila leaned against the entrance door. "It's all right."

Aphtan continued to sob as Scooter softly caressed her back. He ran his fingers through her hair as he used his free hand to hold her tighter. He stroked her cheek as he reached down and kissed her lips. Her lips remained still and closed as she turned her head to the side.

"Why?" she asked without looking at him. "This is the second wound on my heart that you've given me. Why do you want to hurt me?"

"I don't want to hurt you." Scooter grabbed her face gently and made her look at him. "I was fucking around with her long before we started kicking it. I promise I'm not in love with her. I don't want her."

"Why were you fucking with her anyway?" Aphtan shook her head. "Was I not enough?"

"You're more than enough."

"Bullshit," Mila said under her breath.

"Mila, shut the fuck up." Scooter pointed at her. "Your ass needs to be worrying about what your nigga is doing."

"Don't talk to her like that," Aphtan defended her.

Mila shot the bird at him. "Scooter, fuck you. Don't make this Maury Povich situation about me and my nigga."

"No, fuck you. Mind your fucking business," he snapped.

"Handle yours." Mila walked out of the room as she looked at Aphtan.

The silence between Aphtan and Scooter was

thicker than peanut butter. Lips opened with force, but no words managed to form and roll off their tongues. They stood there, stuck in a nasty place with no clue how to get out. It was going to take more than sex to fix their issues.

"I want to be married to you for the rest of my life," Scooter said, breaking the ice.

"You want your cake and eat it, too, Scooter." She leaned her head back and closed her eyes, her back against the island. "I don't know what I want. It's hard for me to trust you. What else are you hiding from me?"

Scooter held his hands up in the air. "There's only one other thing that you don't know about."

"My God," she screamed. "What is it now?"

"I'm back in the game."

"With my father?" she whispered.

"No." He leaned on the island next to her. "It's my own shit I got going."

"How long have you been back in the game?"

"About three years now," he answered honestly.

"You've been lying to me about everything. The places you've been going. The people who speak to us out in public. Where you go when you leave here," Aphtan huffed.

"I didn't lie, Aphtan. You never asked."

"So that makes it okay? You're back in the game. You know what that means? It means I need to be watching my back as much as you watch yours."

"I'm watching your back." He reached for her waist.

"I don't want you doing shit for me." She swatted his hand. "I think we need a break."

"You don't mean that."

"Aphtan," Mila screamed from the living room, "get in here."

Mila's voice startled Aphtan. It was a different kind of yell. It sent chills down her spine. She blinked, and before she knew it, she had run into the living room. The fear in Mila's voice made the blood in her hands rest. She had to find out what caused such an intense yelp.

She looked at Mila who had tears running down her face. Aphtan looked at the television after Mila pointed to it as her father's picture filled the screen. She didn't pay attention to anything else as she sat down and cut the volume up as far as it would go as her ears got hot.

"Alleged drug lord Lester Epps was found dead earlier today at a private lake off of East Highway 11800. Police say signs of foul play were present. Right now, there are no leads."

Aphtan threw the remote at the television, breaking the screen immediately.

"I'm going to ask you this once." Aphtan stood up and walked over to Scooter. "Did you have anything to do with this?"

"No." He shook his head and looked her in the eyes. "I didn't do this. I wouldn't do this to you. Not again."

"I swear I will never speak to you again if you did this." Aphtan's eyes began to run like a body of water after a dam broke.

"I just told you that I didn't have anything to do with it," Scooter pleaded.

"Your words don't mean shit to me right now." Aphtan eased past him as her voice shook. "They don't hold value."

"Aphtan?" Mila chased after her when she ran out of the room.

"I need to get out of here." She grabbed her keys.

"I'm coming with you." Mila grabbed her hand as they walked toward the front door.

"Aphtan, I'm sorry for your loss. Boss was a good man. I never wanted to see him go out like that," Scooter called out as the front door opened.

"Please be gone when I get back. I don't want to look at you right now. I can't do it." Aphtan slammed the door before she and Mila got inside the car and drove off.

"Aphtan?" Mila cut the music down.

Aphtan held her hand up. "Mila, I appreciate what you're about to say. I just need some quiet right now. Just ride, best friend." She cut the music back up as Mila nodded her head in compliance.

The wind blew in Aphtan's face as she let the tears flow as they wished. The cold truth of her being parentless made her hurt to heights she'd never known before. The pain filled her like helium finding a home inside of a balloon, and she was about to pop.

Everything was happening to her at once. Her mother's death, Scooter's betrayal, and now her father's early demise. It was too much for any one person to deal with. She was on the verge of a mental breakdown.

The tears continued to fall for her loved ones. Every tear was a memory that she cherished with her parents. Each tear was a moment, a minute, a second that she spent with them, forming an unbreakable bond.

"Thank you for everything, Daddy." Aphtan stopped at a red light and wiped the tears from her eyes.

"Are you okay?" Mila asked as a large, cold draft chilled the car.

"I will be." Aphtan closed her eyes, taking the wind as a sign that her father was right there with her. "I think I'll be okay." She wiped her eyes one last time and drove to the morgue to identify his body. She wanted to see him one last time before the funeral home got hold of him.

CHAPTER 24

Aphtan closed her suitcase, then she fastened her diamond earrings on her ears. She pranced around her house, collecting everything she would need when she traveled to her father's house. She wanted to make sure she didn't forget anything. She didn't want to have to turn around on the highway. Once she left, she didn't want to return, until it was over.

She eyed Scooter's side of the bed as she tiptoed out of her bedroom with the luggage in her hand. It had been a few days since he left the house. She wasn't answering or returning his calls. She missed him terribly, but they needed time apart. They needed that time to miss each other. Scooter needed that time to realize what he has before it became what he had.

She walked into the kitchen, her mind now on her father. She dreaded attending his funeral the following day. It was hard enough picking out a casket. Planning it wasn't a walk in the park for her, either. She didn't want to go, which was a normal feeling. However, she wouldn't miss the chance to pay her respects to her father. He had taught her so much that outweighed what any book ever could.

"Hello?" Aphtan answered the phone after it rang.

"How are you feeling?" Mila asked from the receiver of the smartphone.

"I'm better than yesterday." She walked toward the door, her purse resting on top of the luggage she was wheeling. "I can't complain."

"That's good." Mila sighed. "You know me and mama coming tomorrow."

"I know." Aphtan opened the door as her maid grabbed the luggage from her. "I'll have a spot in the front for you and Tammy." She hit the trunk button on her alarm to open it so Madeline could put the luggage inside. "You are the only family I have left."

"We are here for you. Call us if you need anything."

"Thank you, Mila. I love you, girl."

"I love you, too." Mila hung up the phone.

"Mrs. Dixon," Madeline spoke as Aphtan got into the car, "do you need anything else?"

"No, thank you." She gave her a twisted, fabricated smile. "If you could be a doll and make sure if Mr. Dixon comes here to call and let me know."

"Yes ma'am." She nodded before walking down the trail to go back inside the house.

The withering heat boiled the pores of Aphtan's skin as she let the top down to her Mercedes. She checked her mirrors before starting the ignition, which commenced without making a single sound. She popped in H-Town's *Beggin' After Dark* into the six-disk CD player, then drove off.

With her Loc shades on, her skin tightened at the thought of returning home as she eased down the divided highway. She didn't know how the visit was going to turn out. All the associates she had once had in the slums of Dallas she had lost contact with so many years ago. She hadn't been home since she was eighteen. Once she finished high school, she left without ever looking back.

The thought that she had not seen her father in months boggled her mind with regret. She would drive down regularly to see him, and they would talk on the phone as much as their busy schedules would allow them. But she still felt bad for not making the commute to the suburbs he called home. *If I had been more involved, would he still be here?* she asked herself.

Aphtan put her turn signal on when she saw the exit to her infamous city. Her heart climbed into her throat when she saw the "Now Entering Dallas" sign. The smell of fresh garbage and piss attacked her nostrils to let her know that she was finally home. Looking around, she could tell she was close to where she grew up. From the smell that snuck into the vents of her car, she was blocks away.

She turned on a street that looked vaguely familiar to her. The once stable projects she loved and respected in her adolescence were in shambles. She couldn't believe her eyes. She pulled up to the entrance as crackheads and prostitutes surrounded her car. She blew the horn to get through as she reached underneath her seat to pull out the gun that her father gave her before she moved. She learned long ago to never leave without her sprayer.

Her hood instincts took over as she parked. With her car still surrounded, her heartbeat was beating loudly in her ears. She closed her eyes as she cocked back on the gun. Her heartbeat slowed down when she realized that her father ran the city; dead or alive. With no fear in her heart, she opened up the door, slamming it against whoever stood next to it.

"Do you like girls?" one of the prostitutes yelled out through the crowd. "I can show you a good time."

"Can you spare some change?" a crackhead asked as his lips crackled with each word he spoke.

"Y'all motherfuckers got two seconds to get the fuck away from my whip," Aphtan screamed as she held the gun up in the air and released a couple rounds in the opposite direction from where she stood. With her sunglasses hanging from her other hand, she peered into the sky to make sure the bullets didn't fall on her or near her.

The crackheads and prostitutes ran for their lives. Unaware of the killer in her blood, they had mistaken her for someone who was lost, but she was far from it. The well-mannered persona she worked so hard to grow into was disassembled in a matter of minutes. Minute by minute she could feel the hood urges in her awaken. In all the ruin throughout the projects, she could still see the beauty in them. That alone gave her a sense of serenity and let her know the hood was definitely a one-of-a-kind place.

She got back inside the car and cut the ignition

off. Curious to go to the buildings she called home for seventeen long years, she locked the doors to her car using the alarm and stepped onto the sidewalk with her gun dangling from her soft hand. The short hair on her head shook with ease with each step that her stilettos took. Pulling down the black dress that was painted on her body, she looked around as fond memories filled her head.

All of her first moments happened in the same projects she was walking through. She had her first fight in the back of the apartment buildings. She had her first kiss by the rusty pale-blue jungle gym that sat directly in the center of the apartments; it was still there, barely standing. She saw her first murder there, played her first dice game, and everything else that an adult grew up and thought about later in life had happened within those project gates.

Aphtan laughed and smiled as she walked around the now abandoned projects. Memories of her and her father filled her head. She remembered some things that she had forgotten. It was hard to believe that those were the same projects that used to be filled with so much life and love. They went from having tons of people standing around doing miscellaneous things to an empty ghost town.

She approached the building that she and her family had called home. The "Q" that once hung from the top of their building was sitting on the stoop. She picked it up before going into the building, which was now missing the tall door that figured in all of her memories. She walked up the stairs while flashbacks of her running up and down those stairs raced through her mind. She closed her eyes and a small lingering scent of Mary Jane still filled the hallways.

Aphtan's eyes turned glossy when she walked into the apartment she once called home. There was a sense of abandonment to the building, old and forgotten. The door hung wearily upon its corroded hinges. The paint on the walls peeled and flaked as though the apartment had a disease of the skin. The boards on the floor were warped through age and neglect. Though the windows were intact, the buildup of grime acted like a natural curtain blanketing the light that entered, making it meager. Webs from productive spiders adorned the corners, the fittings, and anywhere else that they could spin two pieces of silken trappings together.

She closed her eyes as she walked in and remembered where every piece of furniture they owned sat when they stayed there. Tears started to fall as visions of her father passed out on the couch in one of his expensive suits hit the edge of her brain.

"You kept your promise and got us out of here huh, Daddy? Even if it was short-lived," she whispered as she tossed down the metal Q. She smiled as she walked back down the wooden stairs while wiping her tears away and exited through the doorless entry.

"What the fuck are you doing in my hood?" a man holding an AK-47 with a hundred-round magazine clip curved underneath the large gun asked Aphtan as soon as her stiletto touched the unmaintained lawn. "You got a gun? Are you a motherfucking cop?" he screamed as he walked up on her. "Put the motherfucking gun down, you pig bitch."

Aphtan did as she was told as her body turned numb. Her eyes followed the man's every movement as she studied him up and down. Draped in a Polo overall, he stood equal to her height, which was about five-foot-five. His skin tone was bright, and with the slightest pinch, you could tell he would turn red. The tan Timberlands he wore stomped heavily on the concrete sidewalk as he got closer and closer to her. His grayish green eyes stayed glued on her as he reached down and picked up the gun she had tossed to the ground.

"Who the fuck is you?" He pressed the gun to her throat. "I ain't never killed a pig before." He smiled, exposing his mouth full of gold. "Mmm mmm mmm, and you fine, too." He looked at her up and down. "Maybe I'll get in that pussy and then blow your head off."

"I don't know who the fuck you are," Aphtan hissed as she gulped heavily. "But, if I were you, I would get this big ass army gun out of my fucking face and go on about your fucking business."

"You a tough girl?" He kept her own gun pressed against her throat and ran the AK-47 up her dress, exposing her lace panties. "I should put this gat in your pussy and release the trigger."

"Peanut," a voice yelled from behind them, "get that gun out of her face, right now."

"Peanut?" Aphtan said under her breath so only she could hear it.

Peanut's eyes opened wide with fear, and he quickly followed the order he had just received. Aphtan grabbed her throat as she looked past Peanut to see the face of the man who potentially saved her life. With the sun blocking her peripheral vision, she would have to wait for him to get closer before she could see.

The smell of the man's expensive Acqua Di Gio cologne reached Peanut and Aphtan before he did. As he approached, Aphtan finally got a good look at him. Skinny but sexy, the six-foot-four man had the skin tone of a God and the body of one, too. His body swayed as his six-pack dripped with sweat, which was exposed from the opened Polo button-up he had on. Slacks and dress shoes made up the rest of his outfit, which added to his sex appeal. A Rolex gripped his wrist as he tugged at his mustache, which was neatly trimmed.

"Do you know who the fuck that is?" the man asked Peanut as his large hand pointed at Aphtan as he talked to his worker.

"Naw, man," Peanut's voice shook a little. "I thought she was five-oh."

"Nigga, this is Boss's daughter." The man eyes turned and studied Aphtan. "I can't believe you put a fucking gun up to her neck."

"Aphtan?" Peanut turned and looked at her up and down. "The little tomboy I used to shoot dice with?"

"I guess, nigga. I didn't grow up here." The man never took his eyes off of Aphtan.

"Goddamn, Cole. You didn't know Aphtan back then. But if you would have seen her then and then saw her now? You would understand my shock." He handed the gun back to Aphtan. "Sorry for the misunderstanding. You know your pop have to know everybody who enters and leaves his city. You just looked suspicious, that's all," Peanut kept explaining to her.

Aphtan tuned Peanut out as she looked at Cole. She hadn't seen him since the day at the projects all those years ago. He looked the exact same, just more mature, and maybe a couple of inches taller. He looked at her, his stare making her nervous. It was as if Peanut wasn't there. She couldn't focus on anything but him.

"Are you all right?" Cole grabbed her neck to check for bruises.

"I'm good." She jerked her head away from his grip, even though his touch felt good to her.

"I'm sorry to hear about your pop and everything." Peanut shook his head. "He was a true ass boss and there will never be another nigga like him to walk these streets."

"Shut the fuck up," Aphtan snapped as she pointed the gun at him. "I swear to God, if I didn't know you from way back in the day, I would stop your heartbeat."

"Damn, smart girl still hood." Cole laughed.

"I'm sorry, Aphtan," Peanut pleaded as he held his hands up while the AK-47 hung on his shoulder from a strap. "No need to tell Scooter about this. He would have my head."

"This guy." Aphtan walked directly in between Cole and Peanut and shook her head.

She walked at a slow pace until she reached her car. Hitting the alarm, she got in and put her head down on the steering wheel. She couldn't believe what had just happened. Being her father's daughter put her life in danger, but at the same time it was what saved her. She was sitting there in a trance when she heard knocking on her window.

"Who is knocking on my window?" Aphtan asked with her head still resting on the steering wheel.

"It's me." Cole knocked again. "Get out of the car really quick."

"For what?" She leaned up and glared at his muscular stomach that rested on the driver's-side window.

"Just get out of the car."

"I can maybe if you move the fuck out the way." She blew the horn.

He moved aside just enough to let her out. Aphtan opened up the door, and her body brushed against Cole's as she got out. The smell of him made her pussy moist. The sight of him made her knees weak. She noticed herself looking at him for too long, and she glanced away as a diversion.

"What you want talk about?" She leaned on the parked car.

"Long time no see?" Cole looked down at his phone as it started to ring.

There was nothing on his phone that he needed to look at in that moment. He couldn't look at her. He needed anything to distract him from doing so. If he did look at her, steal glances of her beauty, there was no telling what he might do. His heart still fluttered in her presence. She transformed him into a little, shy boy.

"You disappeared." Aphtan pulled at her earring. "You didn't come to my wedding or anything. I haven't even received a phone call from you."

"I didn't agree with you and *him*. So with that being said, I fell all the way back. It's good to see you, though."

"Is that all you wanted, Cole?" Aphtan opened the door to her car to get in.

"I also wanted to tell you that I'm sorry to hear about your father." He reached past her and closed the door. "I've been working with him over the past few years, and he was a good man. If you need anything, call me and let me know."

"I don't have your number."

"You can ask for it."

Aphtan folded her arms. "You can offer it to me."

"You haven't changed at all, Aphtan. You still think everything is about you." Cole walked away.

"And, you're still acting like a little ass brat who didn't get the girl," Aphtan screamed at his back. "Let that shit go, Cole. It's water under the bridge."

Cole turned around and opened her door for her. "I don't give a fuck about you and Scooter. If you want to be with him, that's your business. It doesn't have shit to do with me. Believe me; I'm done caring about that. I don't think about you, Aphtan." He walked away. "Lose that snobby attitude. Don't forget you're from here."

"Since I got out, that means I'm snobby now?" Aphtan asked as she pictured her lips pressing against his.

"Trying to bait me into one of these childish arguments is not going to work."

"I'm not trying to do shit." Her eyes met his as he looked back at her. "You're the one holding a grudge against me because I chose Scooter."

"Shut that shit up." Cole closed the door after she got inside. "Get the fuck out of here."

"Whatever, bitch ass nigga." Aphtan flipped him off and drove away.

"Stuck-up ass." Cole bit on his bottom lip as she exited the gate of the projects. His eyes squinted from the rays blazing from the sun as dust galloped in the same spot where Aphtan's car once was. "Damn, I didn't think she was going to blossom like that." He grabbed on his dick through his slacks. "She got booty and a pretty ass face."

Cole shook off his initial thought about Aphtan when his phone rung in his hand. He smiled at her attitude, which was a turn-on to him in some way. He secured his post in hopes that he would cross paths with her again. She wasn't like any other woman he had fucked with in the past; and that's exactly how he wanted it. The only problem was, she belonged to his brother.

CHAPTER 25

Tsunami looked on as Scooter threw his phone into the wall, making it shatter on contact. Aphtan was avoiding his calls, and she could see it was driving him crazy. She knew he was tired of talking to her voice mail. She could see all over his face the want to talk to Aphtan face-to-face.

"Baby,"—Tsunami picked up the broken pieces of the phone—"calm down."

"Don't tell me what the fuck to do, Tsunami." Scooter fell back onto the bed.

"Scooter,"—she climbed into the bed—"I'm not trying to make you upset." She kissed his chest. "I want to make you feel better."

"You want to make me feel better? Get my wife to speak to me, and maybe I'll feel better." He pushed her off him and onto the floor. "I don't want to be touched right now."

Tsunami put her head into her knees as she sat on the floor. No matter what she did for Scooter, it wasn't good enough. She catered to him. She did everything he asked of her, yet he didn't want her. She was willing to do anything for a man who wouldn't piss on her if she was on fire. Her heart had finally broken.

Anger consumed her thoughts, clouding her judgment. She stood up as her eyes burned a hole into the side of his head. She wasn't thinking rationally. All she wanted to do was make him feel some of the pain she was feeling. She wanted his heart to break into two pieces like hers had.

"Get out," she whispered. "Get out," she said a little louder as he ignored her. "Get out," she screamed as loudly as she could.

"What did you just say?" He got off of the bed and walked toward her. "I'm sorry?" He put his hand to his ear to see if she would say it again. "What did you say?"

"I said to get the fuck out of my house." She rolled her neck.

"Bitch, I'll—"

"You'll what?" she interrupted him. "You'll stop giving us money? You'll stop coming over when you and your wife are mad at each other? You'll stop playing with my feelings?"

"Don't play the victim. Don't act like you didn't know what you were getting into."

"I didn't know it would be like this forever. I thought—"

"You thought what?" he cut her off. "You thought I would marry you and give you my last name?"

She didn't utter a word as her lips began to tremble.

"You know my heart is somewhere else," he said slowly.

She pointed at the door. "All I know is that you need to get the fuck out of my house."

"This is your house? Can you tell me who paid for this motherfucker?"

"Whose name is it in?" She pushed him. "Get the fuck out. I don't want to see your confused ass ever again."

"You may get what you ask for." He grabbed her cheeks, his hands covering her mouth. "If it ain't about my son, don't call me."

"I won't even call you then." She shook away from his grip. "Now get out, Scooter."

Tsunami plopped down on the edge of the bed as she watched the father of her child collect his things. She wanted to yelp out; to scream and tell him to stay. She would rather they make love, ending a night of sex with feeling-induced hugging. But it came with a price she wasn't willing to pay anymore. She had to let him go. She needed to get over him.

She fell back onto the eight-hundred-thread-count sheets as she stared at the ceiling. She contemplated her next move as the light from the spinning ceiling fan made the sparkle in her eyes gleam a tad bit more.

All she wanted was revenge. She wanted to hurt Scooter. She wanted him to feel the pain, to go days without sleeping. She wanted him to finally worry about something. His life was too easy, and she wanted to change that.

Tsunami grabbed her cell phone from the

nightstand. She scrolled through her contacts and stopped at a name she never thought she would call. She needed some information to get to Aphtan. If she couldn't deliver it herself, her best friend would be the next best thing. She stood up as she dialed Mila's number.

"Hello?" Mila answered the phone.

"Black," Tsunami whispered as if someone was listening.

"Who is this?" Mila held the phone away from her face and looked at the screen.

"Tsunami."

"Goodbye."

"Wait," she called out. "I got some information that your girl Lotus may want to know about her husband."

"I don't believe shit you say." Mila got serious. "Why would I shake her world up with some 'he said, she said' bullshit that comes from your mouth?"

"It's about her father."

"What about him?"

"Scooter killed him." Tsunami put her hand over her mouth, knowing that she just opened up a can of worms. "I heard him talking about it with Money," she continued, her mouth running like water from broken hydrant.

"Are you just saying this, Tsunami? You're always talking about something."

She leaned against the headboard. "They're meeting tomorrow night to discuss everything. Tell Aphtan the meeting is at the soul food restaurant on Alexander."

Tsunami hung up the phone and walked into

her closet. She would have to leave town now. Scooter would never hurt his son, but her, and after she told Mila that information, he would take her life.

She took her suitcases out one by one, packing them to her liking. She planned to leave in the middle of the night. When the sun rose and the rays shined through the windows, they wouldn't shine on any flesh. She and her son would be hours away by then.

"Why would you want to do that to Scooter?" Mila hit the back of their child's back to burp him before passing him to Levi. "That's foul. I'm not with that."

"I didn't even have to tell you." Levi played with the baby and kissed him on the forehead. "Don't worry about your best friend. She won't be a part of it. I promise."

Mila sat on the white leather Italian couch as she thought about how close they all were. They were family. She couldn't believe what was coming out of Levi's mouth. Aphtan had enough on her plate. What Levi was trying to do to Scooter would do nothing but add more than what she could handle right now. It would break her.

"Boss isn't even in the ground yet." Mila put her legs underneath her body and sat on them. "Everybody plotting for his spot, and the man hasn't even been put to rest."

"That's the streets for you." He rocked the baby in his arms. "Now is the time to make the move. Don't you want your man to run the streets? Don't you want our son, and the seed baking in your oven, to have a secure future?"

Mila rubbed her belly. "Yes."

"Then get on board with me, Jamila. I don't want to hurt you and Aphtan's relationship."

"What about your cousin?" She held her hands up. "What about the bond that y'all have? You two have been so close for so many years."

"I know." Levi sat down on the end of the couch and put their now sleeping son on one of the soft cushions. "He's like a brother to me. Don't get me wrong, Jamila. It's just that I have kids now. I can't be second fiddle to no one anymore. Being a lieutenant isn't good enough anymore. I need to be king."

Born two weeks apart, Levi and Scooter had been joined at the hip since birth. They were closer to each other than anyone else. They knew things about each other that would go to the grave with them. Levi was willing to give it all up. Scooter was sure to run the streets after Boss's death. He needed to do whatever it took to do it before him; even if he had to go through him to do so. Timing was everything.

"Nobody will get hurt?" Mila slid over on the couch and got on top of him. "Tell me no one will get hurt."

"Aphtan will be safe." Levi grabbed her waist and kissed her stomach. "You and my kids will be safe."

"What about Scooter?"

"What about him?"

"Will he be safe?"

"If he's smart."

"What if he's dumb?" Mila ran her acrylic nail through his beard.

"Let's just say, your friend is going to need your shoulder."

"Levi,"—she put her finger over his mouth— "don't say that."

"You're my wife." Levi kissed her finger. "I can tell you anything, right?"

"Always." Mila hugged him.

Mila's facial expression changed when her face disappeared from Levi's view. She loved him, but deep down she wasn't down for betraying the people that she considered family. Scooter was their son's godfather. He wasn't just another dude from the block. He was family.

She looked into his eyes when the hug subsided, and she saw someone she had never met before. His eyes begged for power, for respect. It made her wonder what else he was willing to give up for that power.

"You all right?" He noticed her face changing.

"Yes, I am. I was just thinking about what Tsunami called and told me," she lied.

"What did she tell you?" he asked out of curiosity.

"She told me that Scooter killed Boss." Mila looked at his face as it changed a little. "Did he kill Boss?" She hit his chest softly.

"Yes, he did." He nodded his head up and down.

"No, Levi." Mila looked off into space.

"Are you going to tell her?"

"Should I?"

"She's your friend." He picked her up and sat her beside him before getting up. "That's your call."

Mila thought about how she would want Aphtan to tell her news, good or bad. As her best friend, it was her responsibility to tell her. Blood couldn't make them any closer. She was going to be the shoulder she leaned on. She had to tell her who killed her father.

CHAPTER 26

"Rude ass motherfucker," Aphtan said to herself, referring to Cole as her gas light came on. Her car cut her music to a halt and beeping sprouted from her speakers letting her know that she had ten miles left. "Shit," she whispered as she zoomed into a gas station.

Aphtan pulled up to a pump as she grabbed her credit card from her Celine bag. She got out and walked inside of the project store, ignoring countless men's advances and comments. She gave her card to the Iranian working the counter through the gate that separated him from the customers and walked back to her car.

"Ms. Epps?" A man in a tailored suit asked as Aphtan put the nozzle inside her gas tank.

"It's Mrs. Dixon now, but who wants to know?" Aphtan studied him up and down.

"We do." A woman approached the other side of Aphtan.

"Who the fuck is y'all?" Aphtan asked with an attitude.

"We are detectives for this beautiful city of Dallas that your father singlehandedly destroyed." The woman held her identification up so Aphtan could see. "I'm Detective Stead and he's Detective Gomez."

"My father hasn't even been dead a good week and y'all already fucking with me." Aphtan spoke with malice in her voice.

Aphtan checked out the identification and the female detective. The tall, light-brown-skinned woman looked to be about twenty-eight and of Cuban descent. She could tell that underneath her clothes, she had the body of a goddess. She was a very beautiful woman.

Detective Stead looked as if she'd only had timid, gentle kisses so far, never being in any real danger. But there was a tiger inside her, a tiger who wanted a long, hard kiss; a tiger who wanted to be in the line of fire. She'd show a little protest, but only to convince herself she was still a lady. But then she'd start to melt and let herself settle like soft-serve ice cream.

Detective Gomez was a different story. He had been in his profession for over half of his fifty-something years. He would know bullshit whenever he heard it. He got his kick from intimidation, and they were a bad cop, good cop duo.

Aphtan studied his knock-off designer suit and his salt-and-pepper hair and goatee. She looked at his eyes, which were partly shut, but were the color of the ocean on an autumn's evening. She noticed every scar and every mole on his pale, pink face.

"Y'all might as well get out of my face, because you won't get anything from me." Aphtan looked forward, ignoring their presence.

"We got so much on your father, little girl, that we don't need shit from you." Detective Stead laughed. "We were just trying to offer you immunity if you could help us further with our investigation."

"Somebody that is innocent does not need immunity. I haven't been here in years. Y'all ain't got shit on me or my father, so cut the shenanigans." Aphtan continued to look forward.

"You don't know what we got," Detective Stead said in a serious voice as she noticed that Aphtan wasn't shaken at all by their presence.

"If you did have something on me, I guarantee you that we wouldn't be talking about it here. Get the fuck out of my face." Aphtan took the nozzle out and placed it back on the gas pump. "As far as my father goes, he's dead. A dead man can't tell you anything. You two are out of luck."

"We still can get all of his property seized." Detective Gomez walked closer to Aphtan. "Your car, your fancy clothes, your jewels were all purchased with drug money. We can have all of this stuff taken away from you, little girl, and it would shatter your world. We know your father was the drug lord of Dallas."

"You don't know shit." Aphtan smiled at him and blew him a kiss. "If you did, you wouldn't be trying to push up on me. And for the record, my husband buys me whatever I want. Also, my daddy owned many companies. If I did get anything from him, who's to say the funds didn't come from one of his lucrative businesses."

"Your husband is Christopher Wayne 'Scooter' Dixon, son of Loon 'Money' Dixon. Trust me, we have enough on him, too. We can get him as well," Detective Gomez assured her.

"Aphtan, if you help us, we can turn an eye on everything your father has ever bought you. We don't have to know about everything your husband has bought you," Detective Stead said in a pleading voice. "We don't want you, we just want the organization."

"What organization?" Aphtan played dumb. "What are you talking about?" She opened up the door to her car to get in.

"Your father trained you well to keep your mouth closed." Detective Gomez grabbed her arm. "But you know we have something on him and Scooter. You're not dumb, so remember that." He let her go. "Nice car, by the way."

"Thanks." Aphtan got in, closed the door, and rolled her windows down. "If you work hard enough you might get one—well, probably not." She waved at the detectives, put her shades on, and drove off.

"That was not how that was supposed to go," Detective Stead told her partner as they walked back to their car, which was parked on the side of the convenience store.

"I know," he agreed as they got inside the car. He pulled his cell phone out and dialed a number as Detective Stead started the car and eased through the alley. "She didn't take the bait." He rolled down the passenger-side window. "She's her father's child, after all. She's going to be hard to break. I can see that now."

* * * *

Cole stood at the front of the projects with his phone glued to his ear. He couldn't get Aphtan out of his mind. He paced back and forth, hoping something would distract him, but nothing worked. Everywhere he looked, he could see her face.

He finished his phone call and put his phone in his pocket. Noticing an unmarked car driving by slowly, he put his hand on his gun. When the window rolled down and he saw it was Money, he let go of his grip.

"I used to protect these same projects." Money got out of the car. "This was my duty as well. This brings back memories."

Cole never looked at him. A simple, "okay" left his mouth.

"Are you going to Boss's funeral?"

"I don't know," Cole answered slowly as his father stood next to him.

"I'm going." Money took a blunt from the pocket inside his blazer. "I want to say goodbye to an old friend." He turned his hand sideways until the face of the watch he wore fell into place.

"You could have done that when you killed the man." He looked over at him. "Aphtan is not going to want you or Scooter there."

"Aphtan doesn't run shit, Cole. This is my city now." He opened his arms as wide as they would go. "This is my fucking city, and I'll go where I please."

Cole put his hands in his pockets. "All I'm saying is that she's been through enough. Why upset her more? The girl isn't stupid. She knows y'all killed her father."

"There it is." Money winked at him. "Your

brother told me you had a weak spot for his wife, and now I see it."

"Your son," he said, referring to Scooter, "need not worry about me."

"What is it about her that drives you two so crazy?"

"I guess it's in her genes. I heard you were the exact way about her mother. You should know. I guess the apple doesn't fall too far from the tree."

"Aphtan isn't half the woman her mother was." Money looked at the ground. "Don't talk about shit you know nothing about."

"I know you didn't come here to tell me this wild love story between you and Aphtan's mother. What do you want, Pop?"

"I want you to work for me."

"Work for you? No, thank you."

"Why not?" Money asked, the blunt being abused by his lips.

"I rather not." Cole put his hand on Money's shoulder. "One of us will end up dead."

"You're going to work for a dead man?"

"I still have some work I have to do."

"What kind of work?" he asked as Cole walked away.

"You'll see soon." Cole disappeared in between the abandoned buildings.

Everything he was planning to do was for Aphtan and no one else. He could easily ignore what Boss had asked him to do. No one would ever know if he didn't do it. The job was more for his satisfaction. He'd been waiting a long time to get Scooter out of the way. There was no way he was going to pass up an opportunity to get it done.

CHAPTER 27

Aphtan arrived in the area of South Lake, a rich subdivision where her father's home was located. She looked throughout the neighborhood. Her father's promise to move to a rich white neighborhood had come true; all she saw were stuck-up white folks. Even the air that traveled inside her car smelled stuck-up.

She wasn't too fond of the neighborhood, even though she had stayed there for a little in her adolescence. Nothing changed; the white women were still walking their show dogs. White men in their too-short shorts were still walking around with the exact same smug facial expressions they had since her family had invaded the neighborhood and changed their white to black ratio from a thousand to zero to a staggering thousand to three.

Aphtan pulled up to the colonial-style house and noticed six cars parked in the large driveway. Three of the cars that lined the circular driveway with its moat with a fountain in the middle of it belonged to her father. The other cars she had never seen before.

Aphtan got out of her car and walked up to the tall white door of her father's house. Without knocking, she walked in; the scent of him lingered in the foyer. She continued to walk through the bottom level of the house to see who all was there. To her knowledge, no one was supposed to be there.

"How are you?"

Aphtan turned around in a jump. Her eyes dashed into the face of her doctor, Verna Coffee. She was confused as to why she was there. It was clear that she wanted answers, from the look on her face.

"How are you holding up?" Verna wrapped her arms around her. "Your father is in a better place."

"Verna?" Aphtan welcomed her hug. "What are you doing here?"

"This is my home." She stepped back and grabbed her face. "Come with me, and I'll explain everything to you."

Aphtan followed her through the dimly lit house. Everything was the same as the last time she was there. She admired the simplicity of the décor as they made it to the all-white family room.

"Please, take a seat." Verna pointed to the seat next to her after she sat down.

Aphtan sat down slowly, reluctantly even.

"I'm sure you have a lot of questions for me." Verna picked the gold-plated bell from the table in front of them and rung it.

"I do." Aphtan looked around and examined the room like she'd never seen it before. "Why are you here? What do you mean, this is your home?"

"Your father is—" She looked down. "—was my lover. We were about to get married."

Aphtan laughed. "Lover? Is this a joke?"

"This of all times is no time for games." She crossed her legs as the housekeeper entered the room. "Would you like something to drink?"

Aphtan nodded her head up and down.

"Bring us a glass of wine," Verna told the housekeeper before giving her attention back to Aphtan. "Your father and I have been in love for so many years. I'm sorry I couldn't tell you this. It was hard being your physician and keeping this from you."

"How many years are we talking? My father was incarcerated for so long. Where could you have met him?"

"In prison." Verna grabbed the glass from the housekeeper when she entered the room. "Be careful," she told Aphtan as she grabbed her glass full of red wine. "This is a white room, after all."

"I'm aware." She sipped from the glass. "I have one of these rooms as well."

"I'm sure you do."

"Back to this." Aphtan crossed her legs. "You met him in prison?"

"Yes, I did." She sat the glass down on a coaster. "I was the on-call physician at the prison. One day, I got a call to come stitch up a man from a brutal fight."

"Daddy got beat up?"

"The complete opposite." Verna smiled softly. "I had to stitch up his fists. Both of them were open deeply. I normally don't speak to the prisoners, but there was something about your father. From that day forward, a bond was created."

"Bumping into me that day at the market wasn't an accident?" Aphtan asked as she reminisced about the day that they met.

"No." She put her hands on one of Aphtan's knees. "Boss told me to keep an eye on you. Being your doctor was the only way I knew how. So I offered you my card."

"Something's not adding up." Aphtan leaned back on the couch, the glass still in her hand. "Wasn't my father locked up hours away?"

"Yes, he was. I moved to where you were to keep an eye on you for him. The last couple years of his sentence consisted of me keeping an eye on you. Even after he got out, I still kept an eye on you for him."

"I was only a job for you?"

"It started out that way. However, the bond we share is real. I couldn't fake that if I tried."

Aphtan looked at Verna as she thought about their friendship. She always wondered why a doctor would take so much interest in her, and now she knew why. She had been a good friend to her, yet something in her wasn't satisfied with just that fact. She was tired of being lied to.

With everything that had been going on with Scooter, she wasn't in any position to lose any more people in her circle. Losing her father was the last thing she could handle.

"How about you go get you some rest? We're burying your father tomorrow." Verna stood up. "Everything is the same. I'm sure you know your way around still."

"I do." She stood up.

"Perfect." Verna gave her a hug. "Your father was

a good man, Aphtan. No matter what you think of him, he loved you with everything in him."

Aphtan forced a half smile before she walked over to the staircase. She walked up the steps as she held on to the steel railings. Nostalgia overtook her and covered her like a quilt. She remembered the first day they had gone to the house. She touched the pictures on the wall as she made it to the top of the staircase.

She closed her eyes and could see her ten-year-old self running full force down the hallway. All the childhood memories that she held near ended under the roof above her head. It was a bittersweet moment for her.

She gently opened the door to her old room and went inside. It was the exact way she remembered it. Boy band posters filled the walls. Everything was bejeweled and pink. The white canopy bed looked lonely, waiting for someone to sleep in it.

She breathed out heavily as she sat on the bed. She grabbed the framed picture of her parents and her from the pale pink dresser. She rubbed their faces with her finger as she remembered the good days when everyone was alive. She lay down in the bed with that image kidnapping her thoughts. With those pleasant memories, she fell asleep.

CHAPTER 28

Aphtan awoke with a yawn, her hair ruffled all over her head. She stretched and yawned again, placing her feet gently onto the chinchilla-like carpet that layered the floor of her old room. She eyed the alarm clock with one eye shut as it read seven a.m; two hours before she was supposed to get up. She stood up, feeling slightly unsteady, and then waddled toward the bathroom.

Upon exiting the bathroom, she noticed an envelope addressed to her sitting on the bed. She looked around her, but the only thing present in the room were the blissful rays of sun that snuck inside the castle-like windows. She grew anxious when the chicken scratch written on the envelope registered in her brain as belonging to her father.

Her stomach turned into an erupting volcano, and the lava was moving toward her chest quickly. She didn't know what to think as she sat down on the bed. Her fingers trembled with anticipation as she opened the envelope and pulled the letter out.

Aphtan sat there until it was time to get dressed for her father's funeral. She read the letter over and over again. It was clear what Boss wanted her to do, but she questioned his decisions. She wasn't cut from that cloth anymore; she just wasn't that girl.

She shook off the thought and put the letter in the drawer next to the soft bed. She slipped into a tight white dress with matching accessories and heels and did her makeup and hair. Everyone else was sure to wear black, but she was never the type to follow traditions.

"Are you ready?" Verna knocked on the door and let herself in.

"Are you ready?" Aphtan stood up and looked the gorgeous woman up and down in disbelief that she would wear red to a funeral.

"Of course, it is a celebration, after all. No need to be sad over something that you definitely cannot change. None of us are gods, you know." Verna walked out of the room. "And, Aphtan, my dear?"

"Yes?"

"You will ride there with me and back with me. Your father wasn't a much liked man, and we have reason to believe that some shit might go down."

"I'm aware of that."

"Well, follow me. We don't want to be late."

Aphtan followed Verna down the stairs and out of the house. Her perfume lingered in Aphtan's nostrils a little more the closer they got to the car. Verna hit the alarm and snapped her fingers at two black SUVs. She got inside, signaling for Aphtan to do the same.

"Who are—"

"They are the men that are going to protect us

from any bullshit that comes our way. They have those army guns, so breathe a little bit. You're safe," Verna cut her off.

The church where Boss's funeral was held was the biggest in all of Dallas. Although it was big, it still wasn't nearly enough room for everyone who wanted to come out and pay their respects. It was like a celebrity had fallen; Aphtan couldn't believe her eyes.

"Is that a news crew?" Aphtan asked aloud.

"Well, this is a newsworthy event." Verna ordered the driver to drive through the crowd and park at the back of the church.

Aphtan walked into the church and didn't recognize but a handful of people. She went to the first row of pews with Verna following and took her seat. She hadn't seen her father in his casket, and when they brought the open box out, she damn near fainted.

"My baby." Verna started to sob.

Aphtan got up and walked up to the casket. She couldn't cry, and she didn't want to. She leaned down and kissed her father's embalmed body. She fixed the tie the funeral home had put on him and smiled at the thought of the man she knew and loved.

"Thank you for everything, Daddy," she whispered. "I got your letter, and I will make you proud." She closed the casket.

"What are you doing?" Verna walked up to Aphtan.

"I want all of these people gone." Aphtan looked out into the crowd. "All of y'all get the fuck out of here. There will be no funeral," she yelled at the crowd.

"There will be no cursing inside of my church." The pastor approached the casket.

"You best not say shit else to me right now." Aphtan looked at the pastor. "Everyone, I promise you, if you're not out of here in thirty seconds, you're not going to like what I do," she yelled out into the crowd.

"Y'all heard the lady. Get the fuck out of here. Right now," Cole screamed as he stood up from the last row of the pews.

Aphtan watched as the church cleared out in a matter of seconds. Cole slowly walked up to her, his eyes never leaving hers. His suit didn't do him justice. It should have been a crime the way he looked in his jet-black suit that fit so perfectly. The gold jewelry on his body played hide-and-seek with the colorful glass that filled the church's windows. His presence always did something to Aphtan; it always hypnotized her.

"Are you okay?" Cole asked as he got in Aphtan's face. "Why did you want it cleared out? Did something happen?"

"My daddy didn't know any of those people, so shit, why should they be here?" Aphtan asked.

"You need to get out of here." Cole grabbed her hand. "Come on."

"Where are we going?" Aphtan asked as they rushed down the stairs of the church.

"Wherever you want to go." He looked back at her and looked in her eyes. "I got you."

People were scattering all about as they walked through the busy crowd. Aphtan only saw Cole in the midst of all of those people. She didn't want to let go of his hand. His touch was so nurturing, so safe to her. She would hold on to him forever if she could.

Feeling her pain, Aphtan could see all he wanted to do was save her from herself. He wanted to let her mourn, but anything other than that, he planned to intercept. All she needed was someone to clear her mind. She wanted for him to make it his mission, no matter the script.

His heartbeat raced faster than the normal pace; she could feel it from his touch as it pulsated through her hand. The beat of her heart was in rhythm with his. They were one at that moment. She couldn't deny it; she was in love with Cole. She could see it in his eyes that he would do anything for her.

"What the fuck is this?" Scooter grabbed Aphtan's free arm as he approached them.

"Let me go, Scooter," Aphtan screamed as onlookers witnessed the debacle about to happen.

"Where are you going?" Scooter asked as she let go of Cole's hand. "Why are you holding this nigga's hand out in public?"

"Chris—" Cole started to say.

"Shut the fuck up." Scooter pointed at him. "I'm not talking to you, nigga."

"Scooter." Aphtan tried to pull away from him, but his grip was too powerful. "This is my father's funeral. Quit making a scene and let me go. Now."

"Aphtan—" Scooter tried to talk.

"You heard her." Cole broke his grip, cutting him off. "Don't touch her if she doesn't want to be touched."

"The only thing saving you right now is the fact that we came out of the same pussy." Scooter got in Cole's face. "I should slap your ass to remind you who runs shit."

"Stop it." Aphtan tried to pull Scooter by the arm.

"What's wrong with your hands, nigga?" Cole asked with clenched teeth.

"If y'all want to kill each other, then do it." Aphtan walked away onto the busy street.

"Aphtan, wait," Cole called out as he trailed behind her.

Scooter grabbed his arm. "Don't cross any lines, Cole," he warned as he let him go.

"I didn't know there were any. I don't see them, big brother." He shoved away from his grip and ran into the street after her. "Aphtan, wait up." He caught up to her. "Stop." He grabbed her. "I'm sorry about that."

"You should be, Cole." Aphtan looked up as he hovered over her, blocking the sun. "I thought you would be the one to bite your tongue. I have too much going on. I'm burying my fucking father today."

"I know." His eyes looked into hers with an intense passion. "I'm sorry. Let's go to my whip and get out of here."

"I kind of want to be alone right now." She closed her eyes. "I just want to scream."

"Scream then, Aphtan."

"What?"

"Scream." He grabbed her mouth and opened it. "It may make you feel better."

Aphtan looked around her as people stood around conversing. She looked at Cole, his facial expression telling her it was okay. She closed her eyes again, opened her mouth, and screamed her tonsils out. She screamed over and over again until her throat got so dry that she couldn't repeat the therapeutic process.

"Do you feel better now?" He used his thumb to catch a tear that was falling from her eye.

"Yes."

"Let's go for a ride." He grabbed her hand and led her to his car.

Notorious B.I.G.'s song "Suicidal Thoughts" blasted from the speakers when Cole started the car after they got inside. He took off his tie and let all of his windows down. Without putting his seat belt on, he bolted out of the church parking lot into traffic. Startled, Aphtan held on to the door with one hand while hitting Cole in his arm with the other.

"Slow the fuck down, nigga." She cut his music down.

"Don't touch my shit, Aphtan." Cole cut the music back up.

"Why the fuck is you so rude?" she asked, cutting the music back down. "Did I do something to you?"

"Just shut the fuck up and ride. Goddamn."

"Fuck that." Aphtan cut the music down a little. "Did I miss something, or was today my father's funeral?"

The brick walls Cole had built up shattered from the pain he heard in Aphtan's voice. Her eyes begged for sympathy because they were filled with so much pain. She had had a soft spot for him since they were teenagers, and not seeing him in years almost made her forget that.

"My bad." He slowed down. "Is this better?" he asked as he shot her a sideways grin.

"Yes, thank you," she replied.

"Where have you been all of these years?" Aphtan took her heels off. "All of these years, and I haven't seen you anywhere."

"I've been out of the way." Cole cut the music completely off. "Plus, when you and Chris got married, I knew it was best for me to stay away."

"Marriage isn't what it's cracked up to be." She leaned back into the seat.

"I'm sure it can be a beautiful thing if you married your soul mate."

"What are you saying?"

"Chris was never your soul mate."

"Was it you?" She put her feet on the seat.

"Maybe." He reached over and knocked her feet off the seat. "Get your crusty feet off my brand-new seats."

"Crusty?" She pushed him playfully. "Boy, you would be so lucky if I let you suck on them."

"Is that an offer?" he asked before he grinned.

"Just nasty." She pushed him again as they both laughed.

"You knew I had feelings for you back then?" He looked at her.

"Yes, I knew."

"Why you play me back then?"

"I saved you, Cole." She put her feet back onto the seat. "You were a good boy. I wasn't as good as you thought. I would have corrupted you."

"Maybe that's what I wanted." He winked at her. "You never know."

"Surely you have a wonderful woman in your life." She hit the button to roll the window down.

He shook his head no.

"Why not?" she asked.

"I can't find another Aphtan Epps out here in these streets." He looked forward as he turned onto a street. "When that happens, or until the original becomes available, I'm good."

"What is it about me, Cole? Why would you wait for me? All of these years, and you still look at me with this hungry desire."

"I guess I'm one of those people who wants what they can't have."

"*Can't* is a strong word. I wouldn't say you can't have me."

"What are you saying?"

She rubbed his leg. "Scooter is out of the picture."

His manhood began to rise and make an appearance in the seam of his slacks. "Aphtan, don't play with me."

"Who's playing?" She grabbed his tool through his pants and started massaging it. "I'd be lying if I said that I didn't want this, too."

"Are you trying to use me to get back at my brother?" Cole pulled into a convenience store.

"Do you care?" She unbuttoned his pants.

"No." He grabbed her hand as she looked at him. "I don't want to be on the list of things you regret tomorrow."

"Then fuck me good."

"Are you serious?" He took off his button-up, revealing his crisp white t-shirt.

"Do I look like I'm playing?" Aphtan massaged his penis more as it grew as hard as it could. "Come on."

Aphtan got out of the car and walked over to the driver's side door. She opened it, grabbed Cole by the shirt, and forced him to get out. She pulled him by the arm until they reached the small public restroom on the side of the store. Aphtan turned the knob, but the door was locked. Cole pushed her out of the way and kicked the door off of the hinges.

He grabbed her, picked her up, and stumbled into the putrid restroom. Lips on lips, they could barely breathe from how passionately they were kissing. Their hands roamed wildly as they explored each other's bodies without interruption. Every touch was intensified by emotion. Every second felt like a minute; each minute felt like an hour.

Cole's back collided against the door of the dingy blue stall as Aphtan attacked him with a sexual desire she'd never known before. She eased downward and pulled his pants down. He stood at attention, making her lick her lips with anticipation. She admired every vein running along the shaft of his dick as she played with his genitals.

He raised her to her feet by her arms. "Let me take care of you."

Cole turned Aphtan around, kissing every part of her body that he could in the transition. His hands assaulted her love box. His fingers entered her pool of lust as her juices flowed onto the tops of his fingers. She cooed while he used one hand to play with the nipple that was fully erect on her firm breast.

His lips met her opening before he flicked his tongue up and down on her pearl. Pre-cum oozed from the head of his manhood while he continued to feed from her all-you-can-eat buffet. Orgasms caused her to scream out. Her cries begged in desperation for him to stop, yet her hands stayed on his head, pushing him toward her and not away from her.

Wanting him to feel her insides, she turned around and sat on the cold, closed toilet seat. He picked her up, slowly biting her breast, as he placed her on top of his long pole. They both moaned, the wonder, the questions that lingered for years finally answered as he went as deep into her as she would allow. His mouth remained on one of her breasts as she rode him the best way she knew how.

Aphtan noticed how mesmerized Cole was by how tight she was. It was something new to him. She could feel from his stroke that he'd never experienced something so good in his life. It was like velvet, and he was ripping into it like tomorrow didn't exist.

"Cole," she moaned as her body shook, "faster."

"Whatever you want." His stroke sped up and mixed with how quickly she was riding him.

Fearing that he would cum too quickly, he raised her off him and entered her from behind. Her back arched perfectly, welcoming his rough stroke. The sound of his balls hitting her flesh invaded their ears while the smell of sex invaded their noses. Stroke after stroke, her waterfalls engulfed him. He was drowning in her identity, in desperate need of a life jacket as her waves proved to be too much for him. Accepting defeat, his body tensed up, and he released his seed deep inside of her.

"That was the best pussy I've ever had in my life." Cole kissed the back of her neck.

"I can agree that was definitely the best sex I've ever had in my life." She fought to catch her breath.

"So what now?" He took his member out of her. "What does this mean?"

"I don't know." She pulled her dress down, covering up her privates. "I haven't even gotten completely out of the situation I'm in now."

"Understood." Cole walked through the stall to find his pants as the door to the restroom swung back and forth loosely. "I don't want you to rush into anything."

"Thank you for that." Aphtan walked over to him and buttoned up his pants after he put them on. "I want to do this every day."

"You do?" He reached down and kissed her lips. "I'll do this every hour for you."

"Finish putting on your clothes." She rubbed the traces of her lipstick from his lips. "I'll be outside waiting on you."

"I'll be right there." He kissed her one more time before she went outside.

Butterflies begin flying around her stomach as she looked up at the sky. It was the anticipation, the rush, now the moment that she only dreamed of. She was finding herself giggling like a little schoolgirl. Her smile expanded from ear to ear. The butterflies felt like she had something inside of her; unconditional love, the most perfect of all feelings. It traveled up to her heart and overflowed it with joy and passion.

Aphtan never would have imagined in a million years that she would end up with Cole. It never crossed her mind. Things were bad with Scooter.

There was no denying it. Yet and still, she couldn't fight the feeling of shame consuming her. Being with Cole was new and fresh. After all the things that had come her way full force in the past few months, she deserved to be happy, despite whom it was with. Whatever it was between them, she was going to go into it head first.

CHAPTER 29

The small black dress hugged Mila tighter than a rubber band around a wad of money. She looked around the empty parking lot of the church. The emptiness was shocking. She walked into the doors as Boss's casket sat closed in the center of the church. The lights from above shined down, welcoming him home.

She walked closer, wanting to show her respects to her best friend's father. She made it to the casket and placed the roses in her hand on top of the high-end resting box. She stepped back and said a prayer for his soul.

"You're paying your respects too, Jamila?" Scooter startled her as she turned around and saw him sitting on the front pew.

"Isn't that why you're here?" She sat down next to him.

"I guess you can say that." He opened the colorful obituary in his hand. "I didn't think this would happen so soon."

"Where's Aphtan?" Mila looked down at her watch. "Shouldn't the funeral still be going on?"

"It should." He set the obituary next to him. "But your friend kicked everyone out before it even started."

"She's going through a lot right now."

"You think I don't fucking know that, Jamila? I'm the cause of her hurt. I don't think we're going to make it."

"There was hope. You killed her mother and she loved you. You had a baby on her and she loved you. And now, look at what you've done, Scooter. Killing the girl's daddy? The last living relative she had left? Really?"

"Who said this was my work?" He raised his eyebrow waiting for an answer. "Levi shouldn't tell you shit when y'all get done doing the do. That pillow talk is a motherfucker."

"I didn't need him to tell me you did it." Mila grinned. "The mother of your child called me and told me."

"Tsunami?" He leaned his back against the edge of the pew.

"I hope that's the only baby mother you have, nigga."

"Messy bitch." He shook his head.

"I guess that pillow talk is a motherfucker, huh?" She stood up and put her clutch into his chest. "You had a good woman, Scooter. You've hurt her and left wounds that will hurt her until she's dead and gone."

"I'm the bad guy all of the time."

"Yes, you are. You've painted the picture yourself." She walked off.

Scooter stood up and grabbed her arm. "What do you plan to do with the newfound information you've received?"

"I'm going to tell her what I know."

"That's not your business."

"She's my best friend." She pulled away from his grip. "It is my business."

"Stay the fuck out of my marriage," he called out as she walked out of the door.

Mila pulled her phone out and dialed Aphtan's number. She got inside of her car as Aphtan's voice mail played in her ear, holding on to the hope of finding her to tell her the news. Aphtan was already shaken, but this was something that she had to tell her.

Scooter stood on the stoop of the church as Mila drove off. He removed the vest he wore and held it in his hand, letting it fall over his shoulder onto his back. His face showed signs of worry like his mind was racing faster than a roadrunner's. It was as if he was about to lose his wife; his everything, for good, and there was nothing he could do about it.

"How were the services?" Money asked while walking up the sidewalk.

"Full of drama, as expected," Scooter replied coldly.

Money looked toward the doors of the church. "Who's in there?"

"It's empty," Scooter answered quickly.

"What's wrong with you?"

"You." Scooter's hands balled into a fist. "I should have never taken those orders from you. Since you've returned, my marriage has been fucked up."

"The war is almost over."

"What war, Pop?" Scooter's voice got louder. "What's the point of having everything if you have no one to share it with? What's the point of running things if you don't have a companion? What is a king without a queen?"

"Those are good questions, son."

"Is it worth it?" Scooter looked at his father as he talked with his hands. "How does it feel to go to sleep alone and wake up alone? That shit has to get lonely."

Money looked back over his life as Scooter's words tackled his mind like a running back with the ball. He put one foot on the stairs while he thought about how love always got away from him. He didn't want to admit it, yet Scooter was right. It was a lonely life to live.

"I don't want that," Scooter continued. "I want someone to come home to."

"There are sacrifices for this lifestyle." Money put his hand on Scooter's shoulder. "You have to figure out what you're willing to lose. You can't have it all. You have to give something to get something."

"I've already given too much."

Money hit him in the back. "Think it over, and let me know what you decide." He walked up the stairs. "Just make sure you're at the dinner tonight, son. Hear everything out, weigh your options, and decide what you want to do."

"I'll be there," Scooter assured him. "Where are you going?"

"To say goodbye to the brother I never had." Money entered the doors of the church.

Money walked up to Boss's casket and stood in front of it. He took two blunts from inside his blazer. He took an engraved lighter out that Boss had given him at the height of their rise to the top and lit the blunts. Setting one on the casket, then one in his mouth, he took a seat in the first pew.

"I never thought I'd see this day," Money said aloud as he puffed on the perfectly rolled stick. "The mighty Boss, dead, in a box. The color of death, however, fits you." He dumped the ashes of the blunt beside him on the ground.

Money tried his best to hold his composure, but he couldn't. Despite their differences, at one time they had had a strong friendship; a strong brotherhood. They starved together, and when they came up in the game, they ate together. Boss was his best friend before he was his enemy. He was mourning for what they once were.

The doors of the church opened as Money finished the remainder of the blunt. He tossed the end of the blunt as Detective Gomez and Detective Stead sat down on each side of him. He ignored them as he continued to stare at the casket. Although he had caused it, he still couldn't believe his friend since childhood was gone.

"He's finally out of your hair." Detective Stead smirked. "The bastard is finally gone."

Money took his gun out and pointed it at Detective Stead. "You can't say that. I can say whatever the fuck I want about Boss, but you two motherfuckers better tread lightly with your words."

"Whoa there," Detective Gomez grabbed his shoulder. "We're on your side."

"You two aren't on my side." Money put his gun away. "I'm on my own fucking side."

"Who would have thought you'd be so sensitive

about a man that you killed." Detective Stead looked at the casket. "This is your work."

"I know what the fuck I did." Money pulled another blunt from the contents of his pockets. "I know exactly what I did."

"Then what is the problem?" Detective Gomez asked.

"The problem is that I need a few minutes to myself to say goodbye to an old friend." Money snapped his hands as the church filled up with his men.

"That's all you had to say." Detective Stead stood up as guns pointed at them from every direction.

"You know where to find us." Detective Gomez stood up as well. "Come find us when you dry your eyes, so we can finish this business."

"I'll come find you," Money called out as they left the church.

Money sat in the pew, asking over and over again in his mind if he had made the right decision. He couldn't help but to ask himself whether it was all worth it. He was about to get his wish. After years of striving and getting rid of the people he cared about most, he was finally about to be king of the streets.

He looked around the church as his workers cleared out. He was alone. He had come so far, and overcome so much, but he had no one to share it with. He stood up and set the remainder of his new blunt on the casket to say goodbye to his old friend. He adjusted the buttons on his blazer, fixed the hat on his head that matched his gaiters, and exited the church in deep thought.

CHAPTER 30

The church got farther and farther away as Mila drove down the busy street. She needed to find Aphtan. She couldn't have gotten far. She wasn't familiar with the area. Still, if she kept driving straight, eventually she'd catch up to her.

She stopped at the red light and pulled her phone out to call Aphtan's phone. Her voice mail flooded her ear as the light turned green. She went through it and looked to her left. She blew out of her mouth when she saw Aphtan coming out of the restroom of the empty convenience store. Mila turned abruptly into the parking lot of the store as the cars all around her honked in frustration at her reckless driving.

Aphtan didn't pay attention to Mila driving like a bat out of hell. Her mind was on the sex she and Cole had just had. Not even the repeated honk of the horn caught her attention. Deep in a daydream, Aphtan was in a trance. Unaware of her surroundings, she stood there, waiting for Cole to come out of the restroom.

"Aphtan?" Mila called out as she got out of the car. "Aphtan?" She closed the door as Aphtan looked at her.

"Mila?" Aphtan stepped a couple steps forward. "What are you doing here?" She looked back at the door of the restroom.

"Looking for you." Mila hugged her. "I went by the church, and Scooter said you left."

"It was too much to take in." She hugged her back. "Most of the people that came didn't know my daddy, anyway. They were just being nosy."

"Are you going to the burial site?"

"When I leave here I am." Aphtan looked at the door of the restroom again.

"What are you doing here?" Mila looked at the restroom. "Why do you keep looking at that broke ass restroom door?"

"I'm not." Aphtan grabbed her by the arm and walked in the opposite direction. "What's up?"

"I had something to tell you. But why are you acting so weird?"

"It's the day of my father's funeral."

"I know that, but this is a different kind of weird. You're fidgety, sweating, and acting paranoid. What's in the bathroom?"

"Not what." Aphtan kicked at the ground with her bare feet. "More of who is in there."

"Bitch, who is in there?"

"Cole." She fixed the earring in her ear before running her fingers through her hair.

"Cole, Cole, Cole." Mila's eyes darted around as she tried to think. "Scooter's brother, Cole? Aphtan?"

"I know." She pleaded with her hands. "It just

happened. He gave me a ride from the church and it just happened."

"It happened in the bathroom of a convenience store?"

"It just," she said as Cole walked out of the restroom and stretched, "happened."

"Damn." Mila observed him. "He done grew all the way up. He's coming, bitch."

"Do you feel better yet?" Cole looked at Aphtan as he approached them.

"A little bit." Aphtan blushed.

"What's up, Cole? I don't know if you remember me or not." Mila waved weirdly at him.

"Jamila." He reached in to hug her. "How have you been?"

"Good, and you?" She mouthed *I always liked him* to Aphtan while she hugged him back.

"Good to hear that, and I'm a lot better now." Cole looked at Aphtan and smiled. "I'll let you two talk. I'll be in the car whenever you're ready to go. Okay?"

"Okay." Aphtan nodded her head.

"That boy is still fine." Mila watched him get into the car. "And from the looks of it, he still has the hots for you." She looked at her with a confused expression.

"What's up?" Aphtan changed the subject. "What do you have to tell me?"

"It's about Scooter," she said quickly. "I debated on if I should tell you or not, because I know you still going through a lot. Even so, I thought that you should know."

"What should I know?" Aphtan put her hands on her hips. "Tell me what the cherry of the top of this beautiful cake is, Mila."

"It's been confirmed that Scooter killed Boss. The streets are talking. Levi has been getting hit up about this left and right. Even he confirmed it to be true."

"I figured he was responsible. The minute he looked me in my face after we saw it on the TV, I knew he was lying," Aphtan confessed.

"You did?"

"You don't stay married to someone for years and not know them. I know my husband very well."

Aphtan's heart fell into her stomach while the acid to break down food attacked it, making it hurt. It was one thing to speculate that Scooter killed her father, still to hear it fall from someone's lips was another. The pain she felt for her mother was back tenfold, only this time for her father. Scooter had murdered both of her parents. She could never forgive him.

Experiencing heartbreak was an understatement. Her heart didn't break. It felt as if an astronaut had taken it to the moon, released it into the depths of space and the uncontrollable pressure from gravity caused it to burst into nothing. No doctor could fix her heart. Only time could do such an extravagant repair.

"I'm still sorry." Mila bit her lip. "That's why I'm glad Levi is doing what he's doing. I wasn't for it at first, but now, I'm down with it."

"What is Levi doing?" Aphtan asked out of curiosity.

"Don't get mad, but Levi was trying to take over the streets."

"Why would I get mad over that?"

"He was trying to go through Scooter to do so."

"That's not my business anymore. Whatever

they do is not my concern. They can kill each other for all I care."

"I just want you to know that I made him promise me that you wouldn't be involved in whatever happened."

"I know you wouldn't do me like that." Aphtan looked over at the car.

"Go handle that." Mila nodded toward Cole's car before hugging her. "You're my girl. If you need anything, call me. I don't give a damn what time of day and night, call me."

"You're my girl, too. I'll keep you up to date with everything that's going on." Aphtan walked toward the car.

"Aph, one more thing." Mila scurried over to where she was. "There's a meeting going down tonight that Scooter is hosting at a restaurant on Alexander."

"Text me the information."

"Are you going to go?" Mila took her phone from her purse to text the information to Aphtan's phone so she wouldn't forget.

"I think I will make an appearance." Aphtan headed toward the car. "I'll call you later."

"Be careful," Mila called out.

Aphtan got inside the car as a plan to get back at Scooter came to her in no time. She was going to make him a victim of himself. He needed to be taught a lesson, and she was the teacher. She would play her role as the trophy wife to her advantage.

* * *

"May I help you?" the clerk asked through the glass window as she looked at Money with one hand on the keyboard.

"I'm here to see Detectives Gomez and Stead," he said before he took a seat.

"May I ask your name?" The clerk stood up so he could see her face.

"No." Money used his hand to direct his workers to sit down. "They're expecting me."

Money sat for less than a minute before the sound of a badge allowing the door to be opened rang throughout the lobby. He watched the door open as Detective Gomez and Detective Stead rushed out one by one. He smiled at their fear. He was never to meet them at their office, but he never agreed to that. He only played by his rules.

"What the fuck?" Detective Gomez's voice lowered while scoping their surroundings. "What are you doing here? You know the deal."

Detective Stead sat down and tapped on Money's knee. "This is dangerous for all of us. You shouldn't just pop up."

"Did I touch you?" Money grabbed the finger antagonizing him and bent it back. "Don't touch me."

"Stop," Detective Gomez ordered while touching the gun in the holster that hung from his waist.

"Or what?" Money dared as he bent Detective Stead's finger more. "You two come shake my world up constantly. Now that I'm here, it's a problem?" He let the finger go. "This is a one-sided friendship."

"Outside." Detective Gomez pointed to the door before bursting through it.

"Are you asking me or telling me?" Money put his hands together as he looked forward.

"Asking." Detective Stead massaged her finger before walking through the door.

Money stood up and walked through the door. The sun bathed the natural oils of his skin as his workers followed behind him. He stood adjacent to the busy street as other detectives, victims, and workers passed and stared.

"You said we needed to discuss business." Money leaned against the rail of the ramp they all stood on. "So, talk."

"First things first." Detective Gomez held his hand out. "Keep your hands to your fucking self. We're not assaulting you, so don't assault us."

"You never will," Money replied. "Get to the business."

"We have a source that tells us there's a meeting going down tonight," Detective Stead blurted out to break the tension. "We want to be on the inside of that meeting."

"Use your source." Money took a blunt out of his front pocket and then a handkerchief from his back pocket to wipe his face.

"Our source isn't invited to the meeting." Detective Gomez grabbed the blunt from Money's hand and flung it. "We need you to wear a wire."

Money shook his head no. "I'm not doing that."

"You don't have a choice." Detective Gomez's hands started to shake.

"Are you threatening me?" Money asked with a growl.

"I'm tired of being nice to your ass." Detective Gomez turned Money around by force. "Loon Dixon, you are under arrest for—"

"Wait." Money moved his hands around as he felt the handcuffs touch them.

"No." Detective Gomez closed the cuffs around his hands. "I'm tired of asking you to do shit for me. It shouldn't be this fucking hard."

"Stop," Money told his workers before they reacted. "I'll do it."

"What did you say?" Detective Gomez made the cuffs tighter around his wrist. "I didn't hear you."

"I'll do it," Money huffed as the weight of the cuffs lifted from his hands.

"Go inside so they can get you wired up." Detective Gomez put the cuffs back in the holder. He leaned close to his ear. "No more bullshit. Trust me, I'll let you rot in a cell while I sleep at night in my comfortable bed."

"You may want to refrain from threatening me." Money walked up the ramp. "I'm very revengeful these days."

"You better not even think about any funny business," Detective Gomez yelled as Money disappeared through the door. "That stupid motherfucker."

"Don't worry about him." Detective Stead put her hands on the rail and stretched. "Hopefully, we can get everything we need tonight to dismantle this whole fucking operation."

"Hopefully." Detective Gomez looked up at the sky. "Because I'm tired of this shit."

CHAPTER 31

Aphtan parked outside of the restaurant as she watched the entire roster of guests of honor go in one after the other. She scooted down in her seat as Scooter removed himself from the car she'd bought him the Christmas before. Staking out the restaurant for twenty more minutes, she got out of the car when the coast was clear.

Aphtan crossed the street, the heels on her feet complementing the plum-colored dress that hugged her frame. Her hair blew from the soft breeze, and her fragrance trespassed inside the noses of everyone close by.

A van pulled up next to her before one of her heels met the sidewalk. The doors of the van opened as Detective Gomez and Detective Stead stared at her. They motioned for her to get in. She looked around before she reluctantly got inside.

"You look very pretty." Detective Gomez looked Aphtan up and down.

"That fragrance." Detective Stead sniffed the air. "What is it?"

"Never going to happen." Aphtan looked at Detective Gomez. "Something you can't afford," she said to Detective Stead. "What are y'all doing in here?" She looked around the van.

"Don't flatter yourself." Detective Gomez cut on the small TVs as the inside of the restaurant showed on the screen. "We're scoping out this meeting."

"We have everything we need. The last piece of the puzzle would be you." Detective Stead adjusted the earpiece in her ear.

"What can I do?" Aphtan fanned herself to stop her makeup from running. "I already told you two that I don't have any information for you."

"We know that you don't want your husband involved," Detective Gomez said as Aphtan held her hands up.

"I don't give a fuck about Scooter anymore." Aphtan crossed her arms. "As long as I'm clear, I'll do whatever."

"You understand your husband will be in the line of fire." Detective Stead looked at her partner with confusion.

"Once again,"—Aphtan looked at them simultaneously—"I don't give a fuck about Scooter these days. Trust me; things are completely different from how they were when you two first approached me."

"That makes this so much better." Detective Gomez rubbed his hands together. "First things first—"

"I didn't hear anything about me being in the clear," Aphtan cut him off.

"You have our word." Detective Stead held her pinky finger up.

"Fuck your word." Aphtan pointed at the note-pad on top of the TV. "I want it in writing."

"In writing?" Detective Gomez grabbed the notepad. "Are you serious?"

"Do you want my help or not?" Aphtan asked.

Aphtan watched Detective Gomez write out a letter saying that she would have immunity in the investigation, considering her cooperation. He dated it, signed it, and handed it to her.

"Let her sign it, too." Aphtan rejected the paper. Detective Gomez handed the paper to Detective Stead, who signed it and passed it to back to Aphtan. "Okay,"—she looked down at the paper—"what do I need to do?"

"We need you to do one thing." Detective Gomez looked at the TV monitor. "Money is wearing a wire, and once everyone in the meeting knows of this, all hell will break loose."

"That dirty motherfucker." Aphtan thought about the rumors of Money being involved with the police. "I can do that."

"Make sure you get in and get out. We're sure bullets will fly. Hopefully they will eliminate each other. We will handle it from there." Detective Stead opened the door to the van.

"One other thing?" Aphtan stepped out of the van. "Cole Dixon."

"Yes?" Detective Stead closed the door halfway.

"I don't want any jail time for him if he gets caught up in this." Aphtan reached in her clutch and pulled her lipstick out.

"I'll see what I can do." Detective Stead shut the door all the way closed.

Aphtan bit her lip as her eyes danced to every

corner of the block while she approached the
door of the restaurant. It soon became too much;
she started pacing rapidly; her breathing and heartbeat began to speed and fill her ears with what-ifs.
She found herself biting her lips, but forced herself to stop. It didn't quite work, as she found herself chewing again a bare minute later, and a cold
sweat had broken out between her shoulder blades.
She was nervous, all right. She was like an ante-
lope that had wandered inside of a lion's den by
mistake.

Aphtan walked closer to the door as she looked
up at the luxurious restaurant sign. The Bliss was
the name. Resplendent in white gloves and a
tuxedo complete with tails, a hostess greeted her
at the door and checked her coat and purse.

After informing the man what party she was
there for, he escorted her to the private room. The
walk included guiding her by placing her hand
gently in the crook of his arm then, efficiently and
effortlessly, seating her in a sumptuous plush mahogany chair at the table.

Scooter, Money, Cole, Levi, and the rest of the
guests in their expensive garments all looked as
Aphtan sat at the end of the table. No one said
anything as wine and drink lists were offered; the
nightly menu was not only recited but described in
detail and appropriate pairings for wines and
beers offered from memory. Orders were placed.

No physical menu was offered. Only four to five
options were available as it was a chef's menu, with
courses at a very high price, with items like aru-
gula salad for the salad course, followed by an ap-
petizer of baked egg, followed by a crudo course,

and then an entrée course such as duck cassoulet, and finally a dessert such as ricotta zeppole, with an after-dinner drink like a rich sweet port wine.

The lights were dimmed. The artfully placed candles in the fresh-flower centerpieces provided a soft, sparkling glow over the entire restaurant that gave it a rich, upscale quality that made you want to linger over a bottle of expensive wine.

The ambiance was warm, rich, inviting, and seductive. The artwork was tasteful. The music from the live piano player wasn't too loud; it was just right. The tables were of a highly varnished and polished dark rich mahogany wood that matched the chairs and exuded wealth and luxury.

The napkins were thick and real linen. The settings were contemporary chic and elegant all at once; made of real china. The silverware was heavy and substantial: luxury for the hand. This was the kind of life Aphtan had become accustomed to as she looked into the eyes of her husband and smiled.

"You look beautiful, Aphtan." Scooter sipped from his glass as part of her face showed from the dim light cascading over it.

"I know." Aphtan took a sip.

"What are you doing here?" Scooter turned his wedding band with his thumb. "Who told you about this meeting?" His eyes glared at Levi.

"I didn't say anything to Mila." Levi puffed from the cigar in his hand.

"I damn sure didn't mention it. I mean, hell, I haven't talked to my own wife in how long?" He looked at Aphtan.

"Not long enough." She winked at him.

"Let's discuss this fucking business." Money hit

the table with anger. "Y'all can discuss this mushy married shit later."

"I agree." Levi stood up. "As most of you know, Boss is no longer with us. The next in line to run the streets is—"

"Aphtan, of course," Verna said as she entered the room with a beautiful purple gown on. "Everyone knows when the CEO of a business passes away or is brutally murdered, then the next person to run the business is the firstborn." She was led to the seat next to Aphtan.

"You can't be serious." Levi sat back down. "Aphtan doesn't know shit about this business."

"And you do?" Money chuckled. "Levi, you're a dope boy at best. You're not a businessman. You don't have it in you."

"Levi, don't embarrass yourself." Scooter put the cigar to his lips and puffed.

"What are you doing here?" Aphtan leaned in to ask Verna. "You're a doctor. Why are you getting involved in this?"

"I'm standing in for your father. I'm honoring his wishes. Trust me, Aphtan." Verna crossed her legs.

"Care to share what's being discussed at the end of the table?" Scooter held one of his hands up. "Whispering is rude, Aphtan. I thought I taught you that."

"The only thing you taught me, Scooter, is how much of a liar you are." Aphtan put her elbows on the table and pointed. "You taught me how weak of a man you are. You hide behind lies for your benefit, because it sure as hell wasn't for me."

"Aphtan, when I met you, you were nothing; a nobody. Look at you now. Beautiful, proud, and proper, I did all of that. I made you, bitch, and you have the nerve to talk to me crazy in front of my peers? I should have left your ass in the projects with the roaches. You're an ungrateful bitch. That's what you taught me."

"Watch your mouth, Chris." Cole put his hand on his gun.

"How can I forget that my baby brother is in love with this woman; my wife. For years, he has wanted my wife." Scooter looked around the table.

"The want is no longer there." Aphtan grinned at Scooter as his blood boiled.

"What did you say?" Scooter gripped the edge of the table.

"You heard her, nigga." Cole pulled his gun out and put it on his lap. "You can drop Aphtan back off at the projects. Just tell me when, though, so I can go scoop her up."

"Are you fucking my wife?" Scooter stood up and threw his glass against the wall. "Answer me, nigga. You man enough to fuck my wife, then be man enough to say it in my face."

Cole stood up and walked over to where Scooter was standing. His gun rested in his hand as he opened his mouth and said, "I didn't fuck your wife. I made love to her."

Scooter pushed him as hard as he could. "You can have that bitch." He pointed in Aphtan's direction. "I hope you two scum ass, trifling bitches be happy together."

"I'm not going to be too many more bitches." Aphtan got up from the table as Verna tried to grab her. "You better address me by my fucking name or don't address me at all."

"You heard her." Cole waved the gun around.

"This is some bullshit," Money's voice bellowed throughout the room. "Enough of this love triangle shit. Another word of it and I'll put all three of you sappy motherfuckers six feet under."

"Money, you shut the fuck up." Aphtan rushed over to him and slapped him in the face. "After what you put my family through, you better not ever threaten me."

Money positioned his hand to slap Aphtan as Verna pointed her gun at him, causing him to put his hand down. "I wish you would." Verna stood up. "I'll shoot your ass and stitch you up afterwards. Try me."

"Verna Coffee." Money looked at her. "You sure this is the life you really want?"

"I know how to make up my mind, Money. Don't speak to me like I'm your average broad," Verna spat.

"Aphtan,"—Money looked at her—"I strongly suggest you get out of town."

"Pop,"—Scooter walked toward him—"don't talk to her like that. I'll handle Aphtan."

"Don't defend me, motherfucker." Aphtan slapped Money again. "I told you to stop threatening me, Money."

Scooter rushed and grabbed Money to hold him back as he tried to get to Aphtan. "Bitch, I'll kill you. You'll be in the ground just like your fucking parents."

"Shut your punk ass up." Aphtan pointed at her chest as she looked around the room. "I'm sure you're all here to discuss business. If I were you, I'd keep my mouth closed. Somebody in this room is wearing a wire."

Frivolous chatter erupted from the mouths of

the other drug lords around the table. Their workers that stood behind them all put their hands on
the guns at their waist. They were ready for whatever happened next. Loyalty had flown out of the
window as those words left Aphtan's mouth.

"It isn't me." Levi puffed from his cigar, still
upset about his request being laughed at.

Cole held his hands up. "It ain't me."

"Sure the fuck isn't me." Scooter released his
grip on Money as he looked at him. His facial expression changed before his eyes. "Pop?" He felt
the wire through his shirt. "Get the fuck out of
here." Scooter took two guns out of his waist,
turned around, and started shooting.

Aphtan fell to the ground as bullets flew in every
direction possible. She crawled as the gunfire intensified. Her dress got stuck on the leg of the table,
and she ripped it to release its hold. She kept going, not knowing who had been shot or not. Her
heart felt like it was on a pogo stick. For the first
time in her life, she feared for herself.

Aphtan watched Money reach out, latching
onto the barrel of the gun, too late to do anything.
She could tell he was in shock from the look on his
face. Then she saw clear white smoke and looked
up at the pistol that was smoking in his weakened
hands.

As his face changed, Aphtan knew he finally felt
the pain. He grabbed his shoulder as if a jabbering
pain almost like a hammer thudded aimlessly with
enough force to make it a reality. And below that,
a river of crimson ran from the blazer he'd just
bought only a day ago. It was blood. He'd been
shot.

Scooter's face changed in an instant as if his heart ached in a new way. His father bleeding out in front of him was something Aphtan wished he didn't see. He continued to shoot as he tried to make his way to his dying father's side. The sympathy she felt for him changed as Scooter pointed his gun at her and shot, but missed. She continued crawling, using the door to get up.

Aphtan's eyes slowly pierced into Scooter's, the love she had for him completely turning into hate. Never in a million years would she have thought Scooter would shoot at her, let alone try to kill her. She could see some regret mixed with remorse on his face, yet the damage was done.

"Go." Verna ran behind her, opened the door, and pushed her through it. "Let's get out of here."

"What about Cole?" Aphtan looked back at the door as they paced through the upscale restaurant.

"He's a big boy, Aphtan," Verna reminded her as they exited the restaurant. "Come on." She pulled Aphtan by her dress as a black car pulled in front of them on the street.

Aphtan got inside the car with Verna following, with Cole on her mind. She prayed he was okay. There was no telling what Scooter was going to do to him. Better yet, there was no telling what he was going to do to her. She could tell he blamed her for Money getting shot. Things were an eye for an eye from now on.

CHAPTER 32

Scooter rushed over to Money as the room cleared. Bodies filled the floor as fabric and other things floated in the air due to being shot. Scooter shook Money's body, but he didn't move. He kept shaking him, with little hope; deep down he knew he was gone.

Scooter watched the man who shared his DNA. He had always wondered how he'd feel if the day ever came, and now that it was here, he felt like a piece of him had disappeared. A big portion of him felt enraged by his death. A larger portion of him was more concerned about Aphtan.

"Did you get hit?" Scooter stood up after closing Money's eyes and looked at Cole. "Are you good?"

"I'm good." Cole walked over to Scooter and stood next to him. "What are you going to do with Pop's body?"

"Call the cleanup man." Scooter turned over the table. "Fuck."

"Calm down." Cole continued to look at Money's

body. "You can't change this, so let's not lose our heads right now."

"Our?" He turned around and looked at Cole. "You don't give a fuck about Pop. You never have. All you care about is Aphtan, and look what the fuck she did."

"She didn't shoot him."

"She might as well have," Scooter screamed as he balled his fist.

"You can't blame her for this."

"She is to fucking blame."

Scooter cursed heavily at him, the words burning on his tongue as he continued to scream. He was taken out of character due to his pain, but soon regained his composure and flung an even worse set of curses and explicit words. He needed to blame someone. He needed his pain to be noticed.

"You need to chill out," Cole advised him.

Scooter turned around to face his brother, his hands trembling. Rage boiled inside his heart, and he clenched his hands, nails digging into his skin. Cole took a step toward him. Scooter held his ground firmly. He could see it in his eyes, he meant no harm, yet his anger made him perceive it wrongly. He could feel his blood pounding in his ears, and his jaw clamped shut.

Scooter unleashed his fury. His arm pulled back, his lips drew back into a snarl as he brought his fist down on Cole, hard enough to draw blood. He didn't know why, but hitting him gave him cold joy, a cruel, merciless mirth. He hit him again, and again, his knuckles breaking his skin. He fell back, and Scooter wiped his blood off his hands, disgusted with it.

"Do you feel better?" Cole spit blood out of his mouth.

Scooter didn't say a word as he paced back and forth in front of Money's body. The door to the private room swung open as Detective Gomez and Detective Stead walked in with their guns ready. They looked around the room as they pointed their guns at Cole and Scooter. Scooter got down on the ground, pulling Cole down with him.

"What do we have here?" Detective Gomez stood over Money's body and spat on his corpse. "You dirty motherfucker. Good riddance."

"You two clowns again." Scooter pressed his knees into the floor as he put his hands behind his head. "Don't spit on my fucking pop again, you stupid bitch."

"Shut the fuck up." Detective Stead pushed the back of his head.

"This is police brutality." Cole put his hands behind his head.

"You haven't seen police brutality." Detective Gomez pushed Cole's hands away from his head. "Get the fuck out of here."

"What?" Cole turned his head to look at him.

"You heard me. Get the fuck out of here," Detective Gomez repeated as Cole stood up. "Don't thank me. Thank your friend Aphtan."

"Aphtan?" Cole looked at the detectives' faces.

"Get the fuck out of here." Detective Stead pulled Scooter to his feet while she looked at Cole. "Don't make us tell you again."

"What about my brother?" Cole took a couple steps toward the door.

"Murder, drug trafficking charges are coming your brother's way." Detective Gomez put his gun inside the holster.

"You can come see about bailing him out later." Detective Stead put handcuffs on Scooter's hands. "Call backup." She looked at Detective Gomez. "I'm taking him down to the station."

"I got it." He pulled his cell phone out as Detective Stead rushed out of the door with Scooter handcuffed in front of her.

Everything slowed down as Cole walked through the door to leave. He left the cleared out restaurant as Scooter was being put in the back of a van. He eased down the street. With what had just happened, there was a war about to break out in the streets. With Money gone, his part of the block was up for grabs. Getting far away with Aphtan was the goal. This was another valid reason to get out of the game.

"Mila," Levi screamed as he opened up the door to their home. "Mila," he yelled again before he fell to the ground.

The shock hit him hard. He felt it, but it wasn't painful. He couldn't believe what was happening. He looked down at his stomach and then his arm, watching as blood began to flood his belly and stain his t-shirt. *I have to get better, I'll make it through this*, he thought to himself. Soon doubt began to flood into his thoughts as his mind began to weave in and out of consciousness. Fear ran through his veins, turning his blood cold.

He crawled through the foyer. He had used the last of his strength to drive there; he was so weak. He tried to apply pressure to the two gunshot wounds, but the blood kept flowing like a faucet. He tried to yell again, but his energy was null. The pain was so intense that just a simple blink made him want to express his emotion with sobbing.

As blood flowed, it came down in tears of red, dripping down his jaw, and the feeling of it was hot and tingly against his neck. It was ecstasy as it spilled down involuntarily. The taste of it was fragile and familiar against his tongue, rasping down his throat like momentous pleasures. Contrary to the usual effect, he became crazy with it, driven mad by the feelings of delirious fantasies.

He made it to the kitchen. The lights in the house were cut off. He fought through the darkness, looking for anything to make a sound to alert Mila that he was there. There was nothing. He closed his eyes. The feeling of his soul leaving his body made him more anxious than he already was.

He reflected on his mortal life, knowing that it would all be gone soon. His eyes bled with pain. His son's face was all he could see. Soft visions of Mila came into his mind as well. Thoughts of him not knowing the child that she was carrying hurt him even more.

He gasped for air, blood continuing to rush out of him. His chin rested on the dark wood and he tried to breathe slowly, hoping it would help. But it didn't. His lungs were abandoning the will to live. His heart couldn't pump properly; the massive amount of blood lost wouldn't allow it to.

The world seemed to go darker as he submitted to his fate. He felt the last breath of air escape his lungs as he desperately grasped any remaining life he had in him. Finally, he felt every ounce of emotion drain from him, as death took his hand and guided him away from the world.

CHAPTER 33

Aphtan gripped the chains that held up the swing set as a cool breeze sent her hair fluttering back. The touch of the metal became icy and strange . . . cold, but not the type associated with weather. She stuck her hands in her pockets, trying to feel secure in the dusk. Even the stars seemed cruel, gleaming like blades against the blackness of the sky.

Suddenly, she jolted back. She spun around in defense, but between the mist and shadowed playground equipment, there was nothing. She steadied her breath and tried to calm the panic she felt rising in her chest. The silence got too eerie, so she started humming a song—though where she'd first heard it, she wasn't sure. But the melody was comforting, and soon she forgot the coldness as warmth enveloped her the way a lullaby does a child.

She sprung up from the swing, another voice whispering the song into her ear. *Just settle down,* she told herself, *it's probably anxiety; I've always been*

prone to panic anyway. Too slowly the other voice
died out, leaving her with a haunting feeling. She
held her arms hard against herself, snuggling their
way to safety in her dress. She couldn't even sit
outside on a swing set without her mind playing
tricks on her. Crazy. That's what she decided to
call herself.

"Hey," Cole greeted her.

"You scared me." Aphtan hugged him. "Are you
okay?"

"I'm good." He pulled away and examined her.
"Are you okay?"

"Yes." Aphtan grabbed his face and caressed it.
"I love that you care."

"I do care." Cole sat down on the swing. "I care
enough to get you out of here."

"Out of where?"

"Here." He used his arms to sway around. "Dallas. We need to get out of Texas altogether."

"Why?"

"Money is dead and Scooter blames you for it.
Besides that, they took him to jail and let me go.
They told me to thank you. Now he's going to
think you set him up."

"I'm not running from Scooter." Aphtan leaned
into the chains of the swing. "I'm not leaving my
home."

"Aphtan, it's not about being a tough guy. You
don't have shit to prove. Scooter will kill you."

"I don't think he will."

He grabbed her waist. "He will kill you. Trust
me, I know my brother."

Aphtan thought about her marriage with Scooter;
their ups and downs. Wondering how their hearts
turned so cold, she couldn't believe how two lovers

could turn into enemies so quickly. A month ago things were good, and now he was ready to take her life.

Getting out of town didn't sound like a bad idea to Aphtan. She had no family, her marriage was over, and the only thing that would keep her in town was Mila. She weighed her options and decided that phone calls and video chat would have to work to communicate with Mila and her godbaby. Her mind was made up to leave.

"We can go." Aphtan fell on top of him.

"Are you serious?" Cole put his head into her stomach.

"Yes." She grabbed his face and turned it to the side as the night sky illuminated it perfectly. "What happen to your face?"

"Don't worry about it." He rose up.

"So what's the plan?"

"Do whatever you have to do, Aphtan. To be honest, you don't have to buy anything. We can replace whatever you have when we get there."

"What are you going to do?" Aphtan put her hand in his.

"Clear out accounts, get money together, and tie up loose ends."

"Where are we going to go?"

"Wherever the wind blows us."

"Okay." Aphtan looked at the street as Verna had her driver flash the headlights. "I'm going to go and tie up my loose ends." She kissed him.

He kissed her back. "I'll meet up with you tomorrow before we head out."

"Okay, baby."

"I love you, Aphtan," Cole called out after she walked up the steep hill.

"I love you, too." Aphtan waved before she made it up the arch of the hill.

"You two must have something special." Verna scooted over as Aphtan got inside of the car and closed the door behind her.

"You can say that." She smiled as big as she could while the car drove off.

"Where to now?" the driver turned around and asked.

"The police station," Aphtan blurted out, the words running like a wild stream.

"The police station?" Verna grabbed her shoulder.

"Scooter is in jail." She rolled down the window, inviting the chill breeze in. "I need to talk to him one last time."

Aphtan walked into the police station as the door closed behind her. Her heart raced in quickening speed as she approached the small window. The glass in front of her was full of fingerprints. Her mouth went dry as the woman with a buzz cut stared at her, waiting on her to speak. The woman snapped her fingers, yet Aphtan was in a daze.

"How may I help you?" the woman asked with an attitude.

"I need to speak to Detective Gomez or Stead." Aphtan rested her hands on the separator between her, the glass, and the clerk.

"Aphtan?" the woman asked as she nodded her head. "Go through the door, and it will be the last door on your left." She hit the buzzer as the door opened. "Detective Stead is expecting you."

Every step, every breath she breathed, seemed

to echo through the halls. Pictures of past and present captains followed her with their eyes. Hallways that ended without a door forced her to retrace her steps. She had no sense of direction. It seemed as if she were going in circles. Some doors were locked, and some doors opened into dark, seemingly empty rooms, but she was unsure and afraid to proceed into the room in case she became trapped.

"Aphtan?" Detective Stead stuck her head out of her office. "I'm in here."

Aphtan's hands went numb when she walked into the daunting office. She opened and closed her hands repeatedly. She even squeezed them to try to get blood flowing back through them as she took a seat. She observed the small office as she waited for Detective Stead to finish writing down something on a piece of paper.

"I need to get Scooter out of jail," Aphtan pleaded as she looked at her.

"I thought you said you didn't give a fuck about him?" Detective Stead leaned back in her chair.

"I don't." She paused. "I just need to talk to him."

"I'm sorry, Aphtan." She continued to write. "I can't help you with that."

"I've done everything that you've asked of me. Everything." her voice grew louder. "You mean to tell me I can't get any information to get him out of jail."

"That's the thing." She continued writing. "Scooter isn't in jail."

"I thought he got locked up?" Aphtan was confused. "Cole told me he got arrested."

"Cole must have gotten his information crossed."

She looked at her phone. "I think if you go outside, you'll have your answers."

Aphtan opened her mouth, but Detective Stead held her hand up to stop her.

"Just go outside," she repeated. "That's all the information I have."

Aphtan got up from the chair and walked through the door as Detective Stead's eyes followed her. Her arms hung loosely, swaying with every step she took. She hit the buzzer on the door to be let out and walked through the main entrance to go outside.

Immediately, she saw Scooter's car parked on the street as the sound of crickets made her aware of their presence. She walked toward the car as she looked for the car that Verna and her driver had brought her there in, yet it was nowhere to be found. The window on the passenger side of Scooter's car was rolled down as she bent down to look inside.

"Get in." Scooter looked at her and then at the open road.

"Where's Verna?" she asked.

"I convinced her and her driver to take a ride." He reached over to the door and opened it. "Get in."

"What If I don't?" Aphtan gripped the top of the door, her fingers playing with the rubber lining.

"I wasn't asking," Scooter yelled. "Now get in the fucking car."

Aphtan got inside the car, the small dress still holding her body prisoner. The heat rushed from the vents onto her silky skin. She wanted to ask questions as Scooter zoomed off, but she was afraid it would come off as pretentious. She decided to let Scooter initiate all conversation.

In spite of what Cole told her, she wasn't afraid. Knowing what Scooter was capable of never escaped her mind, but she didn't think she had anything to fear. Regardless of how they felt at that moment, the love they once had could move mountains. With that fact, no fear consumed her.

"You don't have anything to say to me?" Scooter squeezed the steering wheel.

"What am I supposed to say?" Aphtan closed the vent, the heat becoming too much for her bare skin. "Or rather, what do you want me to say?"

"How about 'I'm sorry for killing your pop, Scooter'? How about 'I'm sorry for working with the feds behind your back.'" He talked with his hands.

"I'll give you one when I get one." She cut the radio completely off.

He bit his bottom lip before he took the fitted cap off and tossed it in the backseat. "You want an apology, and your ass done way more foul shit."

"Like what, Scooter?"

"Fucking my brother, for starters."

"You made me do it."

"I made you?" He cut the heat off and rolled the windows down a little. "Did I open your pussy and wait for him to slide inside of you?"

"You might as well have," Aphtan said softly.

"Are we over?" he asked as he turned into their subdivision. "Tell me now if you want this to be over."

"There's nowhere to go from here, Scooter. I don't trust you. You don't trust me. We've both done things that the other one will never forgive or forget."

Scooter entered the code to the gate of their home before driving up the driveway. He couldn't deny the words that rolled off Aphtan's tongue. Staying together would cause a dangerous case of resentment and problems that he didn't want to deal with. He loved her enough to let her go. It hurt him, but it was something he had to do.

Aphtan couldn't help but look at their beautiful home when they pulled up and parked. She removed her wedding ring as the memories they shared together played in her mind like an old movie. She would never sleep another night within those walls, and the thought of it made her queasy.

"I agree with you, Aphtan." Scooter opened the door as the sensor beeped. Light filled the car as his left leg hung out of the door. "I don't trust you."

"What is a relationship without trust, Scooter?" She set the wedding ring in the middle console.

"Nothing." He got out of the car and closed the door behind him.

Aphtan sat in the now dark car as she watched Scooter sit on the hood of the car and lean back. His eyes gazed into the night sky. She could feel the pain rushing through his body, for the same pain was running through her own. To her it seemed Scooter was more sad than angry. Even though they were over, it still bothered her.

Aphtan got out of the car and joined him on the hood. She leaned back as he scooted over to make room for her. She put her hands behind her head and used them to separate her head and the dirty windshield.

"When did you fall out of love with me?" Scooter leaned on her a little.

"I didn't." She welcomed his touch. "I just fell in love with someone else."

Scooter put space between them. "Are you in love with Cole?"

She closed her eyes. "I absolutely am."

"Why did you choose my blood, Aphtan?"

"It should have always been him," Aphtan answered. "My feelings for you have always been pure and real. Still, it should have been Cole."

"I can't take seeing you with another man. Let alone my brother."

"I get it."

"If you're going to be with him, you need to leave the city. It's taking everything in me not to kill both of you. I figure, out of sight, out of mind." He hopped down from the hood.

"We're planning on it."

"You can come get all of your shit tonight out of the house. Anything I've ever bought you, take it."

"Scooter." Aphtan eased off of the car as he walked toward the door. "Scooter, stop."

"For what?" He turned around and looked at her.

"I just get all of my stuff and we never talk again?"

"I can't talk to you, Aphtan. I can't be your friend if you're with my brother."

"I don't want us to be enemies." She took a few steps toward him

"Too late." He gave her a half smile and went inside the house.

Looking up at the sky, Aphtan gazed upon the moon as it struggled to shine through the thick clouds that covered its glow. Her thoughts stopped completely as a shooting star raced across the sky, its tail following in its wake. It reminded her of a ball of magnificent fire. She closed her eyes, freed the thoughts that filled her mind, focused on what she wanted, and made a wish. A feeling that everything was going to be okay took over her. And, because of that comfort, she went inside the house and packed as many of her things as she could.

CHAPTER 34

It was an interesting phenomenon, the sky. It was like a canvas. The clouds were brushstrokes of white paint along its surface. They told of emotions and stories in the beautiful scene. The day was a particular interesting scene, for it was split in two. To the west was the setting sun, which had a heated pink hue. Not a cloud in sight, yet still, the wind blew from every direction.

Storm clouds blanketed the horizon, intimidating all who lay beneath. The occasional bolt lit up the sky, revealing the bumpy skin of the clouds. Rain fell, the first of the year, leaving a thin, translucent layer of water upon the earth. The conflicting shape of the weather painted a battle; a war in the sky. To the west was calm, clear, and peaceful. The east was violent, dark, and dangerous. The two sides would forever be in conflict.

Mila sat on the front porch with her son in her arms. Tears rushed down her face as she looked up at the horizon. It had been a half day since she found Levi's body, and her heart had run away from her chest.

She hugged her child as tightly as she could. His seeds were the only piece of him she had left. The thought of what to do with his body came unwanted as her eyes released waves of pain. Calling the police would bring about questions that she couldn't answer. The last thing she needed was the police watching her.

Small drops of rain splashed on her exposed legs as they ricocheted from the concrete onto her skin. Some splashed on her face, yet her tears already had dibs on that area. The pain that she felt was new, so frightening and unimaginable that she couldn't think a full thought. Her mind was all over the place as she tried to come up with a solution to her problem.

Her eyes blurry, she rocked back and forth, letting the sound of the light rainfall take her to another place. The understanding that Levi was dead wasn't grasped in her mind. She had looked at his body over and over again. She had even performed CPR on his corpse in a delusional attempt to awaken him from his eternal slumber. All of her attempts were in vain.

A car pulled up slowly and parked in front of her house. She grabbed the gun beside her, unaware of who it could be. Her heart began to race. She didn't know if someone had come to finish the job or not. If Levi owed or did something to someone, it was news to her. She didn't have a clue what he was doing in the streets. She vowed to protect her son, her unborn, and herself with everything in her.

"Mila?" Aphtan's voice made her put the gun down. "Why haven't you been answering the phone?" she yelled out after rolling the window down.

Mila didn't say a word as her crying became uncontrollable. Her body shook wildly as she could feel Aphtan's eyes on her. She watched Aphtan rush from the car, leaving the door open as she walked up the sidewalk that led to the porch. Mila welcomed her hug as she wrapped her arms around her. She hadn't the chance to tell Aphtan what was wrong, but it was clear that she was in pain.

"What is going on?" Aphtan grabbed her godson with one hand, using her free hand to grab her face. "Did that nigga hit you?"

Mila shook her head no.

"What's going on?" Half of Aphtan's body was off the porch, the light rain running down her back.

"They . . . got . . . Levi," she said between panted cries.

"Who got Levi, Mila?" Aphtan rocked the baby in her arms.

"I don't know." She put her head into her hands. "They took him from me."

"What happened to Levi?"

"Go see." She nodded her head toward her front door. "Hand me my son, please."

Aphtan handed her the baby before she walked to the front door. She turned the knob, letting herself into the dark house. The small light from the porch gleamed inside of the doorway, exposing the dried blood on the floor. Levi's body sat as stiff as a board next to the residue.

Aphtan put her hand on her chest. Every ounce of blood that flowed through her veins slowed down. She stepped deeper into the house to get closer to the body. She dodged the blood, stepping over and around each pint that stained the tile. Walking up to Levi's body, she grabbed the small piece of hair on her forehead. She folded her arms and walked back through the front door.

Aphtan sat down next to Mila and laid her head on her shoulder. They had both lost the men that they loved, but in different ways. Mila continued to cry to get her pain out through her tears. Mila realized that nothing Aphtan said would make it better, at least not so soon. Those tears were mandatory; they needed to fall.

"I'm pregnant," Mila continued to cry.

"I know." Aphtan rubbed her belly. "I was just waiting for you to tell me."

"How did you know?" Mila wiped her eyes.

"I had a weird craving for peanut butter and pineapples."

"Eww," Mila said before they both laughed as tears escaped from her eyes. "What am I supposed to do, Aphtan? I'm pregnant with a second child by a man who is dead. My kids will never know their father."

"The only thing you can do, Mila, is live."

"I don't think I know how to do that."

"It will come to you." She played with the little boy's feet while he slept. "It may take some time, but it will come to you."

"I hope so." Mila rubbed the baby's back.

"You can always come with us." Aphtan held up her bare wedding finger.

"Where is your wedding ring, and who is 'us'?"

"I gave it back to Scooter, and we decided to just end it. It will never work again; it's too broken."

"I'm fucked up in my heart and soul right now, Aphtan. But I'm happy for you."

"I know you are." She wrapped her arm around Mila. "And 'us' is me and Cole. That's why I came by to see you. I tried to call you before we got on the road, but you weren't answering your calls."

"You're leaving me?"

"I'm leaving this city, Jamila. I can't do it here anymore. Everything good in my life ended right here in this zip code." She pointed to Mila and her sleeping son. "Y'all are the only good things that remain here for me."

"I understand what you mean."

"You should come with me." Aphtan held her hands out. "You, my baby, and my new baby." She rubbed her belly.

"I can't just up and leave, Aphtan. My mama is here. My kid's family is here. I love the offer, boo, but I can't."

"I understand." She gave her a long hug and stood up. "We're heading out tonight. Once I get my money together, and all of my other stuff, I'll come by and say goodbye."

"Okay." Mila frowned.

"It will be okay, Mila." Aphtan walked down the sidewalk.

"Aphtan,"—Mila turned around to look at her best friend—"can you get someone over here to take care of Levi's body?"

"I'll tell Cole about it." Aphtan continued walking to her car. "I'm sure he knows somebody who can come clean up this mess."

"Thank you. I love you, best friend." Mila waved at her.

"I love you, too." Aphtan got inside the car and drove off.

Mila had an uneasy feeling as Aphtan left her street. The rain had subsided, but a newfound rain began to flow from her eyes. Aphtan felt like the only family she had left. Her leaving was going to be one of the hardest things she'd ever have to deal with. With everything that was going on, she figured it was the best thing for her friend.

CHAPTER 35

Tsunami drew crimson curtains away from the windows and neatly tied them. A few tables curved along the circular walls. Candles rested on the tables, burning with a soft, golden glow, casting flickering shadows across the room. Tsunami crawled back into the bed, her body breaking the petals of the blood-colored roses that were scattered on the sheets. She looked to her right at a man's face that was about to solve all of her money issues.

Getting out of town wasn't as easy as she thought it was going to be. She drove two cities over and realized that she didn't have nearly enough money with her. Turning around, she understood that she couldn't ask Scooter for any money. He never gave her cash. In order to get what she needed, she had to rob him, and she could do that in her sleep.

Tsunami eased off the bed as she tied the robe around her. She looked over at Ralph, the man who handled Scooter's money, as she picked up a rose petal and smelled it. She closed her eyes and let the sweet smell compel her, before she did what she had to do. Fucking Ralph was a small price to pay for the half million dollars that she was about to get from him. She remembered his schedule like her Social Security number. This day, each month, he delivered half a million dollars to Scooter.

She walked over to the nightstand and grabbed her purse. She opened it and pulled out her small gun, the metal ice-cold to the touch. She picked up the champagne bottle on the table and took a big gulp from it. She walked over to the bed as her fingers ran through her hair. She kicked the bed as hard as she could, continuously, until Ralph awakened and jumped up.

"Calm down." Tsunami sat on the edge of the bed and pointed the gun at him. "It's okay."

"Seeing as you have a gun pointed at me,"—Ralph threw the covers off himself—"I doubt that very seriously. What do you want?"

"The half a million dollars you're going to deliver to Scooter tonight."

"What are you talking about?"

Tsunami shot at the pillow next to him. "Don't fuck with me right now. I'm very fucking irritable."

"All right." Ralph held up his hands. "I haven't even picked it up yet."

"I thought you picked it up in the morning time?" She stood up, walked over to the nightstand, and grabbed his cell phone, never taking the gun off him.

"Scooter likes to change up the routine every so often." Ralph looked to his right at his pants, which were on the floor.

"Try to make it to your gun." Tsunami waved

the gun around in her hand. "I dare you, mother-fucker. Because, you see, I have been wanting to blow someone's fucking head off. Try me. Please."

"I'm at your whim." He put his hands behind his head and leaned against the wooden head-board.

Tsunami threw the phone on top of him. "Call whoever you're getting the money from and let them know Aphtan is picking it up."

"Aphtan?" He grabbed the phone. "Scooter's wife?"

"Just do it." She pointed the gun at him. "Put it on speaker phone."

Ralph unlocked the screen on the phone before he dialed a number. Tsunami knew that he wouldn't call her bluff as she watched him look at her up and down. On the outside, she could tell that he thought she was soft. Yet, from the way she looked at him with persistent depth, she warned him not to test her. She was capable of murder. There was no doubt about it.

"This is Ralph," he said into the phone.

"Put it on speaker." Tsunami shot beside him again. "Don't make me tell you again."

He hit the speaker button. "Change of plans." He put the phone on the bed. "Aphtan, Scooter's wife, is coming by to get the money."

"Why would his wife come by to get the dough?" the man on the phone asked.

"I don't know." Ralph continued to look at Tsunami. "This came straight from his mouth. I don't know what exactly it is that he's planning, but do it."

"What will she be driving?" the man on the phone asked.

"A black Mercedes," Tsunami whispered.

"She will be in a black Mercedes." Ralph picked up the phone. "She'll be there any minute now."

"I got it." The man hung up the phone.

Ralph threw the phone on the bed and stood up. "I did what you asked. I'll stay here until you collect your money."

"You'll stay here." Tsunami emptied her clip into his body. "But it won't be alive."

Tsunami rushed to the table and put her gun in her purse before gripping the purse tightly. She grabbed her shoes and dress from the floor and rushed out of the dingy hotel room. Getting inside of her Mercedes, she knew she had to move quickly. She needed to pick up the money, get her son, and head outside of the city limits. Scooter would never suspect her. Aphtan would take the fall for the betrayal. It would be her parting gift to both of them.

A cold northerly wind blew bitterly, chilling Aphtan to her marrow as she walked through the rusty, ancient cast-iron gate. Overhead, dark clouds blotted out the full moon from time to time, casting the centuries-old cemetery into an inky blackness. Yet farther afield, she could see the storm gathering. Lightning flashed in the distance. She hurried along with the chore that brought her out in the middle of the night, following Cole's every move as her hand rested in his.

The deafening silence was pierced suddenly and without warning by the deathly shriek of a blackened crow. Again, it shrieked, and again. Like the screaming of a child or the roaring of some terrible beast, the presence of neither would seem strange in this place. The unending fog hung on the stones of the dead like a heavy, suffocating sheath, casting a relentless misery on all who trespassed through it.

The moonlight casts its eerie shadow on the path that lay ahead. It seemed to beckon with a ghostly glow that none could resist. Pulling, pushing, dragging each victim farther through the mist, each one silenced by the beauty and terrified by the power.

As she moved farther into the cemetery, a fresh chill ran anew along Aphtan's spine. Grayish white headstones dotted the landscape before her. She continued to walk as fear swept over her like a broom.

Everywhere she turned, a silence prevailed, yet not so silent that no noise at all spoke to her unsteadied nerve. Among the trees, the wind whispered and called to her. A bush, its living green now dormant, rattled against some unknown tombstone.

"What are we doing here?" Aphtan asked as she swatted a bug away from her leg. "This is freaking me out."

"We're almost there." Cole kissed her lips. "Trust me, Aphtan."

All of her fears left when he kissed her. The day with Cole had been magical. She was like a little kid at Disney World for the first time; she didn't want it to end. She wanted to ride the ride over and over again, no matter how scared she was. He was helping her get over Scooter's betrayal, and she adored him for that.

Falling in love with Cole wasn't a part of Aphtan's plan, yet she wouldn't take back a second spent with him. He was like an upgraded version of Scooter. Every time he looked at her, it was like he was staring at her for the first time. He made her weak in her knees with every glance.

Aphtan needed Cole now more than ever. Her feelings were real, but her motives were selfish. After being hurt so many times by Scooter, and wanting revenge, when she made her move a war was soon to break out. Whenever it did, she needed as many people on her side as possible.

She faltered over whether she could forgive Scooter, which, deep down, she couldn't. He had caused her pain she never thought she'd experience; like she was exempt from it. Everything that she held near and dear, he severed the bonds she had with it and demolished it before her very eyes, with his own hands. She would never be able to talk to him again, let alone be with him. A divorce was necessary.

"Here." Cole stopped and wrapped his arms around her waist, holding her from behind. "Take a look."

"What am I looking at? I saw my father's grave yesterday."

"Look at the one next to it."

Aphtan looked at the tombstone with her mother's name on it as tears left her eyes. "Cole, did you do this?"

"Of course." He wiped the tears from her eyes. "I know you need a place to come talk to her whenever we come back in town. So I thought, what would be more perfect than you being able to talk to both of them at the same time?"

"Thank you." Aphtan kissed him. "No amount

of money, piece of jewelry, designer bag or clothing could ever mean more to me than this moment. Thank you, Cole. This was so thoughtful
and selfless of you."

"I did it for you, Aphtan."

"I know." She rubbed his chest. "I know you did
this just for me."

"I love you." He kissed her forehead. "I always
have."

"I love you, too."

Aphtan's insides got cool as the words rolled off
of Cole's tongue. Her feelings for him were being
appreciated, no longer going unnoticed. It felt
good to finally hear those words from his mouth.
Being deprived of his love for so long made her a
patient woman, but her patience would have eventually worn thin. Not having to find out how much
longer she could wait made her the happiest woman
in the world.

She could see them building a life together and
starting a family. A new house and children. She
had everything planned out. The first thing on her
plan was relocating. Scooter would start a war the
second he saw them with his own eyes. Cole's and
her safety was her first and most important priority. Anything else came second to it.

"It won't be this eerie in the daytime." He put
his chin on top of her head.

"I hope not." She stared at the tombstones. "I'm
so ready to get out of this town," Aphtan confessed.

"I know." He held her tighter. "Tonight we will
be gone. I have more than enough saved up. Let's
go somewhere where no one knows our names."

"That sounds good." She turned around as the

light from the night sky lit the color in her eyes. "That would be wonderful, Cole."

He grabbed her hand. "This is our chance to start over, Aphtan. No Scooter, no drug business, and no looking over our shoulders watching our backs. It can be a clean, fresh start, with a brand-new life."

"I want that, too, Cole."

"Did you get everything together?"

"Yes." Her voice trembled. "I just hate that I'm leaving Mila. Especially after Levi is gone."

"Aphtan—"

"It's fine," she cut him off. "I know it will be okay."

"I wouldn't mind staying a few extra days, but if anything happens to you." A hint of worry stole his face.

"Nothing will happen." She grabbed his face. "I promise. I actually think I'm ready to get away, though."

"That's what I want to hear." He kissed her passionately as her phone started to ring.

Aphtan answered the phone and put it to her ear. "Hello?"

"You dirty bitch," Scooter screamed into the phone. "You think you'll get away with stealing my money?"

"Huh?" Aphtan walked away from Cole. "What are you talking about, Scooter?"

"Don't act innocent, bitch," he continued to yell. "Where's my fucking money?"

"Scooter, I don't know what you're talking about." Aphtan trailed through the cemetery as Cole followed close behind her.

"If you're going to steal from me, at least be a woman and admit to it," he continued to yell.

"You need to calm down, Scooter." Aphtan remained calm. "I don't know shit about any money. I've been with Cole tonight. I haven't even heard anything about your money. We're about to leave town."

"Not if I can help it," he threatened.

"Scooter—"

"Save that shit, Aphtan," he cut her off. "You think you're going to take my money and run off with the next nigga? You're crazy as fuck. Save your lies. I don't believe a fucking word from your mouth. I have eyes everywhere, and they have instructions to do whatever's necessary."

"What are you saying?" Aphtan stood at the door of the car as Cole held it open for her.

"I'm saying I'm coming for you two with everything I got."

"Scooter,"—she got inside of the car—"I seriously don't know what you're talking about."

"You'll learn." He hung up the phone.

"What was that about?" Cole started the car after he got inside and closed the door behind himself.

"He said I took some money from him." Aphtan put the phone between her legs. "I don't know what he's talking about."

"What else did he say?"

"He said he's coming for us with everything that he has." She put her hands over her mouth and exhaled. "This shit is crazy. I don't have a clue what he's talking about."

"Don't sweat it." Cole looked at his phone as it

started to ring. "We're about to be out of here. Yeah," he answered the phone.

Aphtan checked her surroundings as Cole talked on the phone. Her hearing had become faint and her mouth dry. Scooter meant his words. He always did what he said when it came to threats. That in itself bothered her. It made her uncomfortable in her own skin. She felt like a pair of eyes was watching her.

"I'll be right there." Cole hung up the phone.

"What's wrong?" Aphtan grabbed his knee.

"I just got hit." He punched the steering wheel.

"What do you mean hit?"

"All of my spots got robbed." He opened up the door. "That was the dough I was going to use to get us far away from here." He got out of the car. "I need to take a walk."

"Cole?" Aphtan called out to him as the door slammed in her face.

Aphtan exhausted her brain as she watched Cole pace back and forth in front of the car. The money that she had couldn't take care of them. Verna was missing. There was no way to get any of the money her father had left her. They needed quick money to get away. If they didn't, Scooter would have their heads on a platter.

A lightbulb went off on top of Aphtan's head as she dialed a number in her phone. There was only one way she could make enough money to start them off wherever they were going. She didn't want to, but one night at Pearl Tongue would take care of all of her money problems.

"Hello?" Mila answered the phone.

"Quick question?" Aphtan continued to watch

Cole to make sure he wasn't coming toward the car door. "Do you know who owns Pearl Tongue now?"

"It's one of Levi's homeboys. Why?" Mila asked.

"Can you call him and tell him Lotus is coming out of retirement for one night?"

"Aphtan," Mila gasped. "Why are you trying to strip?"

"It's a long story," she whispered, in fear that Cole could maybe hear.

"If you need money—"

"Stop," she cut her off. "You have two kids to think about, girl. I could never do that. Just call him. Tell him I'll be there by midnight and to spread the word."

"Are you sure about this?"

"I am." She put the phone away from her head as she saw Cole coming. "Do it."

CHAPTER 36

"Up next to the stage is your all-time favorite performer here at Pearl Tongue. After a hiatus, she's back, and as fine as ever. Get the big faces out, because anything else will not do. Please welcome the beautiful, talented pole professional, Lotus."

Aphtan's heart beat ferociously in her chest as her lungs desperately begged for air. Her fingertips went numb as the long black trench coat she wore swept the marble floor underneath her now sweaty feet. Her butter-colored skin sparkled under the lights as her stomach thumped uncontrollably with mixed feelings.

"Fuck." She took a triple shot of Ciroc to help calm her nerves. "You got this," she told herself. "It's like riding a bike. You got this."

Aphtan slowly transformed into Lotus the closer she got to the door that led to the stage. The bass from the music boomed through her ears as a feeling of nostalgia took over her. She looked down at her red-bottomed heels as she leaned against the pale-blue door that separated her from her past.

She couldn't believe that she was about to strip again. It had been six long years since she had been inside Pearl Tongue, which had been her only home at one point in time. It had been all she knew when she was seventeen, and although she hated to admit it, it felt good to be back.

Aphtan leaned her back against the door as the crowd's roars intensified in anticipation. Her straight, red-hair wig hung gorgeously over her shoulders as she signaled for the DJ to play her signature song. She smiled as the familiar tune filled the building and brought back into her mind bittersweet memories that she had tried to forget.

All she could think about was Scooter as she opened the door and walked through it, strobe lights flashing in her eyes. The crowd went crazy once they saw her. The love in the room made her feel good, but making enough money stained her brain like bleach mixing with colored clothes in a washing machine.

She put her finger in the air, telling the DJ to run it back and to start the song over. The scratching of the turntable flushed away her thoughts as she focused on only the pole. She removed the trench coat, letting it fall to the ground, revealing her two-piece custom-made gear that she hadn't worn in years and which complemented her small, well-built frame.

Money covered the stage seconds later. She knew she would give the crowd exactly what they came for. Aphtan grabbed the pole, swaying her body up and down against it as she made her ass cheeks clap to the beat. She released one hand's grip, spun around slowly to build up speed with the other, and climbed the pole with ease until her head was at the very top, almost touching the ceiling.

She posed on the pole, using her upper body strength to change positions. Money kept flying onto the stage as the crowd's cheers and praise competed with the volume of the music. Aphtan continued to make her ass cheeks clap as the door at the entrance of the club swung open wildly. A hint of worry stole over face. Her eyes grew to the size of golf balls as Scooter and his crew walked in.

"Oh, shit," the DJ spat into the microphone. "Y'all get ready. Here's Lotus's signature move."

Aphtan watched them slowly. Her eyes met Scooter's. Fear immediately came over her. She could see the hate in his eyes; the desire to take her life. She positioned her hands, then her legs as they split in the air. She never stopped looking at Scooter as she slid all the way to the ground into a split on the floor.

Scooter stared at her from across the room. He just stared; nothing else. Aphtan could feel his pulse beating in her ears from across the room, blocking out all other sounds except the breath that was raggedly moving in and out of her mouth at regular, gasping intervals. If she could hear it from all the way across the room, she imagined it was deafening in his own ears. Their eyes locked, so now it was apparent that she too was staring.

Aphtan could not take her eyes away from the other set of eyes across the room that were staring her down. Nothing else mattered. The connection had to be held. If it broke, she would die. He would die. Maybe both of them would. Aphtan had never felt so certain of anything else in her life. Aphtan discerned that Scooter could no longer control his hands; they were shaking in an odd trembling rhythm as the color drained from his face. Yet still he stared. He looked as if he was willing himself not to run, willing the connection to hold.

"There it goes." The DJ spun around, tangling himself into his headset. "That's the move that has been imitated by many, but only Lotus does it right. She is the one and only Lotus."

Aphtan eased herself off the ground. Scooter and his crew were now in the front of the crowd. All she wanted to do was get away. She put two fingers in the air to let the DJ know to end the song. She ignored the crowd's disappointment as they yelled for their money back while she gathered the bills from the ground.

Grabbing her trench coat, she put it on and walked quickly off the stage. She could feel Scooter's eyes follow her every move. She opened the door and rushed through it. She paced to the dressing room. Her feet sped up with each second that passed. She ran to her locker while shock consumed her body. Her heart beat inside her throat as she gathered all of her belongings. All of the strippers looked on with wonder as beads of sweat formed all over her face.

Aphtan hadn't thought Scooter would come for her that quickly. It had only been a few hours since he'd accused her of something she had not done. She thought for sure that she could make a quick few grand and be on her way, but as the door closed behind her in the locker room, she knew that wasn't going to happen. She was caught and there was nothing that she could say to save her life.

She turned around; the smell of his cologne

confirmed that it was him before her eyes ever could. A loud ringing formed in her ears as he smiled at her. He winked at her, antagonizing her. A scarce stream of pee rushed out of Aphtan as Scooter removed the gun from his waist and pointed it at her.

"Ladies," he yelled, getting the other dancers' attention in the room. "May we have a moment?"

The dancers screamed as they ran like a herd of bulls at the rise of a red flag. The sight of Scooter meant something bad was about to go down, and they didn't want any part of it. He walked over to Aphtan. Tears rushed down her face without a sound exiting her mouth. He rubbed the small dimple on her cheek while their eyes glared into each other's. He pressed the gun into her chest as she closed her eyes, inviting her end.

"Why?" He pressed the gun as hard as he could into her bare flesh. "Why would you betray me? I gave you everything, Aphtan. I upgraded you. I took you out of this place." He pointed around the room. "Still you betrayed me. I guess a bitch will always be a bitch."

"I didn't steal from you." Aphtan shook her head.

"You don't have to lie, my love." He leaned over and kissed her.

"What do you want from me?" she screamed as she opened her eyes. "Stop playing with me. Kill me if you're going to kill me."

"Can I have a moment to remember you as you were?" He kissed her lips. "I do love you, despite this moment."

"Then let me go," she cried. "I'll leave, and I won't come back."

"You know this game." Scooter pulled the trigger and released a bullet into her chest. "I just can't do that."

As the sweat dripped down her forehead, she pleaded for her life. She pleaded, but her cries weren't good enough. Before she'd even had a chance to pray, she'd heard the bullet scream out of the gun. The connection of metal and her skin was quick.

As the hard, cold, evil lump of metal penetrated her chest, she sighed. She sighed feelings of anger, anguish, and agony. She could feel the life being sucked out of her, and her eyes began to shut. Shut for good. Her life was over. And it didn't even flash before her eyes. It was just gone. Finished. She was about to die.

Scooter caught her body as it was falling and fell onto the ground with her. He let her rest in his arms as blood gushed from her wound onto his freshly ironed button-up. She looked around the room, her eyes wide with fright; no, not fright, but wonder. Was she in the light? Could she see the light at the end of the tunnel?

Her skin turned a pale, opalescent color. Her hair stuck to her forehead. Laying her head down slowly, she looked above her, at the dull roof. And before she closed her eyes, she smiled and took her last breath in the arms of the man she once loved.

"No." Cole stood in the doorway. "Is she dead?"

Scooter nodded his head up and down as he rubbed her cheek. "I didn't have a choice."

Cole walked closer to where Aphtan's body rested. It was as if it took an eternity. His ears popped, like someone had shot a gun right next to his head. His heart paced and raced through his entire body.

Cole's eyes were stuck. The only thing that they could look at was Aphtan in hope that she would move. He put his hands on his head, making his palms rest on his temples. His heart raced faster and faster as every minute passed. His anxiety was reaching a new level.

"You didn't have to kill her, Chris. Come on, man. You didn't have to do this," Cole spoke softly.

Scooter didn't say a word. His face twisted in odd ways, as if regret was eating at him like a disease attacking his whole being. His love for her hadn't been tested until that moment. She was his entire world. Her death wasn't like any other death he'd experienced. The fact that he couldn't undo what he had done made his jaw clench tight with anger.

"Everything got out of control, Aphtan." Scooter rocked her continuously.

"This is wrong, Chris. She didn't have to die like this. She didn't deserve this," Cole spoke in a low tone.

"Shut the fuck up," Scooter screamed. "You think I don't know that?" He hit the center of his forehead between each word that he spoke. "Why are you even here?"

"The last thing Boss wanted me to do before he died was kill you." Cole took out his gun and pointed it at him.

"Your own brother?" Scooter let go of Aphtan and gently laid her on the ground. "Your own brother, Cole?" He walked toward him as his emotions heightened.

"Brother." Cole raised his voice. "You've taken too much from here, Chris."

"What have I taken from you?" Scooter looked behind Cole as his workers pointed their guns at his back.

"Aphtan, for starters." Cole looked at her body and shook his head. His teeth showed because of how angry he was. "She didn't deserve this."

"What did she deserve for betraying me? What did she deserve for fucking you behind my back?"

"She deserved a long life." Cole shot him in his shoulder.

"Lower your fucking guns," Scooter told his workers as he grabbed his shoulder. He applied as much pressure as he could. The pain intensified with each second that passed.

"She would have never worked in a fucking place like this if she was mine." Cole kicked a pair of thongs on the ground in front of him. "She would be here. She would be alive."

"Cole, listen to me. Put the gun down. If you don't, one of us will die."

"You think I give a fuck about your workers?"

"What do you give a fuck about?" Scooter took off his shirt and wrapped it around his shoulder.

"Nothing," he answered coldly.

"What about mama?" Scooter's eyes closed from the pain he was in. "Do you want mama to bury you? You know what that'll do to her."

"I would never want to do that to mama," Cole said as he looked at Aphtan.

"Put the gun down and go home," Scooter pleaded. "No matter what," he screamed at his workers, "don't shoot at my baby brother."

"You can kill me any minute you want," Cole yelled.

"I don't want to, Cole. We are blood. We share the same blood."

"I still have a job to do."

"Boss is dead," Scooter screamed. "Aphtan is dead. There is no job. If you want to kill me, then just say that."

Cole put the butt of the gun to his chin. "Fuck."

Commotion erupted from the hallway of the dressing room as Scooter's workers all fell to their knees. Detective Stead and Detective Gomez rushed into the room with their guns ready. The small lightbulb that was the only source of light for the room flickered wildly. The faint smell of blood danced around.

"Get the fuck on the ground." Detective Stead pointed her gun at Scooter.

"You, too." Detective Gomez pointed his gun at Cole.

"He can go." Detective Stead waved Cole off. "She may be dead, but we still made a deal with her." She looked at Aphtan's lifeless body.

"You heard her." Detective Gomez pointed the gun from Cole to Scooter's workers. "Get the fuck out of here."

Cole walked over to Aphtan's body, picked her up, and kissed her softly on her cold cheek. He carried her toward the door, his eyes on his brother, hate filling his glare. If he ever saw Scooter again in life, it would be too soon. As he walked out of the door, with the dead body of the only woman he ever loved in his arms, he vowed never to have anything to do with Scooter ever again.

"Finally." Detective Gomez put his gun away. "We got this scum." He smiled as he pulled his handcuffs out. "We can finally put this dirtbag in jail."

"Finally is right." Detective Stead put her gun to Detective Gomez's head and released a bullet into it. "I can shut you the fuck up for good."

"About time." Scooter turned around and kissed her lips after Detective Gomez fell lifeless onto the floor. "Detective Stead, it looks like you just committed murder." He grabbed her waist.

"We came here, a fight broke out, and he was shot to death on duty." Detective Stead kissed Scooter's lips. "The perfect lullaby."

Scooter wrapped his arms around Detective Stead. As his hands gripped different areas of her body, it was clear that wooing her had been smart. With her on his side, he would never see the inside of a jail cell. Her loyalty was undeniable. She would do anything to keep him happy.

As he hugged her, a tear fell from his eyes. He had killed his best friend, his wife, and the love of his life. The piece of his heart that went away when she took her last breath was something he could never recover from. No matter who he was with, they would never be her. In the end, as a goodbye was necessary, he couldn't do it. He would spend the rest of his life hating love, because love hated him.

DON'T MISS

I DO LOVE YOU STILL

From *New York Times* bestselling author
Mary B. Morrison comes the seductive, no-holds-
barred novel of a dazzling power couple who play
their scandalous love-hate deceptions one game
too far . . .

Enjoy the following excerpt . . .

CHAPTER 1

XENA

Silence gave sound to the voice inside my mind.

Rolling onto my side, I lay in bed facing the open window. Curtains flapped, whipping a summer breeze that brushed my naked body as though I was its canvas. I inhaled the warm air. I didn't want to be here.

Why was I living with one man, knowing I was still in love with my ex? Exhaling, I turned onto my back, bent my knees, placed my feet flat on the mattress, then stared into the darkness of the bedroom.

Remember why you left him, Xena. I know. But I don't want to be here.

In the beginning, I was happy with my new guy. Doubling back to a former boyfriend, I'd never done that. After all the shit my ex had put me through, I should hate him. I really wanted to, but . . . what

had I proven by trying to hurt him the way he'd
done me?

I touched my stomach. God knew my aching
heart was filled with love for my ex and repentance
for what I'd done. Couldn't stop thinking about it
or missing him. Doubted he'd take me back if I
told him the truth of why I'd left him.

4:50 a.m.

A familiar hand caressed my breast. I scooted,
hips first, to the edge of the queen-size mattress.
Closing the gap between us, he hugged my waist,
pulled me toward him. I resumed my previous position. Stared toward the ceiling fan that clicked
each time it rotated.

Leaning in, he sucked my nipple. Didn't deny it
felt good. My breaths became shallow, wishing it
was my ex.

"Not now," I said, facing him, trying to assume a
fetal position to create space between him and my
parts I knew he wanted to access.

Dragging me closer to the middle of the bed, he
crawled on top of me, began licking my areolas.
His hand massaged my B-cups, then he twisted my
nipple with his fingertips. I didn't want to enjoy
his touch right now, but my body could not deny
the percolating energy circulating throughout my
chakras.

Pop. Crackle. Pop. Noises emanated from the settling of his old colonial home, recently renovated
on the inside.

He used his knee to spread my thighs, then penetrated me. Our morning ritual had begun. *Squeak.*
Headboard. *Squeak.* Frame. His hips thrust back and

forth. No side to side, figure eight, or round and round clockwise followed by counterclockwise the way my last boyfriend used to do.

Our music was the chorus of a love ballad. I liked my current. I had done a good job of separating the sexual act from my feelings for him.

Closing my eyes, I squeezed my vaginal muscles supertight, pretending he was my ex. Shallow breaths deepened into a soft "haaa," as I exhaled into orgasm number one.

"That's my girl. Let it out," he said. Bracing himself on his forearms, he paused, then he sexed me in slower motion. "Give me another one."

The stimulation inside my pussy intensified. I released a bigger climax. For me. Not him.

"Don't hold back, baby. Give me all of my sweet juices," he moaned, shifting his mouth toward mine.

Quickly I pivoted in the opposite direction as he kept stroking. In and out.

"Kiss me, baby." This time he slid his tongue from my cheek to my lips—trailing saliva—then forced it inside . . . lizard-style.

Lust transitioned into frustration with each probe. He was never a good kisser. I cleared my mind. Focused on my task list for the day to calm myself.

Meditate. Go to the market. Meet my contract deadline for our client.

5:05 a.m.

His dick moved back and forth, all five inches in, then all the way out. Lightly he circled the tip of his penis at my opening, glided back in, pulled out. Entering me again, he poked my G-spot. Couldn't lie. Our sex was never wild, but he always made me wet.

Imagining he was my ex, I pulled my boyfriend's ass to me, hugged his shoulders, started groaning loud. "Ah, yes." I told him, "Go deeper inside me, baby." With my ex, I wouldn't have to ask.

"Um-hmm. I love you so." Abruptly his words ended midsentence, then he asked, "I'm not hurting you, am I?"

Nice of him to ask, but he didn't have the proper equipment to inflict vaginal pain. The lump in my abdomen hadn't gotten larger, but it'd been there for almost a year. I shook my head in response to his question. The doctor said it was a fibroid tumor, and that it didn't need to be removed. Nor would the lump prevent me from conceiving.

Escaping into a fantasy of one of the best love-making session with my ex, I visualized his long girthy shaft snaking up the walls of my vagina. The opening of his penis moved about the depth of my pussy as though it were a searchlight looking for my soul. I'd pretend to hide my pleasure point, and he wouldn't stop fucking the shit out of me until he made me scream soprano . . . I missed him so much. Instantly my pussy became hot and my juices flowed like a waterfall for my current boyfriend. I tilted my pelvis up, granting him total access to Niagara.

5:12 a.m.

"You're making me cum early," he said, then added, "You ready?" Delving to his max, inches shy of reaching my cul-de-sac, my new boyfriend froze.

Suddenly his ass jerked backward. *Squeak.* He paused. Thrusting forward, he paused again. *Squeak.* One. Two. Back. Forth. His rhythm grew closer, becoming one continuous motion until he and the squeaking came to a stop. I felt his throbbing shaft, then he collapsed on top of me. His accelerated heartbeat pounded against my breasts.

5:16 a.m.

After rolling him onto his side of the bed, I pulled the spread up to my neck, stared toward the ceiling. Lying next to my current, not a day went by where I didn't miss my ex.

Was Memphis in a relationship? Had he forgotten about me? Did he crave spooning me the way I longed to cuddle with him? Trying to convince myself I'd made the right decision to break up with him, I told Adonis, "I love you, baby." My head understood what my man needed to hear. My heart knew the truth.

Lifting the plush yellow comforter away from my naked body, I scooted away from Adonis, sat on the edge of the bed, gazed over my shoulder.

I didn't choose him. On our first date at Paula Deen's Creek House, he'd told me he wasn't looking for a girlfriend; he wanted a wife. I wasn't in search of a husband. Desperate, I had to get out of my mom's house. Didn't want to move in with my best friend, Tina-Love. Her pussy had a revolving door. Men came and went. None of them stayed.

Adonis was considerate, generous, and in love with me. From day one I allowed things to be his way. Sighing, I pivoted in his direction, touched his face, traced the front of his neatly trimmed hairline. The dark hairs of his crown had started to thin. The softness of his beard against my fingertips flowed to a mustache that arched over supple red lips, which had greeted mine each day since we'd met a year ago.

Every day I told myself to stop reliving my past, each time I replayed the reel of my walking out of Memphis's house, into my mother's. In less than a week I was out of my parents' place, and into Adonis's apartment building. Planting a kiss on Adonis's forehead as he snored deeper and louder, *Please, don't leave me, Z, I'll be back in Savannah twelve months tops* echoed in my mind.

Not wanting to ruin the biggest opportunity of his lifetime, I'd made a unilateral decision. Aborting my ex's baby without telling him we were pregnant was wrong. I knew that.

Chapter 2
Memphis

"I know you have to leave, baby, but I wish you could stay with me a little longer," she professed, trailing kisses along my spine.

She was a sexy motherfucker. First time I saw her I knew straight up I was going to fuck the shit out her. Thin lips. Deep throat. Long wavy blond hair. Ice-blue irises. Tall. Six feet. Perfect size ten. Former high school volleyball Hall of Famer, she'd broken the record for the most game-winning spikes during her four years on the team.

Time was almost up for me here on the West Coast. All I wanted was to get back to the South and confront Xena regarding our unfinished business. I had to know the real reason why she broke it off. Tina-Love pretended Xena hadn't told her.

Yeah, right.

I lay facedown across the massage table Natalie had bought me, fixated on my ex. I'd been nothing but good to her for five years. A brotha had recently turned legal when I'd met Z but the fact that Z—my nickname for Xena—was five years older and salivating ova me kept my dick pointing north every day we were together. An athlete like me could have my choice female. But I wasn't average in any department. Also, I wasn't perfect.

Telling Natalie the same thing Z had told me the day Z walked out of my life, I replied, "You'll be all right." Not certain about my future, not caring about hers.

Natalie dug deeper into my quads. I felt her frustrations. She wouldn't understand, I had a lot riding on Z's love for me.

Olympic Training Camp was coming to an end. I didn't want to return to my hometown a failure in search of a nine-to-five, listening to fans reassure me I could beat Usain Bolt, having my IG followers DMing me not to give up. Sports flowed through the blood in my veins. I would become the world's champion; if Z hadn't abandoned me, I would've gotten an acceptance letter by now to represent the United States in track and field. I know I would've.

Venting to Natalie, I lamented, "I can't comprehend why she ended our relationship. I mean, I-I wasn't going to be gone forever, you feel me? Didn't want any other woman securing her spot. Gave her my all. But it's cool."

The hell it was. Blindsided, I hadn't sensed she was unhappy with my performance in or out of the sheets. A few hiccups here and there were the norm for guys, especially a track star like me. Z had issues, but I wasn't the one who'd fucked her up in the head.

Breaking her silence, I had to ask Natalie, "What do women want? I-I mean her mother was the one who abused her. I'd never mistreat her. You. Any female. Most of y'all have man issues. Can't find, keep, or please one. That's not my fault."

Wanted to add, Why do females do everything for a man thinking that's going to make him love y'all, then when he steps to the next woman y'all feel betrayed when what really had happened was . . . you played yourself. But I wasn't that stupid.

Heard from our mutual friend Tina-Love Z had found my replacement shortly after I'd left Savannah. "I took her off the market first date. Something wifey about her that other women can't compete with. She's better than a Willy Wonka golden ticket. She's more like a gold medal only one man can win, keep, and treasure until he dies. I thought I'd won her for life. I—"

Slap! "Shut upppp! Memphis!" Natalie screamed, commanding my attention. "I'm sick and tired of hearing about your precious Z! You don't call *her* name when I'm sucking your dick!"

Actually, I do. You just don't hear me.

Naked and accessible, I was not arguing with Natalie while I was facedown. Xena Trinity was in a unique category. Passion for me was in her voice, her eyes, her touch, her pussy when I tasted my baby. Penetrating her . . . damn. My dick hardened. She'd never disrespect me the way Natalie had done. Yelling out of control. Z had that silent cry that would break my heart when I saw the sad look on her face. I stared at the twenty-pound barbells on the black carpet of my living room as I listened to Natalie sniffle. Teardrops plopped on my legs, trickled down to my shins.

"I told you when we started this was temporary. Please don't cry." I didn't want to hear it.

"I thought you were over her. Now that you're leaving me you're bringing her up again. Are you planning on getting back with her?" Natalie's fingers firmly glided from my ankles up to my glutes. She squeezed my butt hard with both hands.

Verbally. Mentally. Spiritually. I'd never terminated things with Z. I couldn't, even if I wanted to. Circumstances were beyond my capability. Real love secured home plate. No matter how many pussies I hit, Z had my heart on lock. We had history. Z was forever my girl. All the other females were on first, second, third, the mound. I'd never told her, but Natalie was somewhere in the outfield. Spoiled, rich, privileged white female wanted this middle-class black man's dick to continue making her feel good.

If I never saw her again, that'd be okay.

"What are we?" she questioned. "What's our relationship status?"

You don't wait almost a year to solidify your place in a man's life.

Repeating the same motion, foot to cheek, Natalie had gotten better at releasing my tension, not hers. She'd also grown bitter over the year, wanting what I wouldn't agree to: a commitment. I couldn't take a white woman home to my Jamaican mother. I was going to miss all the generous things Natalie had done for me on a daily. Laundry. Cooking. Stroking my ego and sucking my dick at the same time.

Natalie was upgraded from her tryout spot. She was a free agent. If she traded me the way Z had done, I'd miss the perks. Not Natalie. I hadn't asked her for anything she didn't want to give me. Lifting my head, I readjusted the pillow, lowered my face into the doughnut hole cushion. "What we have is and always will be special."

"Special? And what exactly is my place? Huh?" She stopped touching me.

Sitting up on the table, I placed my hand on her hip, cupped the nape of her neck, pulled her close. "Kiss me." I couldn't lie, she made me feel amazing. "Don't cry. We'll work this out when I get back," I lied.

Slowly she shook her head, then said, "You're not coming back."

"I have to," I lied again. "My things are here."

I'd received an e-mail that boxes were being delivered to my unit. Upon receipt, I was to pack up my personals, print and adhere the shipping labels. Someone would call me to arrange a pickup time and tracking information would be e-mailed to me.

"To get your clothes, Memphis. Really?" Gazing into my eyes, she continued, "I love you. What am I supposed to do without you?"

Natalie sounded like Z, except Z walked out on me. "I've got to get ready for practice. I'll hit you up when I'm done."

Natalie wrapped her arms around my neck. Smashed her clit against my flaccid dick. "I've invested a lot of time into you. I want to go with you to Savannah."

That was not happening. I glanced around my furnished apartment. "Nah. You need to go on your mission trip to Havana. People in Cuba need you."

"And you don't?" she cried.

"That's not what I'm saying. I have to focus on qualifying for the Olympics. When you get back, we'll see where I am and take it from there."

Natalie was a twenty-three-years-young female who grew up in Beverly Hills. Didn't know what a W-2 with her social security number on it looked like. Post–high school she traveled the world on missions to help people. Most women needed something or someone to care for. I'd become her stateside philanthropic recipient.

"You love me?" she asked, lowering her hands to my thighs.

One bedroom, bathroom, living, dining, and kitchen, I resided in eight hundred square feet. Natalie owned, free and clear, a two-bed, two-and-a-half-bath town house here in Chula Vista. Her parents didn't believe in her renting real estate. If I were the type of man to dog a female, I would've had her have me on payroll making weekly deposits into my bank account.

Puckering my lips tight, I shifted my mouth and eyes far to the left, then nodded, thinking . . . I loved her in an appreciative kind of way, for all she'd done. Yeah, that was it. "I do."

Natalie stepped back from the table, then demanded, "Say it, Memphis."

I stood. "For real. I've got to get ready for practice in a few hours." I accompanied her to my door and opened it. "We'll talk things over tonight. I promise."

Standing in the hallway, she said, "A radio producer named Rick in Savannah contacted me about you. He's trying to get me to—"

Natalie was trying too hard to solidify her spot.

Closing the door, I turned the lock, got my cell. Scrolling through photos of Z and me, I bit my bottom lip. Tears clouded my eyes, splattered on my screen. I wasn't a bad dude.

I didn't know if I could ever forgive Z for breaking my heart.